Imagine Living Healthier

MIND | BODY | SOUL

Discover the Power of a Lifestyle Makeover

Bridgette L. Collins

Imagine Living Healthier: Mind, Body, and Soul

Published by Origins Publishing Company
P.O. Box 542671, Grand Praire, Texas 75054-2671

Publisher's Note

This is a work of fiction. It is not meant to depict, portray, or represent any particular real persons. The author has encountered many people through the years as a fitness consultant, and these stories were inspired by some of the things that she has experienced. The characters, places, incidents, and dialogues are based on the author's imagination, or if real, used fictitiously. Any resemblance to actual persons, living or dead, business establishments, events, or locales is entirely coincidental. The health information presented is intended to facilitate the author's account of the characters' lifestyle choices. Information in this book is intended for general reference purposes only and is not intended to address any specific medical condition. This information is not a substitute for professional medical advice or a medical exam. Prior to participating in any exercise program or activity, you should seek the advice of your physician or other qualified health professional. No information in this book should be used to diagnose, treat, restore or prevent any medical condition.

The author and publisher of this book specifically disclaim all responsibility for any liability, loss, or risk, personal or otherwise, which is incurred as a consequence, directly or indirectly, of the use and application of any of the contents of this book.

Readers should be aware that Internet Web sites offered as sources for further information may have changed or disappeared between the time this book was written and when it is read.

Printed in the United States
Cover and interior design by www.KareenRoss.com
Photography by Kevin Brown (www.digitalproshots.com)

ISBN 13: 978-0-9790932-1-0
ISBN 10: 0-9790932-1-X

To My Parents

Mr. Earnest L. Collins and Mrs. Doris J. Collins

This first book is dedicated to you.

I thank God for allowing us to share a vision

that has become a reality. I thank you for your

unfailing love, support, guidance, advice, and

encouragement. And above all, I thank you for

your sacrifices and continuous prayers throughout

my life. I love you – you are the best.

CONTENTS

Acknowledgments

Introduction

PART I

Sarah — Escaping the Emotional Roller Coaster

CHAPTER 1   A Quest for Unconditional Happiness 13

CHAPTER 2   Discovering the Misconceptions of a Healthier

Lifestyle 29

CHAPTER 3   The Health Alarm Rings Out Loud 51

CHAPTER 4   Withstanding the Tests of Temptation 63

CHAPTER 5   Saving A Flourishing Workplace 77

CHAPTER 6   Mixing the Old with the New 91

PART II

Suzanne — Deceptive Lifestyle Truths Revealed

CHAPTER 7   Reflections of Deceptions   .105

CHAPTER 8   Fallout - Treachery or Legacy 123

CHAPTER 9   Passing the Baton through the Storm 141

CHAPTER 10   The Eye of the Storm 161

CHAPTER 11   Surviving the Aftermath 177

PART III

Todd — Surviving the End of Marital Bliss

CHAPTER 12 Picking Apart the Layers of the Masquerade 193

CHAPTER 13 Sorting Through Life's Priorities 209

CHAPTER 14 Stepping Up and Taking Charge 221

CHAPTER 15 The Road to Restoration 241

CHAPTER 16 Superficial or Substance 251

Appendix of Recipes 265

Health and Fitness References 275

About the Author 281

ACKNOWLEDGMENTS

To my creator: I thank God for giving me the vision to address the issue of health, fitness, and spirituality in a unique and entertaining way.

To my friends and proofreaders, Yulonda Fletcher, Debra Murray, and Helen Taylor, for taking time out of your busy lives from day one to read and provide valuable input, and for making this book real and relevant. Your comments, critiques, and opinions were exactly what I needed and allowed sheets of paper to evolve into this book. Thank you so much.

To my friends, near and dear, Sharon Arnold, Valerie Ballard, Carmon Brown, Adrian Drake, Joyce Johnson, Antonia Jones, Vicky Martin, Linda Morrison, Shelby Robinson, Kim Starling, Danyale Warren, and Patricia Webb, for your prayers, love, support, and encouragement during the time of writing this book. Each one of you contributed in a special way to its creation and development. I'm grateful you all are in my life to share this most memorable event. You are truly gifts from God. I love you all.

To all of my relatives, especially Cheryl Freeman, Roy Ellis Nelson, and Amber Robinett, for your love and words of encouragement. I love you all.

To my running partner and friend, Daniel Henderson, for getting me out of my house for our five o'clock early morning running sessions.

To my editors, Anita Bunkley and Mindy Reed, your advice, recommendations, and support helped to shape this book, and I will be eternally grateful. You are the best.

To my tax advisor, Jimmy Turner, for your advice and words of encouragement.

To the managers and employees at the Dallas County Human Resources Department, you all were a constant source of great ideas. I thank you for your support and words of encouragement.

To my newfound friends in the literary world, Richard Carter and Daphine Robinson, for guiding me through the maze of the publishing world.

To my medical expert, Eunice Stanfield, MD., your insight and clarification, knowledge and wisdom helped me make sure I presented it correctly.

To my Pastor, Dr. Frederick Douglas Haynes III, for your leadership and mission to empower changed people to change the world, and the family of faith at Friendship West Baptist Church, for your support and words of encouragement.

To my Lord and Savior Jesus Christ: All I am and ever hope to be is because of you. Thank you for grace, mercy, and unimaginable blessings.

INTRODUCTION

Too often in the midst of life's pursuits and challenges, we embrace lifestyle habits that can place us in a vulnerable position. Unless a revolutionary shift in our priorities occurs, the things we tend to value most continue to be in jeopardy — careers, finances, possessions, and relationships.

This is a book of parables, illustrating possible health crises anyone could face with factual medical information. Its purpose is to unveil the effects of unhealthy lifestyle habits. Through the accounts of Trevor MacElroy, a renowned fitness consultant from Dallas, Texas, you'll meet three of his most inspiring clients. He provides a snapshot of their personal lives… the delays, denials, and disappointments they have experienced with acknowledging and changing the priorities in their lives. You'll witness how Trevor's passion to rescue and save the uninformed, uncommitted, undisciplined, and unhealthy leads to the elimination of self-inflicted health hazards.

First, you'll meet Sarah. Single and thirty-eight, Sarah possesses all the symbols of success. To satisfy the opinions and expectations of her family, friends, and co-workers, she lives a life of pretense. Internally, she is filled with unhappiness and insecurities, and uses an allegiance to food and alcohol as her escape — an allegiance that influences the status of her health. Sarah faces the greatest challenges of her life while struggling to find peace and happiness.

Next is Suzanne, a health conscious newlywed. Her hopes of starting a family are blindsided by a series of health problems. She becomes overwhelmed by emotional and physical challenges, and begins to think she's being punished for her deceptive habits and a secret past. Suzanne's close encounter with a debilitating disease comes at a time when she has to confront her emotions for someone from her past.

Finally, there is Todd, a successful businessman and recent divorcee, who still mourns the abrupt departure of his ex-wife, Joan. After seventeen years of marriage, she left him and their three children for another man. Unable to move pass the pain of betrayal, he spends the following year buried in depression. Upon the advice of a friend, he agrees to join a cycling group to help him move on with his life. As Todd fights for the strength to restore the family he has neglected and survive the end of his fairy tale marriage, Joan reenters their lives seeking reconciliation.

In the midst of life's uncertainties, Sarah, Suzanne, and Todd expose an inner strength that supports their ability to prevail over the repercussions of poor choices. They learn to reject traditions that wreak havoc on households, finances, and relation-ships. They pack-up the lifestyle habits that hindered their ability to achieve a healthy mind, body, and soul, and ship them off to a point of no return.

Trevor's clients are placed strategically through the book to motivate you. Hopefully, you will discover solutions that address and are meaningful to your personal situation. Reading how others coped with the pitfalls of unhealthy lifestyles is intended to inspire and empower you to change the order of your priorities. A revolutionary shift in thinking unleashes an undeniable spirit that will nurture the life God has orchestrated for you.

PART I

Escaping the Emotional Roller Coaster

CHAPTER 1

A Quest for Unconditional Happiness

*A*s the sun penetrated her bedroom window, signaling the beginning of a new day, Sarah sat at the edge of her bed distressed about her life. To those around her, she was the pinnacle of success — high-power career, affluent lifestyle, and active social life. But, in reality, her spirit was filled with stress, frustration, and insecurity.

While staring out her bedroom window, Sarah thought about her day. *Lord, I know I'm supposed to be grateful that I have a good job, but I am so tired of the office politics. Everyday my decisions are challenged. Everyday I'm interrogated by Glenn and Floyd about my marketing strategies. They're trying so hard to make me look incompetent in front of our bosses. Fifteen years in the business, and I've never encountered cut-throat, calculating co-workers like these guys. And worst of all, I've got to pull out, a day's worth of smiles and laughs to go with the flow.*

Eight months earlier, Sarah had joined Bell and Yates Marketing Firm, the fourth largest marketing agency in the country, as a marketing executive. After nine years with Mercer Marketing, she decided to join a Fortune 500 company, and earn an extra $40,000 a year. Now, she was questioning that decision.

She turned the television on to get the traffic report, but was drawn into the headline story, which reported overweight and obese individuals were frequently the victims of discrimination in the workplace. The anchorperson reported that a recent study revealed evidence of discrimination at almost every stage in the employment cycle — getting hired, promoted, disciplined, and fired.

While she proceeded with her morning routine, she took a moment to think about her accomplishments in the workforce over the years despite being overweight. It had been an electrifying fifteen-year stretch. Managing sales and marketing efforts for major organizations, closing deals that resulted in millions in sales — Sarah was one of few African American MBAs at her level working for a prestigious marketing agency. So what if she had been overweight most of her adult life. Her talent and ability to deliver customized marketing solutions always took center stage. Bothered by the notion that others were enduring discrimination because of their weight, Sarah was grateful that she hadn't experienced such ignorance.

As Sarah finished preparing for work, feelings of anxiety began to overwhelm her. *What do people really see when they look at me? Is it me? Or, is it my weight?* Not really interested in what the answer might reveal, Sarah dismissed the question. Desperate to overshadow any unfavorable images, she lived a life of pretense to cover up what she perceived to be a flaw. Driven by the opinions and expectations of family, friends, and co-workers, she lived in a lavishly furnished home in Harvard Heights, an upscale gated community in Plano, Texas. On the advice of a friend and in celebration of her new job, she had recently purchased a brand-new Lexus SC 430, fully loaded. Single and thirty-eight, she spent her free time going out with friends to dinner, happy hour, concerts, parties, movies, plays, and their favorite spot, Club Erotic, for its spoken word, open-mic, live music, and comedian acts. Exhibiting an external appearance of happiness, she managed to hide her internal sadness and succeed at masking her insecurities.

As she grabbed her laptop bag, Sarah thought, *Oops, I almost forgot. I need that marketing campaign for Byer's Retail Consortium.*

I've put a lot into this one. I can really outshine Floyd in the meeting this morning. Sarah had spent weeks analyzing the company, and its' customers and competitors. She was excited about her marketing strategy and the visual presentation she had created. It would be an opportunity to show her talents to the yuppies who were expending so much energy trying to discredit her. *This is the first descent account I've received… It's like Mr. Weisen is trying to help them damage my credibility by assigning me the mediocre accounts — accounts the junior executives should be handling.* Mr. Weisen was the CEO and Chief Creative Officer. Sarah had become concerned about satisfying her twelve-month probationary period, and needed this presentation to earmark her as a top contender in the agency.

I do look sharp in this Ellen Tracy suit. It's a little tight, but that's okay, Sarah thought, looking at the image of her body in the handcrafted, full-length, rectangular mirror. *I love this mirror. It makes me look smaller.*

Sarah set her security alarm and walked out her front door. She paused to think about the possibility of walking during her lunch hour around the building. She had seen some of the other ladies strolling during their breaks and lunch hours.

She then thought about how her peers might react. *I know Glenn will say something to Floyd. They're always talking about people who don't exercise and who need to exercise.*

The persistent thoughts of what others would think kept circulating inside Sarah's head. *I want to lose some weight, but I hate exercising! It ruins your make-up and hair. More than anything, I hate hearing about how necessary it is for one's health. All that stuff about lowering blood pressure and cholesterol… how it makes you feel better. Anyway, working fifty plus hours a week, I don't have time to exercise. Once I leave work, exercising is the last thing on my mind. The only place I'm interested in going is happy hour for a drink or two and a nice buffet with my girls.*

Sarah locked the front door and headed to her car wearing her favorite pair of Jimmy Choo shoes.

It was another hectic day at work, filled with meetings and projects. Sitting in a 10:30 a.m. meeting, Sarah recalled that she forgot to stop by her favorite fast food restaurant for a ham, egg, and cheese ciabatta sandwich. Having seen the advertisement for the sandwich a couple of days ago during lunch, Sarah was excited about trying it. *I can't believe I passed right by Village Bakery and Café. I never eat breakfast, but I'm sure looking forward to trying that new breakfast sandwich. The picture of sliced ham, egg, and melted cheddar cheese layered between the ciabatta roll looked scrumptious. Not to mention their homestyle potatoes. My belly would have been happier with the sandwich. Those donuts Mr. Weisen bought for the meeting this morning tasted stale.*

The meeting was a rehash of yesterday's information, and Sarah's mind wondered back to the news report concerning obesity. The information the reporter disclosed continued to disturb her. Hunger pains were mounting and starting to affect her ability to be attentive to Floyd's marketing concept for the new product. *I wish I could slip out and get a package of those pecan cinnamon rolls from the vending machine.*

Comforted by the fact that in another hour or two she'd be able to eat lunch, Sarah perked up and acted as if she was interested in Floyd's presentation. *I'd better take a few sips of this cola to energize me. I've got to stop yawning. I hope no one notices me. I wish Floyd would speed it up. His presentation is not going to top my innovative and interactive marketing campaign.*

After three hours of tossing around marketing campaigns, the meeting ended. As the one o'clock hour approached, Sarah began to think about where she wanted to eat lunch. She was excited that her marketing campaign impressed her bosses and wanted to celebrate.

"Matt, are we eating at Zarcia's today?" Sarah asked, trying to catch him before he left the conference room. Zarcia's was her favorite Mexican restaurant.

"Sure. I have a meeting with a client at three o'clock, so what about 1:30?" Matt replied, looking at his watch.

"Great! I'll come by your office around 1:15. I'll see if Brent and Thomas are interested in going," Sarah said. "I guess I'll invite Floyd and Glenn. I know they're probably talking about my presentation."

"It's okay. You'll put them in their place," Matt said, smiling at Sarah as she proceeded down the corridor.

Thirty minutes later, Sarah was on her way with the other marketing executives to Zarcia's Mexican Restaurant. Fading in and out of the different conversations surrounding the day's highlights, Sarah remained silent, thinking quietly to herself. *I am starving! I'm glad we're going to Zarcia's. I can get an energy boost from those great tasting tortilla chips and salsa. I hope there's not a waiting line.*

The sight of the parking lot was a sign of relief. She thought about the Mexican traditions that would engulf her belly — the chips and salsa followed by a sizzling pan of fajita steak strips, served with warm flour tortillas, salsa, refried beans, guacamole, sour cream, shredded cheese, and jalapenos.

"Good afternoon. How many are we seating today?" the hostess asked.

"We have six," Matt responded.

"Would you like a table or booth?" the hostess inquired. "We have a nice round booth."

Flashbacks began to invade Sarah's memory bank. She remembered one of her most embarrassing moments. Not too long ago, she and Matt had lunch at another restaurant and decided to sit at a booth. Trying to wiggle inside the booth, she was unable to fit because of the size of her stomach. She remembered vividly how her face became hot and flushed from sheer embarrassment. How her heart dropped in shame. How perspiration began to surface from her skin. How the palm of her hands became clammy.

"I believe we would prefer a table," Sarah responded as she motioned for everyone to follow the hostess to a nearby table.

"They have a great special today," Matt said, reading the menu.

"Fajitas, enchiladas, chimichangas, burritos and sicronizadas," Sarah responded.

"They also have salads, Sarah," Floyd said in a suggestive tone, looking at Glenn.

"What are sincronizadas?" Matt asked.

"They are layered flour tortillas filled with refried black beans, cheese and your choice of meat or vegetables," Thomas replied.

"I think I'm going to try something different today. Give me one of those with meat," Sarah said to the waiter who had been placing water on the table.

"Chicken or beef?" asked the waiter.

"Definitely beef for me. And I'll take the Blackberry ice tea," Sarah said as she handed her menu back to him. "Also, can we each get our own bowl of salsa?"

The waiter nodded.

"I think I'll splurge and get us an order of the cheese quesadillas appetizers," Sarah interjected.

"There's a lot of calories in those tortillas chips and cheese quesadillas," Glenn said, looking at Floyd with a smirk.

"Why don't you put a lid on your mouth, Glenn! The two of you are so immature," Brent said, becoming angry.

Sarah was more concerned with Glenn's attitude than her own health. Her food choices were laden with products high in cholesterol (beef and cheese), saturated fat, sodium, and calories. Sarah could have opted for much healthier choices. She could have skipped the chips and salsa all together, and selected those menu items lower in calories, saturated fat, sodium, and cholesterol, like chicken, black or charro beans, extra lettuce and tomatoes. But, Sarah stuck with her traditions and, in defiance of her co-worker, gorged on a host of artery clogging foods, and that was just lunch.

Back at work, Sarah was now feeling sluggish. The expected energy pick-me-up had a different angle of attack. The beef and cheese she ate contained such large amounts of saturated fats that the effectiveness of her red blood cells to carry oxygen throughout her body was reduced. As the day progressed, Sarah tried desperately to concentrate on her project, but her fatigue was overwhelming. Looking for a late afternoon pick-me-up, she headed to the vending machine for a bag of chocolate covered peanuts and a can of soda.

"Another successful day of workplace maneuvering," Sarah shouted out loud, gripping her steering wheel. Traveling I-75, stalled in traffic, she planned her evening activities. Would she skip classic T.V. to watch reruns of her favorite sitcom and drama show, *Martin* and *Law and Order*? Or, would she chat with family and friends on the telephone, surf the Internet, visit her favorite blogs, or continue working on her new Mainstream Accounting project?

Listening to 94.5FM *The Beat*, Sarah wondered about shedding some pounds in time for her Caribbean cruise. *If I start now, I could be a size eight by July. That gives me about five months to go from a size sixteen to a size eight. I could be half of me!*

Sarah thought about stopping by the amenity center in her community to check out the workout facility on the way home. *It's a shame that I've been living here over four years, and I have yet to visit the center. The community newsletter is always boasting about the state-of-the-art workout equipment, and miles of hike and bike trails. And that fitness consultant, Trevor, sure makes his hiking session sound fun. He always has some informative articles in the newsletter. I would love to meet him.*

Back in the day, Sarah ran track and played recreational sports in high school and college — tennis and racquetball. But visions of sweat pouring down her face and stirring up her acne prone skin haunted her. Even more important for Sarah were those images of exercising without make-up.

Maybe I can exercise just enough so my make-up won't run. I definitely can't workout without make-up. I can't let anyone see me without make-up. And my hair!

Visions of sweaty and matted strands of hair were unbearable. Exercising on a regular basis would entail frequent trips to see her hair stylist. Sarah wasn't proficient at maintaining her hair, so she had weekly standing appointments. *I'm certainly not going to Beverly more than once a week*, she thought. *I'm not trying to spend that kind of time or money at a hair salon.*

Sarah's thoughts were suffocated with a desire to be a smaller size. *It sure would be nice to drop some weight by summer — but, there's just too much other stuff to consider. If only I could wave a magic wand and presto! Instant thinness. I don't want to be rail thin like the model everyone's talking about in the news, but it would be wonderful to be a size eight. I hate feeling like I'm this smaller person trapped inside a cocoon.*

Exiting the interstate, Sarah looked over at the center and thought about stopping to see if Trevor was there. Unable to pinpoint the positives for becoming physically active, she drove on home.

Excited about having a free evening, Sarah unlocked the door to her home, anticipating the joys of her favorite bowl of ice cream — a pint of pecan pralines n' cream. Her evenings typically involved working late or hanging out with her friends. As she began to undress, she noticed that she had a message. Listening to her answering machine, there was a call from her sorority sister, Cathy, about their weekday happy hour outing.

Wow, I hate I didn't get the message earlier — I could have gone by Club Erotic on my way home from work. A drink or two is just what I needed after dealing with those crazies today. Sounds like Marcie, Helen and Leslie were all hanging out tonight, Sarah thought, disappointed that they didn't call her at work. *If I wasn't so tired, I'd go out and meet them. I guess I can wait until Friday.*

Sarah decided she'd get into bed to spend the first half of her evening catching up on three days of soap operas she'd recorded.

Checking her selections in the freezer, she grabbed her favorite, a spaghetti and meatballs entrée. Sarah always kept a well-maintained stock of frozen meals in the freezer — hot pockets, pizzas, burritos, and chicken pot pies. They came in handy on those evenings she worked late.

Removing the tray from the box, Sarah thought, *I sure ate a lot today. I don't need to eat something with a lot of calories!* She began to read the nutritional information. *Okay, it's 440 calories. That sounds good.*

Approving the amount of calories, Sarah continued to read more of the nutritional information. *This entrée sure has a lot of chemicals. Funny, as smart as I am, I can't pronounce any of these words. Wow, 1180 milligrams of sodium.* Remembering one of Trevor's articles in a recent newsletter, Sarah knew the number for the frozen dinner was too high.

She remembered the article saying a frozen dinner should contain no more than 200 milligrams of sodium for every 100 calories. Another article she read stated that consumers should choose frozen entrees with no more than about 600 milligrams of sodium, no more than six or seven grams of fat, and no more than 300 to 400 calories.

I wonder if a hot pocket is better, Sarah thought while retrieving a meatball and mozzarella pocket from the freezer. *This pocket has 810 milligrams of sodium. That's lower than the entrée. I think I'd better eat this one instead. Plus, it's only 330 calories. As long as I don't eat both stuffed meatball and mozzarella pockets, I should be okay. After that huge lunch today and the two donuts, two sodas, and candy,*

I definitely don't need to eat two. Having to prepare meals as a teenager, Sarah did not relish the concept of cooking.

As Sarah waited for the microwave to heat the hot pocket, she thought about her favorite reality show. The one she would watch over her soaps. She could applaud and cheer on, call in and vote for her favorite contestant. The pursuit of the contestants trying to make their dreams a reality always excited Sarah. She admired the determination the contestants exhibited in displaying their talents to the world and hunting down their dreams to stardom.

The hot pocket eaten, and the soaps viewed, Sarah turned on the reality show. She snacked on her pecan pralines 'n cream ice cream while she watched. She imagined having the confidence, determination and commitment to pursue her heart's desire to be a smaller size. *Every door I've opened has positioned me on a staircase to career victory. I've triumphed in a male dominated industry… surely my heart's desire can become a reality. How can someone so talented not accomplish the simple task of weight loss?*

At the conclusion of her program, Sarah felt sadness rather than elation. She decided to retire to bed earlier than usual. A late night person, she often went to sleep around 1:00 a.m. after the conclusion of the late-night comedy shows. Her friend, Helen, always talked about their late nights and the impact of insufficient sleep. Helen worked as a sleep technologist at Parkview Sleep Disorder Clinic. She assisted with the diagnosis and treatment of patients with a wide variety of sleep disorders.

I probably should be getting at least eight hours of sleep according to Helen. Sarah often had difficulty going to sleep at a decent hour. Unable to identify any particular reason why, she learned to survive on whatever amount of sleep she managed to get. Familiar with some of the reasons Helen discussed, she began to think about some of the possibilities: stress, worry, an over-committed schedule, excessive caffeine consumption, alcohol, depression, or an underlying psychological condition.

According to Helen, sleep loss has often been associated with shifts in hormone levels that regulate the appetite, possibly becoming a contributing factor to obesity. I need to strive for seven hours of sleep each night. Helen often says that insufficient sleep forces you to eat more throughout the day…. it's your way of staying energized. A method of energizing that causes you to eat and eat and eat and gain weight, Sarah thought before flipping the switch to her night lamp.

Sarah jumped out of bed the next morning. "It's Friday! Yippie!" she shouted.

Enthusiastic about the end of the workweek, she patrolled her closest in search of a complementing outfit. Fridays were relaxed, and Mr. Turner, the company president, welcomed casual business attire. For the past three months, Sarah had attended outside meetings on Fridays, so she had been unable to wear her casual clothing. Feeling a little bloated, Sarah decided to try on a pair of her favorite jeans. As she suspected, they were too tight. Something about her inability to fit into the jeans simply devastated her. Water sprang into her eyes. The constant denials of a bloated belly, puffy thighs, enlarged breasts and arms drove home the reality that she had gained more weight. A weight gain that was disguised by business clothing made from stretchable fabric and the elastic in her pants and skirts that concealed the expansion around her waistline. Movement towards the bathroom activated a fear to look in the mirror. Reaching for her bathrobe, Sarah was able to avoid reality.

Distraught about her weight gain, Sarah became increasingly agitated. She pondered her options for weight loss. *Maybe I'll ask my doctor for some weight loss pills, or maybe I'll have a tummy tuck or a liposuction procedure. Gastric bypass surgery… stomach stapling… hypnosis… lap band surgery? What about one of those devices implanted inside my body that fools the stomach into thinking it's full? I really would like my breast reduced. What about that three-day diet plan Tiffany gave me last week? With that Hollywood diet I heard about, I could lose ten pounds in twenty days drinking maple syrup, vinegar, and water.*

Terrified about the ramifications of surgery, the impact of weight loss pills, the stringent rules of a Hollywood diet, and Tiffany's three-day diet, Sarah considered her options. *Okay, I can do this... whatever I need to do to get ready for my cruise in July. I just need something to get me jump-started.*

Sarah had plans to travel to Miami to board a luxury cruise ship for a five-day Caribbean cruise. Although she went on a cruise four years ago, this time things had to be different. Reflections of the trip's highlights triggered the disappointment she had felt by not experiencing the fun and exciting shore excursions — jet skiing, parasailing, kayaking, and snorkeling. Hearing others rave about snorkeling in turquoise water and viewing the spectacular coral reef still sailed through Sarah's thoughts. A lover of water, Sarah didn't feel comfortable wearing a swimsuit because of her size.

Anxious to look stunning in a swimsuit, Sarah would pay any price to improve her body image. *What diet can I try? I can stick with anything for a few weeks. Anything except cottage cheese and cauliflower.*

While curling her hair for work, it hit her. She would try the high-protein, low-carbohydrate diet. Two ladies in her building had already lost 35 pounds each after one month. Although Sarah loved breads and pastas, she was willing to sacrifice those foods for all the meat, egg, and cheese dishes she could conjure up.

As the garage door lifted, Sarah projected a new attitude — a new beginning. *I think I'll stop by Village Bakery and Café for one of their on-the-go breakfast sandwiches. I'd like to try the new ciabatta breakfast sandwich, but I know the roll will have too many calories.*

Driving into the parking lot, Sarah was happy about having a quick solution to eating breakfast. Entering the doors, she experienced the sweet aroma of smoked bacon, fresh baked bread, and fluffy omeletes. Viewing the selection of menu items, Sarah ordered two slices of bacon, two scrambled eggs and a 16-ounce cup of coffee. *I can eat this same meal everyday. This will definitely be my breakfast spot on the way to work,* Sarah thought as her bacon and eggs were being fried.

Preparing for a day packed with meetings and work group sessions, Sarah felt invincible. Shuffling through some papers, trying to focus on some research data, she thought about Mary, her research analyst. *Mary sure has lost a lot of weight. I wonder how did she do it? She was large. I wonder if she's in her office.* Sarah decided to pay Mary a visit.

Although Sarah was comfortable with her decision to try the high-protein, low-carbohydrate diet, she wanted to know Mary's strategy for losing weight. She looked great and Sarah wanted to know how she did it.

Sarah found Mary in the copy center and complimented her on how trim she looked. Eager to share her story, Mary talked with excitement about her decision to make some life altering changes a year ago. For years, she knew a weight of 225 was too much for her height of five-feet and four inches.

"I've always suffered with respiratory problems and arthritis in my legs, but it wasn't until my diagnosis of high blood pressure during an annual examination that I was scared straight," Mary said.

Her doctor's explanation of the disease prompted Mary to get serious about her health. Scared of dying an untimely death like her father, who died at the age of 50, Mary knew her lifestyle and genetic connection were precursors that could land her in a coffin sooner rather than later. Eating healthier, eating less and exercising were her ammunition to control and wardoff future health concerns. The results of her efforts had her weighing 150 pounds.

Wow! Mary and I are around the same age. What caused her to have high blood pressure…and arthritis? That's for old people. And respiratory problems? That's a sad situation to be in — she must have been out-of-control with her eating. All I want to do is lose weight. I hadn't thought about diseases and illnesses, Sarah thought as she stood listening to Mary.

After finishing her testimony, Mary invited Sarah to walk with her during lunch. Sarah graciously declined and explained her plans to lose weight following the high-protein, low-carbohydrate diet.

"I'll think about it, but I'm not into exercising," Sarah said.

"Well, let me know if you change your mind. I'll be happy to have you join me for a brisk walk," Mary said, trying to encourage Sarah to get moving.

It was lunch time. A group of the executives were going to B's Deli for lunch. Sarah eagerly hopped on board for the trip. She was excited about the wide variety of protein items. As Matt and the others recapped the highlights of the morning's meeting while walking down the street, Sarah lagged behind, thinking about what she would eat. Focused on eating a light lunch as they entered the deli, she decided on the fried buffalo chicken salad and a diet soda. Matt urged her to try the grilled marinated chicken instead, but Sarah seldom missed an opportunity to eat fried food.

Back at work, sitting at her desk, Sarah worked diligently to finish another marketing report due to Mr. Weisen by the end of the day. Because of delayed submissions from her team, the pressure was mounting. *I've got to have a good showing on this report. Glenn and Floyd seem to be getting the better accounts. And I know their reports aren't as good as mine. I sure wish I worked directly for Mr. Turner. He is fair in rotating the high-dollar clients. I hate he hired Mr. Weisen. If things don't get better, I might talk with Mr. Turner.*

To alleviate her stress, Sarah made a mad dash to the vending machine for a soda. Remembering she was dieting, she chose a diet soda. Upon her return, there was a message on Sarah's desk from Cathy to meet her after work for their happy hour weekend ritual. Friday night happy hours were Sarah's great escape from a week's worth of workplace escapades. She hurriedly cornered her team to get their submissions while spewing out ultimatums, eager to deflect any mishaps that might hinder her opportunity to shine in front of the bosses.

Sarah managed to meet the deadline for submitting her report and now it was time to celebrate the end of another chaotic week. Hanging out with her girls on Fridays presented the perfect opportunity to play catch up. They managed to spend most of their evening handing out trade secrets and marveling over their conquests. Sarah always felt self-conscious about being the largest of the girls. Now she had noticeably increased in size. The pressure was on to shift their attention away from her size. Talking about the folks at work always presented the perfect centerpiece for conversation.

Sarah's favorite cocktail, Peach Margaritas, helped her unravel the internal knots of frustrations and fears. She and her friends always expected an extra shot of tequila from Marvin, the bartender at Happy John's. The elaborate buffet featured seafood, roast, buffalo wings, mozzarella sticks, chicken tenders, and pastas. They had fresh fruit and steamed vegetables, too, but the girls were not interested. Sarah decided that there were enough high-protein choices at the buffet that she could eat with her friends without saying anything about her diet.

Seated in their usual spot, Sarah was the life of the party, making everyone laugh. The waitress placed the napkins on the table and proceeded to take their drink orders. "Hi, my name is Nancy. What are you ladies drinking this evening? We have $2.50 margaritas — well tequila, triple sec and lime juice."

"I prefer a Peach Margarita made with your top shelf tequila. It's been a rough week," Sarah said.

After a few minutes of idle conversation, the girls headed toward the buffet table. Sarah avoided the pasta and assortment of rolls. She concentrated on the buffalo wings, boiled shrimp, and roast beef. Observing her selections, Marcie suggested the pasta with alfredo sauce. Sarah declined, claiming she wasn't in the mood for pasta. But the buffalo wings were irresistible, having a sauce that delivered a mouth-watering, finger-licking taste. She could have easily eaten a plate full. And as the night progressed, she did, along with a couple drinks. Driving home, Sarah knew she had blown her first day.

Discovering the Misconceptions of a Healthier Lifestyle

After two months of adhering to her chosen diet, Sarah was dropping the weight. Looking in the mirror and witnessing her progress, she wondered how long she could continue her meat, egg and cheese lover's style of eating. In the media, opponents were sounding off about their disapproval of the high-protein, low-carbohydrate diet. Based on research and certain studies, they were concerned about the health risks. One concern centered on the link to high cholesterol levels, resulting in the increased risk of developing heart disease. Another suggested that consuming too much protein places a strain on the kidneys, therefore making Sarah susceptible to kidney disease. The last stemmed from the increased risk of cancer — the theory being that high-protein diets lacked the protective vitamins, minerals, fiber and antioxidants associated with carbohydrate-containing foods (whole grain bread, pasta, and rice). Although she was thinking about those things, none of it really mattered to Sarah, because everyone at work was telling her how wonderful she looked. Even Glenn and Floyd had complimented her. The praise was worth it all.

The time for Sarah's annual physical examination had arrived. For the past five years, her doctor had encouraged her to lose weight. *My doctor is going to be really surprised,* Sarah thought as she approached the window to sign in. As she began to sign the appointment book, she was greeted instantly with praise — the staff commenting on her new look.

"Come on back," Nurse Wrigley said. "You are looking good, Sarah. You know the routine… we're going to get your weight first, then your blood pressure, pulse, and temperature."

Going through the doors to get on the scale, Sarah removed her shoes and jacket for true accuracy. Astonished at the number displayed on the digital scale, Sarah leaped inside with joy. She was thirty-seven pounds lighter than the year before. Sitting on the examination table waiting for the doctor, her eyes sparkled with pride. Moments later, Dr. Thomas walked in surprised and amazed at the notations Nurse Wrigley had indicated on her chart. He praised her for the new look and wanted to know what happened. She described the high-protein, low-carbohydrate diet she had implemented, going on further to explain her process. Dr. Thomas stopped her in mid-sentence. He began to explain the possibility of how such diets restrict healthful foods that provide essential nutrients.

"While they may result in quick weight loss," Dr. Thomas said, "they have not been proven effective for long-term weight loss, and they don't provide the variety of foods needed to adequately meet nutritional needs. People who stay on these diets very long may not get enough vitamins and minerals, causing them to face potential health risks. It never ceases to amaze me… the never-ending convoy of miracle poisons… I mean potions. Not to mention powders, pills, and drinks advertised… infomercials… and magazines. You just can't allow yourself to get caught up in the promises. If you're really serious about a healthy weight loss plan, then eating less, eating healthy, and balancing food intake with physical activity is the way to go. You also need to make sure you're getting plenty of rest and drinking plenty of water. Always remember… anything worth having is worth doing what's necessary to get it." After the discussion, Dr. Thomas proceeded with conducting the examination

— prodding and probing to determine any health problems. At the end of the examination, Dr. Thomas completed the paperwork for Sarah's blood work. He informed her if any concerns resulted from her blood work, his office would contact her to schedule a follow-up appointment.

Back at work, Sarah was concerned about the conversation she had with Dr. Thomas regarding her diet plan. *I sure don't want any health problems — maybe Mary can offer me some of her pointers,* Sarah thought.

"Hey lady. How's everything going?" Mary asked, as Sarah entered her office. "You're looking great. I guess your program is really working for you."

After explaining the reason for her visit, Sarah revealed her doctor's concerns with the high-protein, low-carbohydrate diet.

"I, too, was concerned when you told me what you were doing a couple of months ago. For me, the only sensible way to lose and maintain a healthy weight permanently is the old-fashion way like your doctor mentioned," Mary confirmed. "I have to admit that I probably wouldn't be on this course if I hadn't been diagnosed with high blood pressure. It has truly changed my lifestyle."

"It's just so hard trying to commit to eating healthier," Sarah said, getting up to look outside Mary's window.

"Understanding why I was overweight has helped me to stay on track with my new lifestyle choices. I used food to deal with emotions resulting from family, work, finances, relationships, and unhappiness with myself on a daily basis. Living paycheck to paycheck, barely managing my monthly expenses. The bill collectors calling. Robbing Peter to pay Paul. Wanting to get married. Worrying about if I'd ever get married. They all caused me to binge on food. Food was the only thing that comforted me. I found refuge from life's pain, betrayals, problems, disappointments, and rejections in a bowl of banana split ice cream, an order of chili cheese fries, a chili cheeseburger... honey buns and oven baked cinnamon rolls. You name it — food was my escape from the emotions poisoning my mind. Potato chips were my biggest evil… eating whole bags of sour cream and onion, barbecue, cheddar and sour cream potato chips late at night. Then there was Mrs. Murray's Dutch Apple Crisp Pecan Pie. I've eaten a whole one on more than one occasion."

"You look so together," Sarah said, moving toward a chair.

"Most of us look like we're together," Mary said. "The fact is that you don't find many people who appear maladjusted. We all act like everyday, ordinary people. But, when we exit these doors at five o'clock, some of us head to live a life filled with spousal drama, kid drama, family drama, financial drama, relationship drama, internal drama, and childhood drama. We all have some coping mechanism — some addiction that can range from eating… illegal or prescription drugs… drinking alcohol… sex with multiple partners… smoking… partying… infidelity… excessive spending habits… abusing love ones…… something! For the millions of us who suffer from being overweight or obese, it's typically food. When I was drowning in depression, I thought everyone was celebrating life while I was hurting. I've come to realize that every-one is going through something, whether they admit it or not," Mary went on. "Not that it matters what others are going through. I don't get caught up in appearances. I've always looked like I had it all together, but the reality of what was going on probably would shock those who thought they knew me."

"You're so right about that," Sarah responded.

"Working on a job that offered no opportunities for advance-ment caused me to binge on food. Committing myself to a relationship with a long-time boyfriend… a relationship that was going nowhere caused me to binge on food. There were the constant reminders from my mother that my sister was the favorite daughter. Listening to her rave about my sister's marriage and successful career caused me to binge on food. I used food as a comfort when dealing with unfavorable situations in my life. The biggest emotional hurdle was defeating the hostility I felt against my mother for her years of cheating on my father. And most paramount in my life was the fact that my father died an unhappy man because of her unfaithfulness. All the things I've mentioned caused me to overindulge and make poor food choices. Cookies, chips, candy, ice cream were my best friends — my emotional support system. And those choices for deliverance from the horrors of my life led to my health predicament," Mary said.

"You definitely hid your turmoil very well," Sarah said.

Mary admitted to being an expert at disguising her pain. "I was living my own personal *Phanthom of the Opera*. Disfigured internally, every morning before heading out the door, I'd put on my mask that concealed my struggles. With the mask on, I became a master at hiding reality from the world. I was proficient at looking lovely and doing lovely things. All for the benefit of others. One day it all became too overwhelming for me, and I couldn't keep the mask on. And you know what? It was okay. Sure... the ugly reality was unveiled, but it was okay. The mask had to be removed in order for me to deal with the ugly. I had to dismiss the attitudes, thoughts, and actions of others to love myself enough to deal with the ugly. Single and forty-two, with many good years ahead, I had to get myself out of the emotional crossfire." Mary went on to share that once she confronted those reasons that prevented her from loving herself, her life changed dramatically.

Sitting at her desk, Sarah deliberated over Mary's words. Fortunately, she didn't have issues like Mary. Sure, work consisted of long hours, demanding bosses, high expectations, but what job didn't? It was the price one was expected to pay for the big bucks. Relationships? Sarah hadn't been on a date in years. With two wonderful parents and two older brothers, Sarah didn't have family drama. *Yes, I love myself... however, the privileges of having a perfect body... I won't dislike myself if it doesn't happen. Those who know me already love me. The new acquaintances will either learn to love me regardless of how I look or not.*

Sarah was telling herself what she wanted to believe, but others' perceptions of her mattered more than anything.

Finishing her meeting a little early, Mary stopped in and invited Sarah to lunch. She recommended walking to the cafeteria about five blocks from the office building. Other than the deli, a block from the building, walking was out of the question for Sarah. She was accustomed to driving two blocks. While walking, Mary talked more in depth about her lifestyle changes.

"In case you don't know, breakfast is the most important meal of the day. It sets the stage for what's going to happen the remainder of the day. At the start of your day, you're charged and full of energy, a feeling that comes from a good night's sleep. However, as the day progresses, your initial surge of energy is zapped away. More than likely, you will experience tiredness, poor concentration, and irritability. All the effects of someone running on empty... someone with low blood sugar... someone who didn't fuel up. A continued cycle of skipping breakfast can possibly be an added variable in the equation affecting your ability to manage your weight," Mary said, while signaling that it was okay to cross the street. "Skipping breakfast causes you to spend the rest of your day trying to play catch up, and that usually results in overeating."

"I've just started eating breakfast," Sarah confessed. "What do you eat?"

"I typically start off with a bowl of whole grain cereal with soymilk, and fresh fruit like a banana or orange, or a slice of whole-wheat toast, low-fat yogurt and fresh fruit. And for lunch, I'll eat a protein, carbohydrate, and fiber, such as a portion of grilled chicken or fish, black-eyed peas, and collard greens. A steady stream of food throughout the day, spaced just right, will keep your engine going," Mary suggested.

"What do you mean by keep my engine going?" Sarah asked.

"Our bodies needs a certain amount of calories and nutrients each day for normal functioning. Denying your body a sufficient number of calories will throw your system into a survival mode, slowing the metabolism and encouraging the storage of the food you consume as fat. You have to eat in order to lose weight. So try and eat four to six small meals a day and that will be a good way to keep your metabolism going," Mary said. "It has worked for me. I realize that we're all different and that my solutions may not be the answer for you. But, once you become committed, you'll find out what works for you — either through your own revelation or with the assistance of a health professional like a registered dietician."

"I'm trying to be committed," Sarah said.

"Once I finally decided to commit to changing the priorities in my life, I started doing some research on the types of foods I was eating. The results of my findings were astonishing."

"Okay, I'm not that smart about this kind of stuff. What is metabolism? I hear the word all the time," Sarah asked.

"Well, as we all get older, we can blame that process of being unable to burn those calories on metabolism," Mary said. "Simply stated, your metabolism is the way your body burns up all of the calories from the food that we eat. The speed at which our body burns up calories is called our metabolic rate. Your sex, height, weight, genetics, age, lifestyle, and body composition will affect your metabolism, and it's metabolism that plays a significant role in weight management. The faster one's metabolism, the more calories they are likely to burn, and the less likely that they will be overweight. That's why it's so important not to skip meals," Mary responded. "The main thing is to keep your engine going with the right foods. Secondly, you've got to exercise."

"Okay," Sarah replied.

"Before I kicked my boyfriend to the curb, eating and entertaining were the hallmark of our lives — a facade for maintaining common law blitz. Seven years of dinner parties and vacations financed by my shallow income and payday loans placed me on a road to ruin... a collision course emotionally, financially, and physically."

"Wow," Sarah said with amazement.

"It was during the time of my diagnosis with high blood pressure that I woke up from my fast moving road to destruction. Let's just say I woke up from the nightmare I mistook as a dream. I thought I was with someone who really loved me, but he was a leech sucking the life out of me. Don't get me wrong, I'm not wallowing in the past... I'm just identifying how insecurity, pain, disappointment, and betrayal can cause you to grab a hold of someone or something harmful..."

"I've also learned that life is rife with failures and disappointments, but you've got to get up and get back on the trail of pursuits," Sarah said. "You might be riding in the dark for a while, but the sun will rise, providing direction to a triumphant end. That truth has motivated me on my rise up the corporate ladder."

"You have to keep remembering that, especially when you hit a tough stretch, not to revert back to unhealthy habits. One thing I would encourage you to do is start analyzing the foods you've traditionally eaten. If I guess right, you'll discover the potentially hazardous effects of your favorite foods," Mary said.

"Since I've always been a healthy person, it never crossed my mind to analyze my foods. I've never had any health problems. I never get colds," Sarah said. "Everything I eat, I basically ate during my childhood — fried chicken, fish and pork chops... steak... meatloaf. Nevertheless, I've started looking at the frozen dinners I like to eat..."

"Frozen dinners... the average one is loaded with sodium, preservatives, and chemicals. Now, I'm real careful about the ones I bring into my home. There's a new line that one of the leading frozen food manufacturers has that offers a wide selection of entrées with whole grain rice and pasta. One of my favorites is the Rosemary Chicken with roasted chicken tenderloins in a garlic-rosemary sauce, spinach and brown rice. It's made with 100% whole grain rice... no preservatives... no artificial flavors... and no trans fat."

"Sounds good! You're really on the right track," Sarah commented.

"A combination of information I've researched, and my cousin Kelly has gotten me to this point. Kelly is a registered dietician for Barley's Wellness Center over on Crossland Lane in North Dallas. She facilitates a healthy eating class at six o'clock on Thursdays... If you're not doing anything after work on Thursday, and would like to attend one of her sessions, I can call her when we get back to the office. She's facilitating a series entitled, *Getting Back to Basics: A Guide to Healthy Eating.*"

"I had planned on going with some friends to a new club in North Dallas, but I guess I could go another time. I definitely would like to attend the class," Sarah said. "Is there a cost to attend?"

"No. The classes are absolutely free," Mary said. "I'll call her as soon as we get back."

As they entered the cafeteria, Sarah was happy to have Mary with her. "Mary, I normally get the chicken fried steak with the cream sauce, mashed potatoes with gravy, and fried okra," Sarah said.

Visions of clogged arteries roamed through Mary's mind while listening to Sarah. She calmly suggested the grilled fish, mashed potatoes without the gravy, and the steamed broccoli without the cheese sauce. "Try and avoid the extras like gravy and sauces — they are generally high in calories, carbohydrates, fats, and sodium," Mary said, trying to assist Sarah with making moderate changes. Sarah preferred the green beans, instead of the broccoli. Mary was semi okay with her choice, but pointed out the fact that often products like canned green beans, collard greens, and spinach have a large amount of sodium, unless there's a statement 'no salt added'. "Vegetables that are fresh generally do not contain as much sodium, unless it's added by the eater. I'm also certain that the cafeteria is not purchasing the 'no salt added' version of canned vegetables."

Back at the office, Mary contacted her cousin and arranged for Sarah to attend the class. Kelly had been a registered dietician for over ten years. Mary enjoyed Kelly's classes because she offered practical solutions for balancing daily demands with healthy habits. She brought close to home the hazards of unhealthy lifestyle practices. A proponent of cooking meals at home, Kelly's program included a cooking demonstration every third Thursday. Participants who attended the first two classes of the month could write the name of their favorite dish on a card and place it in a box. Kelly would pull one card from the box at the end of the second session of the month, and on the third Thursday, she would demonstrate to the class how to modify the ingredients to create a healthier version of the meal.

"Hi Sarah. My cousin has added your name to the class for Thursday," Mary said, while entering Sarah's office. "The class begins at six o'clock. By the time we get off work and fight traffic to get to North Dallas from downtown, we should be right on time."

"Thanks, Mary. Let's meet at five o'clock out front."

"Okay," Mary said. "I'll confirm our plans again with you on Wednesday."

Sarah and Mary met as planned after work. As expected, the traffic was heavy. After forty-five minutes, they arrived at Barley's Wellness Center. The center had a comprehensive program for individuals wanting to lose weight and/or incorporate better nutritional habits.

Walking into the classroom, Mary introduced Sarah to Kelly. "Hi Kelly. This is my friend, Sarah."

"Hi Sarah. I'm glad you were able to come out tonight," Kelly said. "The class is informal. This is an opportunity for the class participants to get clarification on how to incorporate and/or improve their eating habits."

"That's exactly what I need. I'm glad I was able to come tonight," Sarah said. "Mary had a lot of good things to say about your class."

"She's probably a little bias, since I'm her cousin. Have a seat and we'll get started in about five minutes," Kelly said.

While Kelly was assembling her handouts, a tall, dark, handsome, and charismatic male entered the room. Sarah recognized his face immediately. He was the fitness consultant in her fitness center's newsletter. Moments later, Kelly introduced Trevor MacElroy as her invited guest.

"Mary, that guy coaches a hiking session at the amenity center in my community," Sarah whispered to Mary.

"Really," Mary replied. "He sure is good-looking."

"Good evening, everyone," Kelly said, as she motioned for the participants to have a seat. "I invited a dear friend of mine, Trevor MacElroy, to come and share his wealth of knowledge with us tonight. He has been in the fitness business for over fifteen years. He is the owner of Faith-Based Fitness Solutions, a fitness consulting agency in Dallas, Texas. He conducts fitness workshops throughout the Dallas/Fort Worth metroplex — recreation centers, hospitals, nursing homes, churches... everywhere. And you may have heard him on the radio, Heaven 79.5, on Saturday mornings. For me, his most impressive accomplishments are the marathon races he participates in all over the country. Anyone who can run 26.2 miles in one session is alright with me. Trevor, please feel free to say hello to the group."

"Hello, everyone. And thank you Kelly for inviting me. It is truly a pleasure and a blessing to be here tonight," Trevor said, standing tall, authoritative. "Don't mind me; just go about your business as you would normally do here."

"For the newcomers, I like to start out with testimonies. Hearing how others have overcome their struggles can inspire you to do the same. It's important to remember that you're not alone in this battle to do the right thing," Kelly said.

"I'll share," a white lady in the back of the room sounded out.

"Okay. Everyone, Alberta is going to share with us," Kelly said, acknowledging the lady by name.

"I've had the hardest time giving up fried food. I've been attending these classes sporadically for over six months. And during the six months, I've continued to eat hamburgers, fried pork chops, fried chicken nuggets, fried zucchini... It's hard for me tonight," Alberta said as she began to cry. "Each week I come into this room portraying someone who's doing the right thing. I'm tired of lying to the group. I want to come clean tonight, and let the group know I'm ready to commit to making the changes I've been talking about for the past six months. I'm ready to let go of those demons holding me captive. Demons that keep convincing me that food is the only thing I can count on to console me... to make me feel better... to make me happy when all is dark in my life. I feel like I've continuously let myself down, as well as all of you in the group."

"I'm glad you've decided to come clean tonight and recommit to the promises you've made to yourself," Kelly said, looking around at the solemn faces. "Commitment is important. Commitments are a part of life. Some we keep, and some we don't. If you ever expect to reach your goal, you must be committed to the end. You must be able to overcome the interludes of life that distract you from staying the course. Commitment helps you to establish internal standards.   And with those internal standards comes accountability and responsibility. If you ever expect to conquer unhealthy habits, you must be committed to implementing the changes necessary to do so. Does anyone have any suggestions?"

"I occasionally splurge and eat some of the foods I like, but only once in a while, not every day. Fried chicken was a big weakness for me. Then my friends told me that it's only the skin that's harmful, and that if you remove it, you're okay," Mary said.

"Trevor, please feel free to jump in anytime you'd like," Kelly said.

"First of all, the average person is not going to remove the skin from fried chicken. And secondly, that's a misconception. You can't just take the skin off and think all is well with just eating the meat. Sure, a large percentage of the fat for chicken is the skin, but it's much bigger than that," Trevor said. "The main concern is the process by which the meat is cooked... deep fried... immersed and bathed in the oils. The meat immersed in the oils is just as harmful as the skin. Just look at a piece of chicken after it sits at room temperature. It will develop a white waxy buildup — the same buildup that has the potential to clog the arteries inside your body. The arteries are responsible for transporting oxygen attached to red blood cells. Even if you deep fry your meats with canola or olive oil, it's still too much oil going into your body. To sauté with olive oil is one thing, but to deep fry with it, is another. Once all that oil penetrates the meat... it remains there. And when ingested, it goes directly inside your body, eventually connecting with your arteries. I'm not saying you can't ever eat fried foods, but when you do, it should be on occasion."

"I've been reading information about calories, fat, sodium, cholesterol, and the big whammy… CARBOHYDRATES! There is so much hype about carbohydrates. Eat them. Don't eat them. You can't walk down the aisles of a grocery store, turn on the television, or pick up a magazine without seeing something about CARBS. What do you make of it all? Carbohydrates, fat, and calories. Tell me your assessment of them?" Sarah asked.

"I will start with calories, because they are what get us into trouble," Kelly said. "The body needs calories for energy. But our pattern of eating too many calories — and not burning enough of them off through activity more than likely will lead to weight gain."

"How do you know the number of calories to eat per day?" another lady asked.

"One of the things I do for all class participants is calculate their caloric intake. For my newcomers, if you complete a food record form, I'll conduct a nutritional analysis for you that shows what percent of the food you eat is fat, carbohydrate, or protein," Kelly said, while placing the forms on a desk. "For others, there are so many calorie calculators on the Internet. You just need to do a search for calorie calculators. You enter your height, weight, sex, age, level of activity, and presto! The number of calories you should consume per day will appear. The number will increase depending on daily activities."

"How about the number of carbohydrates?" the lady asked.

"Mildred, aside from the nutritional analysis, I will tell you how many carbohydrates, protein and fat grams you should consume based on your caloric intake, using the commonly referred ratio of 40/30/30 — 40% of calories should come from carbohydrates, and 30% from proteins and 30% from fats. For example, let's say you want to maintain a body weight of 150 pounds, basically you need to eat 1500 calories daily. Therefore, 40% — 900 calories of your food should come from carbohydrates. Nutritional labels refer to carbohydrates by grams. Here's how to do the math: 40% of 1500 calories is 900 calories, and 900 calories divided by 4 calories per gram equals 225 grams of carbohydrates per day," Kelly said, while writing the information on a flip chart.

"Okay, I understand. Before I lost my first 37 pounds, I weighed around 205 pounds. A weight I didn't want to maintain," Sarah said.

"The key is to start thinking about both the quantity and quality of calories," Trevor said. "Most foods and drinks contain calories. Some foods, such as broccoli, contain few calories - (1/2 cup of cooked broccoli contains approximately 47 calories). Other foods, like chocolate covered peanuts, contain a lot of calories (250 calories for a pack). I've had clients tell me they eat at least two packs in a day — a whooping 500 calories per day in candy alone. Five hundred calories in candy is too much quantity and too much poor quality. Start monitoring the calories in your foods by looking at the nutrition label. Don't only pay attention to the number of calories, but also the quality. Depending on your daily allotment of calories, 500 at a setting might not be bad... only if it's 500 of the right type of calories. For example, at breakfast, a bowl of oatmeal and a glass of soy milk, with some fruit, as opposed to a honey bun and a cola, or a blueberry muffin and a grande maple macchiato with whole milk."

"That's exactly what I need to start monitoring more closely... quantity and quality of CALORIES," Sarah said.

"Crackers and chips are the worst. It's not until you get the calculator out that you realize how much damage you're doing," Kelly said.

"I usually eat a whole roll of Ritz crackers — the ones that contain four rolls in a box," a woman named Priscilla admitted.

Kelly pointed to the table where various packages and containers of food were displayed. She invited Priscilla to join her.

"When you look at the nutritional label on the box, a serving of five crackers equals 80 calories. There are thirty-five crackers in one roll. Now let's add that up!" Kelly said, handing Priscilla a calculator.

"Eighty divided by five equals sixteen. One cracker is 16 calories. Eating a whole roll that consists of thirty-five crackers multiplied by sixteen is 560 calories," Kelly said, looking at Priscilla.

"WOW!" Priscilla shouted.

"Just think… if your daily caloric intake is 1500, you've already consumed over a third of your calories eating crackers, and that doesn't include the spread you might add onto the crackers," Mary said, looking at Priscilla's expression. "Even more scary is that the calories are empty calories… offering no substantial nutritional benefits."

"Another one of my favorite foods is barbecue potato chips," Priscilla said.

"Here's a bag of potato chips," Kelly said, reaching for the bag. "Eleven chips are 150 calories. Eating whole bags of chips and other high calories foods will play a pivotal role in weight gain."

"What about carbohydrates?" Sarah asked.

"Carbohydrate is the new term for starch. I remember back in the day, my grandmother telling us not to eat too many starches. She always said that a balanced meal consisted of a meat, starch, and vegetable. Nowadays we eat two to three starches in one setting, and with our huge portion sizes, it's too much," Trevor interjected.

"At one of my favorite restaurants, I usually order the potato soup for an appetizer, and the Honey Grilled Chicken that comes on top of a bed of rice pilaf, served with sour cream mashed potatoes. According to your analysis, I guess eating the potato soup, rice pilaf and sour cream mashed potatoes constitute too many carbohydrates," another lady asked.

"That's entirely too many CARBS! Carbohydrates provide us with energy. Most foods contain carbohydrates, which the body breaks down into simple sugars — the major source of energy for the body. So don't get caught up in the low-carb madness. It's the types and amounts you should focus on. Based on the 1500 daily allotment, I said 900 of those calories should come from carbohydrates — 225 grams. Using the same cracker example…

that same five crackers per serving contains 10 grams of carbohydrates. Priscilla add that up, please!"

"Okay… thirty-five crackers divided by five equals seven, and seven multiplied by 10 grams equals 70 grams," Priscilla said. "I get it. So 225 grams minus 70 grams leaves me with a remainder of 150 grams."

"The main point to come away with is that 70 grams represents about one-third of your daily allowance," Trevor said.

"There's no telling how many carbs were in my potato soup, rice pilaf, and sour cream mashed potatoes," Doris commented. "What are some of the other things we should consider?"

"Please understand that your body needs carbs contrary to all the controversy. What you want to do is stay away from the BAD CARBS and an excessive amount of carbs. Good carbohydrates are high in fiber… contain essential vitamins and minerals… and low in calories. They include fruits, vegetables and whole-grain products like whole-wheat pasta, whole-grain rice, and whole-wheat bread. Bad carbs are processed carbohydrates where the essentials have been stripped away and replaced with fat, better known as refined products. They include white bread and other products made with white flour, like pancakes. They are your cakes, cookies, donuts, and candy bars. They are in your fried foods… foods that are battered and breaded," Trevor said. "Although the good carbs are great, moderation is still key, because CALORIES COUNT."

"I've started choosing wheat over white," Sarah said.

"That's a great start!" Trevor confirmed.

"My ex and I were big entertainers. When we hosted our parties, there was a range of catered foods depending on the theme — spinach, cheese and artichoke dip, mozzarella sticks, honey BBQ wings, cheddar and bacon potato skins, chicken quesadilla rolls, pepperoni pizza bites, chicken breast tenders, shrimp cakes, crab cakes, stuffed crabs, lasagna…," Mary confessed. "As you can tell we loved to eat. When I decided to change my ways, I knew my biggest challenge would be hurdling the obstacles — the foods I loved so much. For my own sake, I knew I couldn't waste energy dwelling on the obstacles, I had to move forward with extinguishing unfavorable habits."

"I can't fathom giving up those same favorites," Sarah said.

"Well, just so you'll know... I've learned that the consumption of those foods combined with all the other stuff I was eating daily was setting the stage for a volcanic reaction in the form of disease and illness," Mary admitted.

"To put it another way, she was eating a waterfall of foods that were creating an incubator for disease and illness," Kelly added.

"Okay, specifically tell me about the spinach, cheese and artichoke dip. My friends and I can eat bowls of the stuff with tortilla chips at happy hour," Sarah admitted.

"Calories, fat, and sodium can vary depending on whether you purchase your foods from a restaurant, the frozen food section or precooked meals at the grocery store... or even prepare the food yourself from a recipe. Two tablespoons of the pre-packaged spinach dip from our neighborhood restaurant has 40 calories, 2 grams of carbohydrates, 2.5 grams of total fat, 135 milligrams of sodium," Kelly revealed, while reading from the empty container. "Sounds like you and your friends eat a lot more than two tablespoons? Combine those numbers with the calories, carbohydrates, fat, and sodium in tortilla chips — your consumption is probably well on its way to being over one-third of what your daily allotted intake consist of. One mozzarella stick is approximately 110 calories, 7 grams of carbohydrates, 6 grams of total fat, 260 milligrams of sodium. That's just one stick. How many sticks would you eat?"

"Depending on the variety of appetizers we'd order, probably around four," Sarah said.

"With your four sticks, you're already at 440 calories, 28 grams of carbohydrates, 24 grams of total fat, 1040 milligrams of sodium," Kelly said, reading from an empty box of frozen mozzarella sticks. "Do you know the daily recommended allowance for sodium?"

"I read in one of Trevor's articles that the recommended allowance for sodium is around 2300. I've just never really thought much about it until recently," Sarah said.

"Most of the people in this class know I had high blood pressure. Although there are many reasons for high blood pressure, I know that my diagnosis came from eating foods high in sodium," Mary admitted. "Along with the stress in my life."

"As the consumer, you've got to be knowledgeable about the ways sodium can be disguised. You've got to read the food labels to scout around for the other terms used for sodium… sodium nitrite, sodium saccharin, sodium caseinate, monosodium glutamate, trisodium phosphate, sodium ascorbate, sodium bicarbonate (baking soda), sodium benzoate, sodium stearoyl lactylate, and other sodium-containing ingredients, including salt (sodium chloride)," Kelly said, while passing out a handout regarding terms used for sodium.

"If you're eating mostly in a restaurant, you really don't know how much sodium you're consuming," Alberta commented.

"Absolutely," Trevor agreed. "A news report recently aired about the menu selections in well-known restaurants. They reported on how many of the restaurants advertise their special meals — appetizers, entrée, and desserts — designed for individuals who are dieting and/or watching what they eat. But, what actually ends up on the plate may or may not be healthy. They talked about how they visited eight restaurants, and ordered some of the meals from the menu. What was interesting is that they ordered a healthy version and the regular version of a meal. For example, they ordered the healthy Oriental Chicken Pasta Salad and the regular Oriental Chicken Pasta Salad. The meals were bagged and taken to a laboratory for testing. Each meal was blended and analyzed for nutritional truths."

"Most of the restaurants now have the nutritional value of what you're getting in their healthier selections. They tell you the number of calories, carbohydrates, and fat," Doris interjected.

"That's true. However, it's what they don't tell you that can cause significant health problems. The findings from the news report revealed that most of the restaurants were accurate in advertising the nutritional value for their healthy menus. However, the report revealed that you do need to be careful about those who offer low-carbohydrate menus. Ordering a steak with vegetables can appear low-calorie and nutritious. But that steak contains a lot of saturated fat. That lobster soaked in butter sauce can also carry a large amount of fat. I shutter to think about the volume if you have steak and lobster together," Trevor said. "Also, if you think about it, you never see the sodium content listed on a menu. I know sodium content is listed on the websites of restaurants I visit. On the news report, the average sodium levels for an entrée ranged from 1,100 to 3,000. And what most don't consider is that those ranges are for the main entrée. It doesn't include that cup of soup, bisque, or gumbo you might order with your entrée, or that appetizer or that dessert. It doesn't include what you've eaten for breakfast, lunch, snacks…"

"Whew, this is going to be more difficult than I suspected. I'm almost afraid to eat," Sarah said.

"Don't be afraid. Restaurant eating is what it is. The only way you can really control what you eat is to prepare your food at home. Restaurant eating should be done on limited occasions if at all possible. If not, concentrate on eating salads with the dressing on the side. Always order baked or grilled. Try and avoid the soups, bisque, gumbos, and white pastas," Trevor said.

"Okay. What's the real deal? How does one really lose weight?" Sarah asked. "How does one actually get the weight off and keep it off? How can I combat the syndrome of starting power, but no staying power?"

"Initially, we all establish goals to lose weight… 50 pounds… 30 pounds. Well, first one must understand that they didn't gain the weight overnight, so they can't lose it overnight. A lot of times we buy into the promises of the various weight loss programs, but the only sure way is through a solid plan that includes changing our eating habits and exercising. And getting plenty of rest and drinking plenty of water. There has to be a commitment to a plan and the key component is PATIENCE," Kelly said.

"I had to learn patience," Mary admitted.

"The basic law of weight loss is that one must take in fewer calories than what their body needs. Like I mentioned earlier, you must determine how many calories your body needs. In order to lose a pound of body fat, you must burn approximately an additional 3,500 calories a week above and beyond the number of calories needed to maintain your current weight. You have to figure out how to go about burning off the 3,500 calories in a week. If your daily calorie requirement is 1800, then a calorie deficit of 500 calories a day will aid in weight loss. There are two basic methods for creating a deficit. You can eat 500 fewer calories, or integrate a combination of eating fewer calories along with exercising," Kelly said.

"I've chose to create my deficit with a combination of eating fewer calories (200) and exercising at least 45 minutes on most days," Mary said.

"That's good! Depending on a number of factors — your body weight, the fitness activity, and the intensity — you can burn over 400 calories," Kelly said. "Once you learn more about weight loss, you'll understand it better."

"Hopefully," Sarah said.

"Once you achieve your desired goals, you can eat additional calories to complement your exercising. You can eat roughly 100 calories per 30 minutes of exercise."

"That's good," Doris said. "More opportunities to eat."

"More opportunities to eat healthy," Kelly clarified. "In terms of mathematics, if you're trying to lose weight — let's say you want to lose 20 pounds, that means you'd have to burn off an extra 70,000 calories (20 multiplied by 3,500)."

"Seventy thousand!" Sarah shouted.

"A safe weight loss goal is 2 pounds per week, and that's roughly about 7,000 calories a week. Based on that estimate, it would take you around 10 weeks. We'll just say about 2 1/2 months to lose 20 pounds. There are a lot of other things to consider. I've only discussed the highlights," Trevor said.

"More. Great," Doris said with sarcasm.

"I think we'll stop here tonight. Go ahead and fill out your favorite dish cards. We'll have something scrumptious next week. For those of you who haven't experienced the healthy cooking portion of our class, you're in for a surprise. You'll learn creative strategies for making some of your favorite foods healthier. Spaghetti made with ground chicken and whole-wheat pasta. Spinach quesadillas made with whole-wheat tortillas and fresh spinach. Fish tacos made with fresh Atlantic Salmon or Tilapia, romaine lettuce and tomatoes, rolled in whole wheat tortillas."

Kelly asked Trevor to make some closing remarks.

"I thoroughly enjoyed the discussion. I have some cards if anyone is interested in contacting me after tonight. Please don't discount the importance of exercise."

After the class, Sarah thanked Mary for inviting her. Just as they prepared to go their separate ways, Mary invited Sarah to attend the upcoming Sunday morning worship service at her church. Sarah stated she wasn't big on church, but she would consider it. Moving in opposite directions, Sarah hoped she hadn't offended Mary. *I appreciate her helping me out, but I don't need to be pressured about church and religion. I had enough of that as a kid. I know if my parents don't worry me, she shouldn't.*

CHAPTER 3

The Health Alarm Rings Out Loud

*I*n a matter of weeks, Sarah had made significant improvements to her food intake. She acquired knowledge about the foods she traditionally ate. With the passing of the weeks also came a voicemail to contact Dr. Thomas' office for a follow-up appointment. *I wonder what's the problem. It's been seven weeks since my blood tests. I'm sure Dr. Thomas will be pleased with the modifications I've made to my daily lifestyle habits.*

Sitting in the waiting room, Sarah visualized lower numbers on the scale. Nurse Wrigley called her to the back. Taking off her shoes to ensure accuracy, Sarah stepped on the scale. To her surprise, she had gained ten pounds. Walking back to the examination room, she thought, *the only thing that could have led to my weight gain was the changes in my foods. It must have been the oatmeal and whole-wheat pasta. Those carbohydrates. Everyone says they add weight and now I believe them. After seven weeks, I should have lost at least another fourteen pounds.*

Dr. Thomas walked in with her chart under his arm. "How's everything going?"

Upset that she had gained ten pounds, Sarah responded with irritation, "Everything was great until I stepped on the scale." Sarah discussed the changes she had made to her diet. Listening to the quivering in her voice, Dr. Thomas complimented her. He then went on to discuss her test results.

"I apologize for the delay in contacting you, but your blood work indicated that you have high cholesterol."

Uncertain about what high cholesterol really meant, she asked the doctor for an explanation. Dr. Thomas went on to explain that one's blood cholesterol level has a lot to do with their chances of getting heart disease. "When there is too much cholesterol (a fat-like substance) in your blood, it builds up in the walls of your arteries. Over time, this buildup causes hardening of the arteries, meaning the arteries become narrowed and blood flow to the heart is slowed down or blocked. The blood carries oxygen to the heart, and if enough blood and oxygen cannot reach your heart, one may suffer chest pains. If the blood supply to a portion of the heart is completely cut off by a blockage, the result is a heart attack." He also stated that decreased blood flow to the brain could cause a stroke, as well as other illnesses and diseases.

"What causes high cholesterol?" Sarah asked Dr. Thomas.

Dr. Thomas wouldn't pinpoint any one particular reason, but stated that the food in one's diet that contains saturated fat, trans fat, and cholesterol could make blood cholesterol levels go up. "Saturated and trans fat are the key culprits, but cholesterol in foods also matters. Being overweight is a risk factor for heart disease and it also tends to increase cholesterol. Not being physically active is a risk factor for heart disease. Or, it could be due to a genetic factor."

Sarah just couldn't accept Dr. Thomas' information as true. Questioning the validity of the tests, she attempted to suggest that the equipment used for the testing was faulty. "You said you've had some problems with the lab company… what if the test results are inaccurate?" Dr. Thomas urged Sarah to accept the information she had been given and to continue the healthy style of eating she had started, along with medications he was going to prescribe.

"Sounds like you're on track with eating healthier. The bottom line is that you've got to start exercising. And that entails exercising on a consistent basis... three to five times per week. To get started, walk about twenty to thirty minutes per day, and gradually build from there," Dr. Thomas stressed as he recorded his notes. "I'm going to give you a pamphlet on high cholesterol. It will help to guide you in your continued process to eat healthier, including how to avoid dairy products high in fat like ice cream, whole milk, butter... how to trade them in for low-fat dairy products like soy or low-fat milk and yogurt. And how to reduce your intake of high fatty meats like beef... hamburgers, roast, and sausages."

After scheduling another follow-up appointment, he handed her the pamphlet and Sarah angrily exited the office.

On her way back to the office, Sarah called her boss, Mr. Weisen. She knew she wouldn't be able to concentrate on work. She wanted to wallow in self-pity. *I was healthier leaving things the way they were. All this trying to lose weight must have triggered something inside my body.* Lying on the sofa, Sarah decided to read the pamphlet. The pamphlet reinforced the regimen Dr. Thomas prescribed for reducing her cholesterol levels.

Maybe I should take Mary up on her offer to exercise together, Sarah thought, walking into her kitchen. The pamphlet stated that regular physical activity would help lower bad cholesterol and raise good cholesterol levels. Plus, it could also facilitate weight loss. "Maybe I should contact Trevor," she said to herself.

Weighing her options, she decided to call Mary to discuss the news from her doctor.

Mary could hear through the telephone the distress in Sarah's voice. Understanding Sarah's feelings, Mary encouraged her to remain positive. On the advice of her physician, Mary started exercising. She joined a cycling group and rode with them at White

Rock Lake after work and on weekends. She also participated in a jazzercise class twice a week.

"Why don't you call Trevor? He seemed like a really nice guy. And sounds like he knows a lot about fitness," Mary suggested.

"I don't know..." Sarah said, hesitantly.

"Since tomorrow is Saturday, why don't you meet me at White Rock Lake at seven-thirty in the morning? We could walk together and talk more about you contacting Trevor," Mary said.

"What about your cycling group?" Sarah asked.

"I can miss riding with the group for one Saturday. Do you have any plans... sorority meeting or something else going on?" Mary was willing to help Sarah get started with becoming physically active by whatever way possible. "You could also go with me to my Christian jazzercise class sometimes. My class is seven o'clock in the evening on Tuesdays and Fridays."

"Actually, I am free tomorrow. I would love to meet you at the lake," Sarah admitted. "What exactly is jazzercise?"

"My Christian jazzercise class combines dance, exercise and the beat of today's hottest Christian music into a fun total-body conditioning program. It's designed to enhance your cardiovascular endurance, physical strength and flexibility."

"I'm not ready for a class setting just yet," Sarah said. "I'll meet you at the lake. What should I wear? I don't have any workout clothes. Just warm-ups."

"You will definitely get overheated wearing warm-ups in May. Why don't you go by Catherines, Sports Authority, or Macy's? They all have great prices on walking shorts and tops," Mary said. "Also, you do want to get a good sports bra that provides support for those of us with a DD, EE, FF and so on cup sizes. I don't know your size, but walking through the clothing section at Walmart the other day, I noticed that they carry 42D."

"I didn't know Walmart had stuff like that," Sarah said.

"Walmart has everything. They are Danskin bras, which is a pretty popular brand."

"Great, I'll go by there after work. Are the workout clothes at Catherines, Sports Authority, or Macy's cute and stylish?" Sarah asked. "I have some cute pink and green tennis shoes I would like to match up."

"I don't know about cute and stylish, but they all have a wide selection of workout attire. I was impressed with the fact that Sports Authority has plus sizes," Mary said. "I don't think your pink and green tennis shoes are going to be appropriate walking shoes. You definitely need to go by Luke's Locker to get guidance on appropriate walking shoes. We don't want you to develop any foot or leg problems because of inappropriate footwear. Luke's Locker is over off Maplewille Lane."

"Okay. One thing for sure... I definitely don't want those biking shorts that ride up on you," Sarah said.

"It's all about fabric. Good workout clothes are made with technical fabrics that are comfortable and adjust to the outdoor temperature. They don't irritate your skin. And they remove the water... that is, sweat away from your skin, keeping you dry. You definitely don't want to exercise in cotton, like a cotton t-shirt."

"Why not? A cotton t-shirt was the choice attire back in the day. Cotton absorbs the sweat. Plus, I already have a bunch of cotton t-shirts from my travels."

"Cotton, when it gets wet, tends to get heavy, cling to your skin, and weigh you down. And that's not good for the exerciser who's trying to move quickly without any distractions. You want to wear attire that's going to keep you dry and not irritate your skin," Mary said.

"How will I know if the clothing is made from technical fabric?" Sarah asked.

"A statement will be on the garment's tag or label, saying something like, 'rapidly moves moisture away from the body to the outer layer of the fabric, where it evaporates,'" Mary said. "Or, you'll see short phrases, 'keeps you dry... breathable... moves moisture from your skin... wicking.'"

"That's good to know," Sarah said.

"And it's the same for socks. Don't wear cotton socks. Your socks should be a synthetic brand that removes moisture from your feet, keeping them dry also. Wearing shoes that are too tight and cotton socks can cause you to form blisters on your feet."

"I see. I'll go by Catherines or Macy's this evening, also," Sarah said. "They are both on my way home from work."

"Great. I'll see you in the morning."

"I almost forgot, what about your hair? How do you keep it stylish and healthy looking everyday? Don't you sweat?" Sarah asked.

"My hair is always drenched when I finish exercising. I wear a breathable mesh wrap to hold it in place and I keep it on until my hair dries. Depending on your hair, frequent washing, blow drying, and hot curling can wreak havoc. That's why good hair products are important," Mary responded. "I'm using the entire line of KeraCare hair products. I go to my hair salon every six to seven weeks for a relaxer. During the interim, I use KeraCare's moisturizing shampoo and conditioner once a week. I also use their *Silken Seal* when I hot curl my hair. It provides protection from the heat. Their other moisturizing oils and crèmes are also particularly good. Everyone's hair is different and requires different techniques and products for maintenance, so check with your stylist for recommendations. And always remember that drinking plenty of water everyday helps with moisture."

The following day, Mary and Sarah met at the lake as planned. Mary started the conversation by telling Sarah how her life had changed with exercise. In the beginning, she also refused to exercise. But, once she shifted her focus to figuring out what she liked, rather than what she disliked, she was on her way to her health transformation. Her discovery of cycling and jazzercise exposed her to more than just exercise — it opened the door to a relationship with God. Aside from improving her physical strength, she gained the mental strength to overcome the internal struggles she had battled for years. For once in her life, she had the courage to follow her inner voice.

"Okay. So, what other advice do have for me starting out?" Sarah asked, as they began walking.

"You have to find an activity that you like and will stick with. For me, it's cycling. I love being outdoors, enjoying the scenery. Communing with nature," Mary said, handing Sarah a bottle of water. "In the beginning, I had some challenges to maneuver around. For instance, I was a much larger size when I started. I had to overcome the fear of what others thought about me — a big girl exercising amongst the skinny folks. I had to learn to focus on enjoying myself. Then there was the difficulty I had locating large padded biking shorts. Luckily for me, they sell large, comfortable double padded seats."

"Um..."

"You want to get in the habit of carrying water on your exercise sessions to replace water lost by perspiration and to prevent dehydration," Mary said. "What I've found helpful are the water fuel belts that fit around your waist. Once again, in the beginning, I couldn't find one to fit around my waist. But now, I'm good to go."

"Where would you purchase one?" Sarah asked.

"You can get them at Sports Authority. I'm sorry... I forgot to mention it yesterday. A lot of them feature convenient pockets to carry your keys, money and identification. They don't bounce. Most include a 20-ounce water bottle. And most expand out more, giving the larger individuals more room."

After thirty minutes of health talk, Sarah and Mary were back at their cars. Sarah inquired about the worship services at Mary's church. She wanted to attend next Sunday's service. Elated beyond words, Mary eagerly wrote the directions and the church's telephone number on a piece of paper, and encouraged her to visit their website.

Driving back home, Sarah felt better than she had in years. Not only did she feel better physically, she felt better about herself. *I need to get a registration form for the company's 5K event. I think I'll participate this year. Maybe I can hire Trevor to help me get ready.*

Over the years, she either made up an excuse or planned a trip out of town on that Saturday. This year would be different. *Great! There's the grocery store. I need to start cooking more of my meals. I can try and make the chicken spaghetti dish we ate in Kelly's class. Maybe I can make this idea of cooking fun. I just need to stop being lazy and making excuses.* Sarah had been carrying around the ingredients to the recipe in her planner for weeks. Sarah's trips to the grocery store were typically for snack foods, sodas, and frozen dinners.

Kelly's discussions about the amount of hidden sodium and other unfavorable products in restaurant foods prompted her to make additional changes. *It couldn't be that much trouble to cook at least three times a week, plus, I could take my lunch.*

Gathering all the essential ingredients, she almost forgot to get some vegetables — zucchini, squash, and broccoli to steam and add to the meat sauce. Kelly talked about how adding vegetables to a meal enhanced the nutritional value. While checking out, the cashier commented on all the healthy stuff she was purchasing. Sarah explained to the cashier that she was practicing healthier eating habits.

On her way home, Sarah called Mary to get further guidance on making the spaghetti, "Hi Mary. I'm sorry to bother you on this beautiful Saturday afternoon."

"Hey lady… what are you up to?" Mary responded.

"I'm on my way home from the grocery store. I'm going to make the chicken spaghetti Kelly prepared in class."

"Great!"

"I purchased everything on the list of ingredients. The 'no salt added' tomato sauce, mushrooms, garlic, bell pepper, onion, oregano, basil, fresh tomatoes, and seasonings to make the meat sauce. I never realized how much sodium the name-brand tomato sauces have…" Sarah said astonished.

"After being diagnosed with high blood pressure, I had to look for ways to avoid excess sodium. That basically meant shrinking my intake of processed and restaurant foods. I had to start eating whole foods, which meant I had to cook soups, stews, sauces and other foods from scratch, rather than buying them canned, frozen or packaged."

"I find that my food isn't flavorful until I add salt," Sarah said.

"We do need sodium to live. It helps our bodies maintain fluid levels, electrolyte balance… and it regulates muscle contractions and nerve impulses among other things. The problem is that we're consuming more salt than what the body needs. It's just like cholesterol. Our bodies make it and need it, but we're consuming more than the body requires. The three ounces of meat for lunch and dinner is what's safe for our daily intake. But, we overdo it. That chicken fried steak you mentioned during our first lunch together was four times the amount anyone needs at one setting. More than likely, you were accustomed to eating the entire serving of chicken fried steak, plus some other major meat for breakfast and/or dinner. The repeated daily installments of hefty meat servings, mixed with other animal products like milk, cheese and eggs, possibly led to your high cholesterol."

"I hear what you're saying. So, what now? I'm getting ready to cook chicken spaghetti. That's meat! Cholesterol!" Sarah said. trying to listen to Mary and concentrate on her driving.

"Always remember… it's about portion sizes. You shouldn't eat more than three-fourths cup of the meat sauce with a cup of the whole-wheat pasta. Be sure to pile on the mixed steamed vegetables. And remember… you don't have to eat meat at every meal," Mary emphasized.

"Okay, I'm set to do this," Sarah said. "I'm at home… driving into the garage… hold on while I reposition my earpiece and get these bags out of the car."

After a few minutes, Sarah was situated in her home. The original conversation was really the prelude to what Sarah wanted to discuss with Mary.

"Mary, I've been thinking about your invitation to your church. I feel like my life is missing something. I can't explain it… but I have a yearning to do something different. I've thought about the pain you told me about with your ex and your family, and it triggered some memories I had buried in my past. I thought they were buried, but they never really go away. I tried over and over to understand my allegiance to work, material things, food... and not myself. When I come to that proverbial fork in the road in regards to work and things... and pleasing others, I always make the right turn. The best decision. When it comes to myself, I always take a left turn. The wrong decision. It's like I don't see myself worthy of good."

"I was like that, Sarah," Mary said. "I guess that's why I remained in an unhealthy relationship for so long. I didn't see myself worthy of anything different. A relationship with Christ Jesus helped me to understand that I was loved and deserved the best. I had to let go of the anger I was harboring. A few Sundays ago, my Pastor preached about 'Having the Character of Christ.'"

"Have you forgiven your mother and your ex?" Sarah asked.

"I can't be like Christ if I don't forgive those who have hurt, misused, and abused me. Don't get me wrong, forgiveness didn't come easy, but through prayer and the Word, I did it."

"Visions of the past are starting to haunt me more frequently. Events from my childhood that I've tried to suppress are constantly in my thoughts."

"What could be that haunting that you've held it in for so long?"

"When I was a little girl, I remembered being fondled by older cousins and the sitters my parents entrusted to look after me."

"How were you fondled? Did you report it to anyone?"

"I don't think I realized what it was until I was older. I remember one of the older boys in the neighborhood having me perform unnatural acts on him. His sister and I were playmates."

"Do you mean oral sex... anal sex? Where were your parents? Your brothers? How old were you!"

"My parents were workaholics, always gone... working late... and my older brothers were always gone, participating in sports."

"How old were you?" Mary asked.

"I had to be anywhere from six to eight years of age. I don't remember. The sexual encounter with the older cousin happened when I was around nine or ten. That's the one that haunts me the most. And that cousin was a girl. She was around eighteen or nineteen," Sarah said as her voice began to tremble. "I've never shared this with anyone else. For years I've tried to block it out of my mind, but the memories won't go away. They just keep running around, and around, and around!"

"Have you thought about counseling? I know carrying around a secret of that magnitude for so long can be overwhelming. You should consider joining a support group. You would be in an environment to speak freely with others who have experienced and overcome the same horrors of sexual abuse."

"I've thought about it. I just think I need a diversion in my life. After listening to you, I think my diversion has been food. Living the high life. Pushing myself to be successful. I often feel guilty and ashamed. Why did he make me put my mouth on his private areas? Why did she touch my private areas the way she did? It hurts to think about it. Above all, I know romantic relationships have been influenced; I'm unable to trust others."

"Whatever happened to the boy and your cousin?"

"The boy and his family moved out of the neighborhood. My cousin on the other hand is still around. We only see each other every few years... at some family gathering or funeral. I often wonder if she remembers what she did to me. I could never say anything about it. She's seen as a model person. Heavily involved in the church and all. And I know disclosure of the secret would send shockwaves throughout my family."

"I've learned that you can't erase the past. And you can't get stuck in time. No situation is beyond the restorative powers of God. God has the power to annihilate the horrors you experienced as a child. If you trust God to reach in and remove your hurt, pain, burdens... your life can be different," Mary said. "First, you must accept Christ Jesus as your personal savior and believe in the Word given to us."

"That's exactly what I want to do. What times are your church services?" Sarah asked.

"Eight and eleven o'clock on Sunday mornings," Mary said. "To be honest, I had to separate myself from those things that caused me to be angry and resentful. After relying on the Word for guidance, I was able to confront the fears that tormented me. I've forgiven my mother and we have a better relationship. Our mother-daughter collision course has changed into a crusade for peace and understanding. Conner, my ex, on the other hand is angry with me because he no longer has mental control over me. But, that's okay. The point is that I've moved on, and now I'm living a life that's pleasing to God."

CHAPTER 4

Withstanding the Tests of Temptation

eeks later, Sarah had a new lease on life. She had solicited the services of Trevor to help her get on track with a healthier lifestyle. A devout Christian, he helped Sarah to create balance and reduce the distractions in her life. Each day was filled with anticipation, rather than despair. No longer held hostage to her insecurities, there was a freedom to unveil the real Sarah. Not just physically, but she had matured spiritually, emotionally and socially. The gift of obedience and discipline allowed her to eliminate what was harmful in achieving a healthy mind, body, and soul.

Sarah recognized that through prayer and faith her life could prosper in areas unimagined. She eventually united with Friendship Missionary Baptist Church and became involved in ministry work. The gratification she experienced from serving and helping others surpassed the people and worldly possessions that were the focus of the first half of her adult life. She was beginning to recognize and accept the purpose of her existence.

It had been months since Sarah hung out with her girlfriends, but now it was time for their cruise. The telephone rang. Sarah looked at the caller I.D. and recognized the number as Cathy's. "Hi Cathy."

"Hi Sarah. We haven't heard from you in a while. Is everything okay?" Cathy asked. "We've missed you at happy hour. Marvin has been asking about you. We didn't know what to tell him since we haven't heard from you. And I know you've satisfied your twelve months probation at Bell and Yates. We definitely needed to celebrate that."

"Everything is great. I did make probation, but I had to step back and take a look at the direction my life was heading. I had to get my priorities in order. I didn't realize it at the time, but I was headed down a road to disaster," Sarah admitted.

"Okay," Cathy said, hesitating. "Are you still planning to go on the cruise with us?"

"Yes, I am," Sarah responded.

"Great! Marcie is getting the alcohol together. Do you want her to get you some Cognac? She is going to get a bunch of assorted miniature bottles."

"Actually, I've stopped drinking alcohol. That was one of the most significant changes I had to make in my life," Sarah said, waiting for Cathy's reaction.

"Okay," Cathy said with a slight pause. "We'll just plan on drinking by ourselves. The travel agency mailed our cruise information to Marcie. Let's plan on meeting at the airport on Thursday at six o'clock in the morning. The flight for Miami leaves at 8:30."

"Sounds good. What are you packing?" Sarah asked.

"Mainly shorts and tank tops. I know we'll need evening attire for the Captain's dinner. Also, we'll probably need some casual wear if we decide to attend some of the special shows. I've heard the shows are like the ones you'll find in Las Vegas — showgirls, dancers, comedians, and singers. The good thing for us is that the shows are included in our cost. Are you bringing a swimsuit? What about extra money for the casinos?"

"I haven't been shopping yet, but I'm going to try and find a swimsuit," Sarah said. "I doubt I'll be spending money in the casino."

"Okay, we'll see you on Thursday. Don't forget your dancing shoes. Maybe we'll get to do the Electric Slide or the Macarena in Grand Cayman. And I will be sporting my itsy bitsy teeny weeny black and white striped bikini," Cathy said proudly.

The cruise came at a pivotal time in Sarah's life. It could turn out to be the "deal breaker". Up until this point, she had managed to stay on track with her healthier lifestyle transition, but that was partly because she had removed herself from her social traditions — happy hour with her girls and all-you-can-eat buffets. Now she would be faced with dancing and partying — activities known for pulling her into a scene of heavy drinking and excessive eating.

A week later, Sarah, Cathy, and Marcie met at the airport to catch their flight to Miami where their cruise ship to Grand Cayman and Ocho Rios, Jamaica would embark.

Standing in line waiting to check in their luggage, Cathy and Marcie were astonished by Sarah's new look. "You look great, Sarah," Cathy said, admiring Sarah's noticeable weight loss.

"Hi ladies. It's good to see you guys," Sarah said, embracing Cathy and Marcie.

"You've lost weight!" Marcie replied. "A lot of weight! How did you do it? Did you go on a diet or something?"

Sarah wasn't a size eight, but she had settled quite nicely into a size twelve. "Actually, I just decided to take that quantum leap forward to lose weight and get healthy," Sarah admitted. "This is the best I've ever felt about myself."

Enjoying the onboard experience of their fun ship, *Imagination*... those words of encouragement handed down from Trevor a day earlier, directed Sarah's every move. Uninhibited, she explored the adventures of kayaking on secluded shorelines, snorkeling and jet skiing in clear waters. Committed to healthier habits, she resisted the tempting grand gala buffet, ice cream parties, 24-hour pizzeria, bars and clubs. She awoke each morning at 6:00 a.m. and headed to the workout facility. For the first time in her life, she felt comfortable mixing with others. In the past, she had felt self-conscious about her size, but now things were different. She finally felt that she fit in. Preparing for the company's 5K walk and run dominated her thoughts. She knew she had to stick with the training schedule Trevor had developed if she was going to walk and jog during the event. Cathy and Marcie, on the other hand, spent their days partaking in the daily cruise rituals… drink specials, the captain's afternoon cocktail parties, and the nightly club scene.

"It's nine o'clock. Time to get the party started! There's a party on the main deck. We only have one more night after tonight," Cathy said, looking through her closest. "Sarah, are you going to the midnight buffet with us? We can alternate between the dance and the midnight buffet!"

"No, I think I'll retire early so I can hit the gym in the morning," Sarah said.

"It's a seafood buffet. I know you're watching what you eat, but how fattening is seafood. Lobster, king crab legs, shrimp, crawfish and lobster bisque, shrimp scampi, seafood gumbo, clam chowder, mussels, and scallops. All of our favorites included in the price."

"Stop! Stop! Don't say another word! Seafood! You're treading on my favorites. I just can't do it. Since my health transformation, I've been attending a healthy-living class on Thursdays. And I have a fitness consultant, Trevor, who has taught me so much about the foods I've traditionally eaten…" Sarah said while fluffing her hair and sighing. "Seafood and the assorted dishes have a lot of calories. It's hard to conceptualize the amount of calories, fat, and sodium I was consuming when we ate at Nick's Seafood Circle."

"I thought seafood was low in calories," Marcie said.

"Seafood is low in fat, calories and carbohydrates," Sarah said, "and according to my dietician, cold-water fish like salmon and mackerel are packed with omega-3 fatty oil, the good fat known for promoting a healthy heart."

"Okay, so that all sounds good to me," Marcie responded.

"It would be good if we ate those foods straight... baked, broiled, grilled or steamed... not battered, breaded and fried. The preparation of potentially healthy seafood items can quickly turn from good cop to bad cop... high in fat and sodium, saturated with cocktail sauces, tartar sauces, and heavy cream sauces. When you combine everything that we eat in one setting at a buffet, it's a lot," Sarah said. "At Nick's, the fried seafood platter with fish, shrimp and clams with fries, hushpuppies and coleslaw is a great example of high calories — based on my tally that platter is around 1,240 – 1,600 calories and over 70 grams of fat depending on the portion size. The fried calamari is around 360 calories and 12 grams of fat per serving. I don't want to consider the volume of sodium. I don't know how we even managed to walk out. Then there were the drinks. Alcoholic beverages can carry up to 600 calories and a lot more depending on the alcohol and ingredients used in our specialty drinks. That's calories in addition to those we've consumed while eating. And you guys know we generally averaged two to three drinks."

"What do you mean?" Cathy said, assisting Sarah with straightening her hair. "How do you know those numbers?"

"I've been using calorie counting tools from the Internet and a little handbook I purchased at the grocery store. I've discovered that those seafood buffets carry a huge amount of calories. Mix all of that with a few drinks — it's a health torpedo in waiting."

"That's pretty strong... a torpedo in waiting," Marcie responded. "Give me a break."

"Is that why you stopped drinking?" Cathy asked.

"Yes. Once I increased my knowledge about calories overall, especially the calories in alcoholic beverages, I stopped," Sarah said, pausing before she continued. "To be honest, my reason for eliminating the alcohol was much bigger than the calories and the fact that they presented more harm than good to my body. Bottom line... I was using the alcohol as an escape from the things hurting me inside."

"Hurt... what hurt! You've got it going on," Cathy responded. "I wish I was a top marketing executive... and all of those success stories you tell us about."

"The stories... the eating... the drinking were the diversions I used to mask my unhappiness and insecurities with self," Sarah added, contemplating whether or not she should share the horrors of her childhood with Cathy and Marcie.

"What about your infamous V.S.O.P cognac?" Marcie asked.

"Some information I found on the Internet indicated that one ounce is about 69 calories. I can't bring myself to imagine how many calories I've inhaled after an evening of hanging out. I remember one time drinking almost an entire bottle."

"I remember that night. You stayed in bed all day the next day," Marcie said. "How do you know that the information on the Internet is true and accurate?"

"I don't know, but it's the best estimate I have. With any information on the Internet, they explain that they do their best to provide the most accurate information on beverages and food items, but that the nutritional facts for alcoholic beverages is extremely difficult to attain or research. For me, it basically provides a frame of reference. Those margaritas made with our top shelf tequila, triple sec and lime juice average around 550 calories."

"I understand what you're saying, but I'm not giving up alcohol, nor my fried seafood, gumbos, or bisque any time soon," Marcie added firmly.

"Continuing healthier habits is my path to a longer and better life," Sarah said. "For too long, I allowed unhealthy habits to chip away my ability to live longer and healthier."

"I'm curious to know what other things you have discovered," Cathy asked.

"For starters... you know the honey BBQ buffalo wings we love so much... three pieces are 190 calories and loaded with fat, cholesterol, and sodium. The numbers were about the same for our favorite cheddar and bacon potato skins and chicken quesadilla rolls," Sarah shared. "I found out that I was slowly setting myself up for a myriad of disease and illness. The bad stuff was entirely too much for my body to continue to handle. My warning sign came with a diagnosis of high cholesterol."

"High cholesterol... my mother and father have high cholesterol. You're young... how did you get it?" Cathy inquired.

"There could be a number of reasons, but I believe for me it was my diet. Once I took an inventory of the foods and beverages I was consuming daily, I discovered that I was knocking on death's door. Or, at least marching toward a band of health problems."

"Wow! I guess I'd better start thinking about making some modifications," Cathy said.

"You just might consider that. If both your parents have high cholesterol, you are probably genetically predisposed to inherit it. Now is the time to start making changes so you can reduce your risks," Sarah said. "High cholesterol can lead to cardiovascular disease, the number one killer of women."

"How did you make your changes?" Cathy asked.

"Believe me it was hard in the beginning. I gravitated towards the gimmicks of weight loss programs that promised quick results. That was in part because my initial primary focus was to lose weight. I looked and explored every option for getting the weight off quickly. My friend at work, Mary, and my trainer, Trevor, helped me to shift my focus. I'm now more concerned about being healthy on the inside. By changing the order, my outside becomes a reflection of my inside."

"What about seafood nights at your house?" Cathy asked.

"Okay, brace yourself... I discovered that the same high caloric numbers exists for our favorite shrimp cakes, crab cakes, and stuffed crab. One shrimp cake is 160 calories, one crab cake is 170 calories, and three ounces of stuffed crab is 170 calories. If we ate the recommended servings, we would consume approximately 500 calories and a lot of fat, cholesterol, and sodium. If my memory serves me correctly, we generally ate two to three times the recommended amount. Keep in mind, those figures do not include what we ate for breakfast, snacks, and lunch. And don't forget the alcoholic beverages!"

"You've definitely given me something to think about. Everything I eat comes ready-made from the restaurant or the grocery store," Cathy admitted.

"Everything I eat is pre-packaged and pre-cooked... it's quick and convenient for me to stop by the grocery deli and get a rotisserie chicken that will last me for about two days — a half one day and the other half the next. Plus, some tasty sides. Or, I can get the pre-packaged meals — battered, breaded and pre-seasoned and ready to cook in the oven or heat in the microwave — chicken fritters, buffalo bites... nuggets, tenders, or strips... plus some sides," Marcie said. "Why would I spend my evenings, after a nine hour day at work, slaving over a stove?"

"The only reason I can come up with is that it's healthier. What I discovered was that the shortcuts were hazardous to my health. Everything I gravitated towards was buttered, sautéed, fried... in a cream sauce or au gratin, all of which in most cases, denotes foods high in saturated fat, cholesterol, and sodium," Sarah shared.

"I eat at the cafeteria most days for lunch. That's healthy, right!" Cathy asked.

"What do you eat?" Sarah asked.

"The other day I ate the chicken & dumplings, praline topped sweet potato, fried okra, and a tossed green salad," Cathy said with excitement. "Wasn't that a medley of healthy selections?"

"The total meal sounds high in calories. Personally, my old recipe for chicken & dumplings wasn't healthy. The main ingredients like cream of chicken soup is high in sodium. Whole milk is high in fat. Biscuit baking mix is high in sodium and fat. Chicken and eggs are high in cholesterol. I don't think the recipe for the one at the cafeteria is going to be very different. Just think, those ingredients mixed with the ingredients in the praline topped sweet potato and fried okra is a lot. The tossed green salad was probably your best item, and that depends on the extras and salad dressing you used."

"You're sure putting a damper on this trip!" Marcie said.

"Don't get me wrong, eating chicken & dumplings every so often is okay. But, don't eat chicken & dumplings, praline topped sweet potato, fried okra, a tossed green salad and a roll on Monday. Chicken & sour cream enchiladas, refried beans, and spanish style rice on Tuesday. Chicken tetrazzini, candied sweet potatoes, mashed potatoes and gravy, and cornbread on Wednesday. Chicken fried steak, mashed potatoes and gravy, corn, navy beans and garlic toast on Thursday. Southern fried fish, macaroni and cheese, hushpuppies, and turnip greens on Friday. It's just too much. And once again, you haven't even considered your breakfast, snacks, and dinner on those days. And don't forget happy hour! It's all about your CHOICES!"

"So, what are we supposed to do? Those are the things we like to eat," Cathy said.

"I'm not saying you can't eat those foods. The key is to work at discovering ways to make the food you like to eat healthier," Sarah said, "and eating the right portion sizes."

"Okay, now that you've said all of that... how do we make changes? That's what we need to know. HOW!" Cathy asked.

"It's all about substituting unhealthy items for healthy items. The only way you can make sure that happens is to start preparing the food yourself."

"You've been exercising the entire trip. What's that all about? I guess you really didn't come to hang out with us?" Marcie suggested.

"Exercise and healthier eating is like Batman and Robin, the two complement one another. True enough, you can lose weight by reduced eating or excessive exercising, but the combination of the two have prove most effective for me. I'm not into some extreme makeover, but I'm going to do what's necessary to safeguard my body from future health concerns. Some people dive into an exercise program and end up crashing. Trevor started me on a moderate program of walking and jogging. To keep me motivated and on track, I've made a commitment to participate in some of the local races, like the 5K walk/run event my company is sponsoring."

"The last thing I have time for is exercise," Marcie responded. "I'm restoring my home, and each evening I'm dealing with these non-responsive contractors. After working all day, and trying to combat their shanenigans, the last thing I want to do is exercise," she confessed.

"Just admit it, you don't want to exercise. Time is not the problem. If you can find time for happy hour two and three nights a week, and your other social gatherings, you can find time to exercise," Sarah said.

"Happy hour relaxes me," Marcie said. "There's effort involved in exercise. Effort that requires effort. After dealing with drama all day at work, the last thing I want to employ is more effort."

"I know what she means. Trying to get my business off the ground takes up a lot of my time. Most nights, I'm working into the wee hours trying to prepare bids and proposals," Cathy added. "The stress of trying to achieve a steady stream of income is what consumes me. The jaws of failure knocking at my back door can be overwhelming when I'm alone at night. Marcie's right... those two nights of happy hour relaxes me. After an evening of drinking, the only thing I can do is jump in bed."

"Once again, those two or three nights of happy hour can be replaced with an activity that provides real value to your life," Sarah confirmed. "Plus, it will probably help you save money while you create that steady stream of income. It's all about what's important to you. Once you really understand the scope of a healthier lifestyle, you will do what's necessary to achieve it. We often talk about stress. Exercise relieves stress. The body's release of good chemicals, the happy chemicals, helps to combat the pressures of life. Aside from those two nights during the week, you can find an hour on a Saturday and Sunday to exercise. Making simple modifications to your daily routine can accommodate an exercise program. Personally, I was expending time with activities that didn't advance me. Happy hour, the latest T.V. shows, and social gatherings dominated my life. The things I pursued added no value to my life."

"So, I guess with your newfound revelations, hanging out with us at happy hour added no value to your life?" Marcie said angrily.

"All I'm saying is that I wasn't happy doing what I was doing. Drinking was a way to mask the pain I felt inside. Pain I had denied and dismissed," Sarah shared. "The whole transformation has created in me an awareness of God's expectations for my life. No longer consumed with things and people, I've committed myself to being a servant. I've realized that I had to connect and redirect the traditional programming of inactivity and poor eating habits. The hazards that lie in restaurant foods helped to solidify my position. Keep in mind that we're approaching forty, quickly. When you're younger, your body is resilient, able to rebound from sickness and illness. As you get older, the effects of an unhealthy lifestyle begin to catch up with you. You might not make it out alive."

"Aren't you the rain on our parade, or better, the rain that ruined the deck party. I'm not ready to put in motion some major transformation just yet. All that research about food and exercising is not important to me at this point in my life," Marcie said, while preparing to head out the door. "Sarah, I've heard enough. It's time to party. I'll wait until I get back home to start considering changes. I'm on this cruise to eat, drink, and be merry!"

The cruise ended two days later. Although they didn't make it to Jamica due to Hurricane Allison, they had a memorable time on and off the ship. Sarah would never forget hanging out in Grand Cayman, exploring Seven Mile Beach, visiting the turtle farm and the town of Hell. And working out in the state-of-the-art fitness center, experiencing a soothing massage, and walking and jogging around the outdoor track enjoying the spectacular ocean views. Among many of her discoveries, Sarah recognized the path she was pursuing was different from that of Marcie and Cathy. Their lives had taken different turns, and she knew it would be their last trip together.

Sarah decided to visit her parents in Missouri City, Texas on her way back home from the cruise. While getting a bottle of perfume at First Colony Mall, she ran into an old flame.

"Wow, you look good!" Donavan exclaimed. He looked Sarah over from head to toe.

"Hi Donavan, it's great to see you!" Sarah replied.

"It's been a while. How have you been doing?" Donavan asked.

"Actually, I'm doing great. Life is good. I'm a marketing executive for Bell and Yates Marketing Solutions," Sarah stated. "What about you?"

"Everything is great with me. I'm still in retail management, plus I started a landscape business about four years ago. Business is good. I'm making a lot of money," Donavan boasted proudly. "How much are you making now? I know it's a lot."

"That's a little personal, don't you think?"

"Girl, we're like family. Back in the day, we always talked money. All we talked about as kids was making a lot of money, driving fancy cars… getting out the hood."

"$165,000."

"$165,000! You're doing real good! From the looks of your finger, you're still single. I can't believe no one has snatched you up."

"Yes, I am. Still single, that is. Don't get caught up on the $165,000. That's good money. Dad often says he would have been rich earning that kind of money in his day. What he doesn't understand is that I should be earning a lot more. Even though I'm top in my field, I'm treated differently. My male executive counterparts are earning $195,000. And I have to work twice as hard to get the better accounts."

"That's a big disparity," Donavan commented. "It's just so good to see you. How long are you going to be in town?"

"I'm just here for a day."

"I've got somewhere to be in an hour," Donavan said, looking at his watch. "Can I call you sometime? I know we ended on a sour note the last time we communicated. I tried and tried to contact you to apologize, but… Anyway, hopefully we can talk about old times. I am sorry for the way things turned out, and hope you give me an opportunity to make up for my past bad behavior."

"Sure, call me. We can play catch-up; although, I feel like I know everything based on your brief synopsis," Sarah said, smiling at him. "Here's my card with all my numbers."

"Great! Man, you look good," Donavan said, hurrying off.

As Donavan walked away, Sarah remembered how much she loved Donavan years ago. She also couldn't help but remember how he broke her heart with his lies and dishonesty. *Why am I focusing on something I shouldn't? We haven't seen each other in years. I'm already putting too much into one meeting. The past is the past. Maybe we can revive that old friendship. Mary says I can't be like Christ if I don't forgive those who have hurt, misused, and abused me,* Sarah thought to herself, walking out to the parking lot.

CHAPTER 5

Saving A Flourishing Workplace

*B*ack at work a few days later, Sarah noticed significant changes in their workforce. She noticed that her fellow employees were having a difficult time physically managing the daily routines of life. Those wheezing noises Joey made walking down the hallway; the panting sounds of Rony working at his desk; the way Miruth gasped for air while strolling to the elevator; the oozing of perspiration from Jerry's face while he explained the results of his market research, were all sounds and visions of ticking time bombs. Potential heart attack or stroke were imminent. It was no wonder, with the sounds of opening candy wrappers, potato chip bags, cookie packages, and the clicking of soda cans that consumed the office area all day. The aroma of freshly popped popcorn left a buttery and salty scent throughout the hallways during the mornings and afternoons.

The company had already begun talks about increasing the employee's portion of health care coverage because of the exorbitant increase in claims. Sarah knew she had to do something, so she decided to visit with Mary.

"Mary, do you have a moment?" Sarah asked, while walking into Mary's office.

"Sure, I do," Mary replied. "How was your trip?"

"It was great. I don't mean to cut you off, but I've been noticing the changes in everyone on my floor and in the building. Everyone is getting larger. I guess I didn't notice it when I was larger. But now I'm noticing how most of the people here eat junk all day, like cookies, candy bars, chips, sodas, and ice cream sandwiches. I even saw Stephanie eating fried chicken legs for breakfast Monday morning," Sarah stated in disbelief. "I overheard her saying it was the only thing she had at home that was quick and convenient. The next day I saw her eating leftover Chinese food for breakfast. I'm talking chicken, fried rice... smothered in Soy sauce. I couldn't believe it. BREAKFAST!"

"I've been thinking about it, also," Mary admitted, "and the snapshot of their future is not good. I saw Jeffrey eating a plate piled high with fried gizzards a couple weeks ago for breakfast... with biscuits and syrup."

"I don't like talking about folks, especially after remembering the days when I was overweight and I had to endure Glenn and Floyd's hurtful insinuations and listen to them make unfavorable comments about others. But, what if we pitch a program to Mr. Turner to promote a worksite fitness program for employees? The company could offer regular health and fitness programs that provide help with stress management, nutrition, fitness training, and smoking. For fitness, you and I could spearhead a walking program during lunch. Mildred and Jennifer in accounting can also assist with the walking. They've been walking during their lunch hours for months. A comprehensive program would encourage employees to focus on healthy lifestyle choices," Sarah said, eager to get started. "Plus, we might be able to shut Floyd and Glenn up by recruiting them to provide tips on racquetball techniques or something."

"I was reading the other day that approximately 65% of all adult Americans are overweight or obese. That translates to six out of ten Americans. I really don't think people realize how alarming that figure is. And more importantly, how much our lives are out of balance," Mary said.

"You're absolutely right. It's estimated that $100 billion per year is spent treating obesity related health problems in the U.S. But not only has the adult population increased, now depending on which health website you research, an estimated sixteen percent of our kids and teens ages six through nineteen are overweight," Sarah said, becoming discouraged as she revealed the statistics.

"The health experts knew we were headed for trouble over two decades ago, but probably never thought it would mushroom to this level," Mary said.

"The worksite fitness program would not only help our employees, but also their families," Sarah said. "I know Mr. Turner will be in favor of the idea, since he exercises. I'll contact his secretary this afternoon to set up an appointment. Meanwhile, on our lunch break, maybe we can lay out the specifics of the program before meeting with him."

"Great, I'll look for some graphics to add to the presentation. You know Mr. Turner is a visual person," Mary said.

"You're right. Thanks, Mary, for being the kind, caring, and compassionate person you are. Without you, I would still be trapped in a life of pretense trying to mimic someone I wasn't. Now my life is different — I'm no longer only consumed with myself. What's important is living my life the way God has arranged it. And that's helping others to escape that dark place where I came from," Sarah said with gratitude.

"You're welcome, Sarah," Mary said. "I'll see you at lunchtime."

A few hours later, Sarah and Mary met at their favorite lunch spot: Hudson's cafeteria, one of few places in the area where they could eat a balanced and nutritious meal.

"Hey lady." Mary waved for Sarah to join her.

"Sorry I'm late. I had to take a last minute telephone call," Sarah said, while sitting down with her tray. "I'm glad the serving line wasn't long."

Mary admired Sarah's selections. "Baked fish, mashed potatoes without gravy, and steamed broccoli. I'm impressed."

"Just trying to stay on track," Sarah responded. "That peach cobbler was tempting."

"They do have the best homemade peach cobbler. So, tell me about your trip."

"It was great! I went kayaking, snorkeling, and jet skiing. You must plan on going next year," Sarah said. "Maybe we can go together."

"I'm going to start saving my money now," Mary said. "Did you meet any guys?"

"Unfortunately not. The highlights for me were the water sports, tours and hanging out in the gym every morning."

"You… hanging out at the gym. Not the girl who doesn't want to be seen, mess up her hair, or ruin her make-up."

"Yes, me," Sarah said. "Trevor has helped me to get on track. My weekly sessions with him keep me energized about my health and fitness. I'm thinking about taking swimming lessons. I've been contemplating getting micro braids, so I won't have to worry about doing my hair. Anyway, I stopped off to see my parents on the way back and ran into an old boyfriend, Donavan. We spoke briefly… hopefully, we'll talk again soon. Girl, he looked really good and he went out of his way to compliment me," Sarah said, smiling.

"Sounds promising," Mary added.

"I'm not going to read anything more into it than what it was… two friends seeing each other after many years," Sarah said.

"Is he married?" Mary asked.

"With Donavan, you wouldn't know. He's not the most honest person in the world. We're actually childhood sweethearts with a lot of history. He married in his early twenties. I ran into him a few years ago. He convinced me we could have something special. He told me that he and his wife were no longer together. After a month of conversations on the telephone and emails, I found out that he was still married and that another lady was pursuing a court order to have him undergo a paternity test," Sarah said.

"Sounds like he's a busy and deceptive fellow," Mary replied. "Why on earth would you want to invite someone like that back into your life?"

"That incident was several years ago," Sarah said. "I'm sure he's not like that anymore."

"A leopard doesn't change his spots, Sarah," Mary said. "What happened?"

"I found out he was married when his wife sent me an email. Her claims extended from him being a poor father, never spending any time with his children, to infidelity," Sarah said. "I ended our communication immediately afterwards. A couple of weeks after the incident, he sent me a letter apologizing for his deception. The letter stated that he was sorry for not being upfront with me and that he was in the process of divorcing her. He begged me to accept his telephone calls, but I just couldn't. I was too hurt."

"How did she get your email address?" Mary asked.

"I guess she was monitoring his computer activities or something," Sarah said.

"Did he ever divorce her?" Mary asked.

"I don't know. The letter stated that he was moving out, but he was waiting for the right time. He said he knew I wouldn't have anything to do with him if I knew he was still married. And he knew right. He called a few more times after the incident, leaving messages trying to explain, but I wouldn't have anything to do with him. He's always been a very materialistic guy, so it sounds like he didn't want to divorce her and give up their lavish lifestyle — 5,000 square foot home, sports and luxury cars, and who knows what else they had in Houston."

"How many children does he have?" Mary questioned.

"He and the wife... or ex-wife have a son, and he had a son with another lady while in college," Sarah answered.

"You never know... maybe he's done some growing up," Mary said. "But it sounds like you need to tread carefully with rekindling a friendship or romantic relationship."

"Right now, I'm just going with the flow. We'll chitchat and email each other for now and see where the conversations lead. I know the type of person I'm dealing with, and that's one who finds it hard to be honest," Sarah stated. "Before I forget, I've scheduled a meeting with Mr. Turner for tomorrow afternoon."

"Good, that gives us plenty of time to prepare the presentation," Mary said.

"So, what do you think constitutes an effective fitness program?" Sarah asked.

"We could start out with a health fair. Something like, *Know the Status of Your Health.* We can play around with the slogan. It sounds a little corny. A health fair would offer health screenings and assessments. Secondly, we can conduct monthly roundtable health discussions, where employees can come and learn creative strategies for implementing healthier lifestyle habits. We could invite Trevor and Kelly to come and lead the discussions. Something to the point so employees can understand the impact of their food choices and the importance of exercising. And what about a stair climbing session during the week?" Mary said, eagerly anticipating Sarah's response.

"Those are some great ideas. Write them down," Sarah said. "I like the idea about Trevor and Kelly coming. For the walking program, I thought we could set a goal of participating in some of the charitable walking events in addition to the company sponsored 5K. Maybe we can get Mr. Turner to pay for all or a part of their registration fees."

"How do you feel about having the employees track or monitor their progress?" Mary questioned.

"I'm not too fond of the idea, because sometimes people tend to flee from activities where they must write stuff down daily. I know it helps them establish accountability, but...," Sarah concluded, "it can be one of several suggestions. Maybe we can have our own version of a 'Biggest Loser' weight loss program."

"I like it -- a weight loss contest," Mary said. "We need to make sure we keep the primary focus on educating employees and healthy lifestyle solutions. If we emphasize balance, fun, and excitement — eating healthy, controlling portion sizes, drinking water, exercising and implementing simple changes, such as eating a variety of fruits and vegetables, I'm sure it will motivate more people. Also, we might be able to get Kelly to conduct a healthy cooking class on Saturday mornings. What about *Getting Back to Basics* as the theme?" Mary said.

"I like it. That's it!" Sarah shouted.

"Mr. Turner is going to be particularly interested in how the program will benefit the company."

"Okay, how about this — First, it reduces absenteeism. Second, it enhances staff productivity and creativity. Third, it reduces health care claims. Fourth, it improves employee morale, confidence, and decision-making qualities," Sarah said.

"How do we sell the notion that a program will help reduce absenteeism?" Mary asked.

"Reports show that healthier employees spend fewer days away from work due to illness, which in turn saves employers thousands, and even millions of dollars on productivity. An effective program will also help reduce depression and help employees manage their time and stress levels better. It will help employees figure out how to balance work, family, and a healthier lifestyle."

"What about the point of reducing health care claims?"

"I read an article that stated 70% of health care costs related to illness are preventable — costs that are linked to lifestyle habits. A health promotion program might help to reduce the escalating costs of health care for the company and the employees. The cost of our premiums, co-pays, deductibles, and medicines are increasing every year. Even if we get some sort of raise, we don't see it because of our health costs. And if we, by chance, see a raise, we can't enjoy it if we're spending it on health-related matters."

"A solid program is exactly what we need," Mary said, confirming the idea. "I'll add the graphics to the points we've discussed and send you the layout by email. Oh yeah, keep me posted on Donavan."

"Okay, I will," Sarah agreed. "Oh yeah, we need to figure out some sort of 'quit smoking' program. I'll do some research."

The next day, Sarah and Mary were anxious about their meeting with Mr. Turner. One of his extraordinary traits was his desire to help people. A man known for assembling winning teams, he was likable, friendly, and genuinely interested in others. Under his leadership, the company had made billions.   And what his employees liked most was that he shared the credit and the wealth.

"Good afternoon, Mr. Turner," Sarah and Mary said, both extending their hands.

"Welcome ladies," Mr. Turner replied. "I understand that the two of you are interested in starting a fitness program."

"Yes, Mr. Turner," Sarah said quickly. "We know the company considers its employees its valuable resource, and we believe our proposal for a health and fitness program will complement that spirit."

"The company is dedicated to the well-being of its employees. I'm a runner myself. I have come to realize that individuals who have an appreciation for better health, and are physically active, are able to endure the ups and downs that come from the daily obligations of family, work, and society," Mr. Turner said. "I regret that the company hasn't taken a proactive role to improve and maintain employees' well-being."

"Mr. Turner, we've developed a proposal for your consideration," Mary said enthusiastically.

"Great, I tell you what. Let me have a few days to review the information and I'll have my secretary contact you with further instructions," Mr. Turner said. "I need some time to visit with our human resources director to make sure the program you're proposing doesn't violate any federal laws like HIPPA or ADA (Health Insurance Portability and Accountability Act or Americans with Disabilities Act)."

"Thanks for taking the time to visit with us, Mr. Turner," Sarah said.

"I thank the two of you for your loyalty to Bell and Yates," Mr. Turner said. "Sarah, could I see you for a moment?"

"Yes, Mr. Turner," Sarah said. Mary continued on out the door.

"I just want to tell you how pleased I am with your performance here at Bell and Yates. I know you didn't get the best accounts when you started, but I needed to see how you would handle the small stuff. And you really demonstrated your skills and abilities to us. You are very talented and a true asset to this company. I look forward to more of your creative, innovative, and interactive campaigns," Mr. Turner said. He shook her hand in appreciation.

"Thank you, Mr. Turner. I appreciate your praise and acknowledgement… it means a lot coming from you."

Mary was waiting in the hallway for Sarah. "What do you think, Sarah?" Mary said. Sarah was still beaming from his praise.

"I don't know — he seemed to favor the idea. He's a hard person to read," Sarah said.

"I guess we'll just have to wait for his response," Mary said. "We hadn't thought about compliance issues and federal laws."

As the weeks passed by, Sarah and Donavan's conversations intensified. Between talks about family and friends, their conversations escalated to finances, marriage, sex, and children. Sarah kept replaying a most recent conversation with Donavan, where he apologized for hurting her… *I have been dishonest with you in the past, and if you recall, just last week I again acknowledged that. I also said to you that my plans were to handle things different with us this time. I'll never hurt you like that again. I'm a different person. And definitely a much better person.* Thoughts of deceit and heartache kept circulating inside Sarah's head, but she remained positive.

"Hi Donavan," Sarah said into her cell phone. She had received several text messages from him earlier that day.

"How was your day?" Donavan asked. "I've been waiting for your call."

"Did you receive my text message earlier today?" Sarah asked.

"Yes, I did. But, I wanted to hear your voice," Donavan responded. "So, how was your day?"

"It was okay. Just another day filled with meetings. My boss, Mr. Weisen, was in a temperamental mood. Seems like lately the slightest thing sets him off," Sarah said. "I think he must be going through something. What about you? How was your day?"

"I spent my day thinking about you," Donavan said.

"Okay," Sarah said, hesitant to comment any further. "I never received your address. I want to send you something."

"I forgot. I'll be sure and send it to you before the day ends," Donavan replied. "I've got a meeting tonight. I'll email you later."

"Okay," Sarah said.

Sarah was a little concerned with Donavan's abrupt departure, but didn't want to start being suspicious every time he said something that didn't meet her expectations. She wondered if he was, for some reason, avoiding giving her his home address.

A month had passed, leaving Sarah and Mary to believe that Mr. Turner was not interested in supporting a health and fitness program. To their surprise, they both received an invitation one Tuesday morning to join Mr. Turner for lunch. His secretary had made reservations for lunch at one of the exclusive seafood restaurants west of Dallas that overlooked Joe Pool Lake. He met them in the lobby at noon.

"Good afternoon, ladies," Mr. Turner said, walking toward Sarah and Mary.

"Good afternoon," they both replied.

On the drive together, Mr. Turner raved about the restaurant. "It's a good place for fish and seafood," Mr. Turner said. "They have a daily fresh fish special and seafood dishes that are both delicious and healthy. I'm sorry, I didn't think to ask — do you eat seafood?"

Sarah and Mary both responded favorably and expressed their gratitude for the invitation. Castlepoint's Seafood Restaurant exuded a relaxed environment that was perfect for their meeting. The high, arched ceilings inset with skylights and thick beams of polished oak, panoramic lake-view windows, and massive fieldstone fireplaces created just the right ambiance.

Mr. Turner recommended the grilled salmon, garlic spinach mushroom mashed potatoes, and asparagus. During the meal, Sarah and Mary shared Mr. Turner's sentiments for the exquisite taste and quality of the food. Mr. Turner talked about how he overcame his weakness for unhealthy foods. Then the discussion about the program started.

"I agree with the suggestions outlined in the presentation and would like for you to work with our human resources department to get things moving. I've discussed your ideas with Andy Barton, our human resources director. His office will assist you with the dissemination of information. I would like to see a quarterly newsletter that provides tips on nutrition and exercising. I don't think the fact that one lacks a healthy lifestyle prevents them from being an outstanding employee. But, I do believe that fit people are less likely to get sick, are more energetic, exhibit more self-confidence, take on more leadership roles, have better attitudes, and are less stressed," Mr. Turner said, while signing the credit card receipt. "I often listen to my colleagues complain about society looking to employers to solve social ills, and they wish employees would exercise some personal responsibility. However, I believe if employers don't get involve, we'll continue to pay mightily in health care costs. And a good start for us will be replacing those Fridays pizza parties with healthier foods, and substituting those boxes of donuts and pigs-in-a-blanket with yogurt and fresh fruit."

Back at work, the ladies put the wheels in motion. They met with Mr. Barton to solidify the plans for the health and fitness program. Their plans included introducing various stages of the program one behind the other. Stage one, a fall health fair. Stage two, a lunch n' learn program on Tuesdays that provided an educational vehicle for promoting good health practices. Stage three, a group walking and stretching session on Monday, Wednesday, and Friday during the noon hour. Mr. Turner agreed to purchase pedometers for each participant. To supplement to the walking program, the company would offer on-site opportunities, such as group classes for yoga, pilates, and resistance training by certified instructors after work.

Stage four included a company softball team; discounted memberships at a local health club, recreation center, or YMCA; special programs for persons with disabilities; and a smoking cessation program. Sarah and Mary worked non-stop at brainstorming ways to implement a program that encouraged employees to eat more fresh fruits, vegetables, whole grains, and low-fat dairy products.

Sarah and Mary's desires to help others achieve healthier lifestyle habits were well accepted and appreciated. The fall health fair was a huge success. A number of employees participated in the lunchtime walk and stretch sessions. Employees could no longer hold on to their trademark excuse of "I don't have time to exercise." The pedometers were a big hit. With pedometers strapped to their waist, employees were more inclined to get up and move around to reach the monumental goal of 10,000 steps in a day. The Tuesday lunch n' learn program, facilitated by Trevor and Kelly, provided education on how to implement better eating and exercise habits. And to reinforce the company's commitment to healthy habits... healthier snacks were placed in the vending machines, certified instructors were hired to conduct evening yoga, pilates, and resistance training classes, and memberships to local health clubs were subsidized.

Sarah never imagined that her lifestyle changes would impact others. Happening to hear that news report about discrimination of obese individuals in the workplace had changed her life forever, as well as the lives of others indirectly. She had acquired the freedom to live a balanced, creative and innovative life. Now, she was helping others to acquire that same freedom. She knew it was divine intervention.

"Congratulations on your time at the company 5K! Forty minutes is GREAT!" Mary said, walking into Sarah's office. "You are an example of what can be achieved with an attitude of commitment, consistency, perseverance, determination, and patience."

"I am truly filled with joy and finally walking in peace," Sarah said.

CHAPTER 6

Mixing the Old with the New

*A*fter two months of telephone calls, emails, online photo exchanges, e-greeting cards, and text messages, Sarah began to examine the direction of her relationship with Donavan. Everything seemed to be copasetic with him, but she couldn't be sure. After all, she was a different person than who he remembered. Could he be happy with the new and improved Sarah? A long-distance relationship filled with issues of trust, fidelity, and loneliness ransacked Sarah's thoughts. Could she handle not having her special someone nearby? What about having to spend those special days apart... Valentine's Day... birthdays and holidays? What about the expense of traveling back and forth from Plano to Houston? The closer they became, the more often they would want to see one another. How could she overcome the geographical barrier? Who would eventually ask the million dollar question to relocate? Would she end up trapped in a web of unhappiness?

The telephone rang. "Hi Sugar Cakes."

"Hi Sweetie," Sarah answered.

"On your advice... I started exercising at the gym the other day."

"Great!" Sarah responded. "Did you go for your physical exam?"

"Yes, I did. The doctor did a lot of blood work. I should have my results next week."

"Okay."

"You know... at the gym they try and sell you their brand of nutritional drinks, bars, pills, and wafers. I like the bars. What do you think about them?"

"I occasionally use a sports bar as a snack before and after my workouts. When I started getting into the health thing, I used them as a meal replacement. After talking with Trevor, my fitness consultant, I've discovered that having them as a meal replacement can be dangerous, because they're not the same as natural foods," Sarah said.

"You are sure tight with this Trevor," Donavan questioned. "Are you sure he's just your fitness consultant?"

"Yes, Donavan," Sarah said. She frowned in confusion. "Anyway, even though the claims on the packaging list a fleet of vitamins and minerals... they don't take the place of those essentials that are in fresh fruits and vegetables, whole-grains, and low-fat dairy products. That's why I consider them as a snack food... and even keeping with that thought, I only select the ones that indicate they are made with natural foods like fruit, rolled oats, and nuts."

"What about supplements?"

"If you eat highly fortified foods... breakfast cereals, fruits and vegetables, along with vitamin and mineral supplements, you might be prone to overload."

"What do you mean... overload?"

"According to Trevor, supplement overload can lead to imbalances, which can lead to health problems. Some people like to take a multivitamin — plus extra calcium, zinc, potassium, and selenium — plus eat energy bars and highly fortified orange juices.

The over indulgence of it all is potentially dangerous. For example, someone interested in taking iron as a supplement should consult with his or her doctor. Insufficient iron in the body can cause problems, as well as too much iron. Too much iron may increase the risk of cardiovascular disease, particularly for men. Blood tests that check hemoglobin, hemotocrit, and serum ferritin are the best indicators for whether a person needs an iron supplement."

"I understand."

"Supplements should complement what you're already eating. Too many of us would rather take a pill or capsule. Unfortunately, that pill or capsule doesn't begin, in most cases, to supply the body with what it needs… at least not by itself. Don't get me wrong, I'm not saying not to take supplements; I'm just saying they should be done under the guidance of a physician or other professional medical personnel. You can develop toxic levels if you're ingesting too much of one thing…"

"You've really gotten into this health stuff," Donavan said. "On a different note, I would like to come and see you."

"When?"

"I can come in a couple of weeks."

"Great, I have a semi-formal event on September 20th. Maybe you can come and escort me," Sarah said, waiting for a response. "There are some other things going on as well that weekend. I believe there's an art festival."

"I'll make all of the arrangements," Donavan said. "Maybe we can go to the art festival, rent some movies… action, romance, comedy… whatever you're feeling. I guess we won't be going to *The Pancake Haven* for breakfast?"

"We can go," Sarah replied.

"Won't it interfere with your healthier eating? I remember you loved their three egg omelet with the apple-raisin pancakes…. and the spinach quiche."

"I definitely don't eat like that anymore. But, don't worry, I can find something on the menu that fits my nutritional budget."

"I admire your dedication and discipline."

"Thanks for your understanding and support."

"I sent you something in the mail."

"You've got to stop sending me things. Everyone is still talking about the roses you sent last week… then there was the gift card you sent me to buy something new to wear. And when are you going to send me your address? I've been asking you for over two months now. I want to send you something for your workouts."

"I just want to spoil you. Just be okay with it. It's my way of lobbying for our future. And about the address, I'm going to send you my P.O. Box. Since I might be moving, I want to send you the business address… something permanent."

"You don't have to spoil me. And moving where?"

"We'll talk about it when I get to town."

Sarah met Donavan at the baggage claim area a couple of weeks later. Sarah tried desperately to contain her excitement as they embraced. Not only was she excited about his visit, she was elated to have him escort her to the event. Back in the day, they went out to parties together, but nothing of this caliber.

"So, are you hungry?" Sarah asked.

"Nope. Actually, I ate lunch at the airport before I left," Donavan said, looking for his claim ticket. "Wait just a second; my luggage is on carousel B."

"Okay," Sarah said as Donavan walked away, admiring his muscular build.

"So, where are we headed to first?" Donavan asked, returning with his luggage.

"Since you've eaten, we'll go to my house and let you chill out until tonight."

"Great! We can play catch up!"

Donavan and Sarah were curled up on her sofa.

"Oh, by the way, here's a little something for you," Donavan said, handing a small rectangular box to Sarah.

"What's this?" Sarah said, accepting the box. "Oh my goodness. Little blue bag… little blue box. Could it be jewelry from my favorite jeweler?"

"Open it up," Donavan said with urgency.

"You really shouldn't have," Sarah said, admiring the sterling silver charm bracelet. "I've been admiring this bracelet for the longest. You really shouldn't have Donavan. How did you know I wanted this one? I don't remember mentioning it."

"Just accept the gift. A kiss on the cheek will be acceptable as your sign of appreciation. That is, acceptable for now."

"Thank you, Donavan," Sarah said, as she leaned over to express her thanks to Donavan.

"Just wait and see what I have planned for your birthday. Oh yeah, I received my blood results last week."

"Is everything okay?"

"Let's see. I actually have the lab report," Donavan said, looking in his planner. "Under comments, Dr. Sears wrote 'all okay.'"

"What were your numbers?"

"Let's see. Total cholesterol is 277. Triglycerides 142. HDL (Good Cholesterol) 109. LDL (Bad Cholesterol) 140."

"What did you say your total cholesterol is?"

"It's 277."

"That's not good. The desirable level for cholesterol is less than 200mg/dl. A range of 200-239 mg/dl is borderline high risk, and over 240 mg/dl is high risk," Sarah said, looking at Donavan with concern. "I think you'd better call your doctor first thing Monday morning and ask him about that 'all okay' comment. I wouldn't want you to suffer a heart attack or stroke."

"I'm sure that'll never happen."

"A lifestyle of unhealthy habits is like a walking time bomb… and you never know which unhealthy habit is going to ignite the fuse."

"Anyway… there's always medication available…"

"Just keep in mind that some medications impair a man's ability to perform his sexual duties… IMPOTENCE! If I were you, I wouldn't be thinking medication as the solution."

"What!"

"That's right. I know you don't want that to happen."

"Let's change that subject. I don't want my mind to travel somewhere it shouldn't this weekend. What about my triglycerides, HDL and LDL levels?"

"I don't want to speculate about your numbers. I do know that a normal triglycerides range is less than 150. And a normal HDL is greater than 40. You need to ask your doctor about your LDL. A normal LDL is less than 100 and yours is 140. I'm not saying that's terribly bad, but you need to get a handle on it before it gets too far off track. Stop eating fatty meats like bacon and pan sausage," Sarah suggested. "The LDL cholesterol is the one that carries most of the cholesterol present in your blood. It contributes to the plaque buildup in the walls of your arteries, setting you up for arteriosclerosis, which is hardening and narrowing of the arteries. The HDL cholesterol is the one that scour the bloodstream, collecting excess cholesterol and transporting it back to the liver to be used or disposed of."

"I know about cholesterol, but what are triglycerides?"

"From what I've researched, triglycerides are the main form of fat in foods and are an important source of energy. Triglycerides come from the foods we eat and are also manufactured by the body. In terms of food, our liver will process them after eating. It's perfectly normal for our blood to contain certain levels of triglycerides. However, if we consume excess calories from the varied sources like carbohydrates, fats, protein… and alcohol, our body will transform the excess calories into triglycerides for storage as body fat. Your doctor can provide you with more information. That's about as much as I understand about them. You need to check on your cholesterol levels, especially the LDL. The triglycerides and cholesterol are all tied together somehow. I had high cholesterol levels myself a few months ago. My doctor gave me a pamphlet on cholesterol and a pamphlet about implementing healthier lifestyle habits. My levels are now within the normal range."

As the evening hours approached, Sarah and Donavan began to get ready for an exciting night. Walking out from the guest bedroom, Sarah was taken back by how handsome he looked. Trying to maintain her composure, Sarah hurried off to finish getting ready.

Eight o'clock quickly arrived and butterflies began to rumble inside Sarah's stomach. This would be their first semi-formal affair together. Sarah knew Donavan would blend in with her friends, and that was one of the traits she remembered loving about him. She didn't have to worry about holding his hand the entire night. He was very secure with himself. She could mix and mingle with the freedom of knowing he would be okay.

"What are we eating tonight?" Donavan asked, while staring across the room at the buffet table. "Raw veggies, fruit. Looks like the chef is carving roast beef and turkey. The pasta with alfredo sauce looks good."

Trying to keep from being so obvious, Sarah felt a miraculous force of gravity pulling her closer to him. She just wanted to touch Donavan, and before she realized it, she found her hand resting on his chair's arm. "I think I'll have a small portion of the pasta with some of the turkey. Definitely the fresh broccoli, carrots, and cucumbers…"

"I think they're ready to start serving our table," Donavan said, standing up. A perfect gentlemen, he scooted his chair out from the table and motioned to assist Sarah out of her chair.

As they moved about the ballroom, Sarah introduced Donavan to her associates. After eating dinner, they danced and mingled with others.

Before his arrival, Donavan had expressed an interest in capping the night off at one of the local jazz clubs. Sarah located a swanky place on the Internet that was dark and intimate — Jazz Imagination.

"Are you ready to leave and move to the next venue?" Sarah asked.

"I'm ready when you're ready," Donavan responded. "Where are we going?"

"I don't go clubbing, but I found a nice jazz club on the Internet across town. I think you'll enjoy it," Sarah said.

Driving to the club, Sarah and Donavan reminisced about the old days — old friends, school, family, and the neighborhood they both grew up in.

Finally, they arrived at Jazz Imagination. Walking inside, Sarah and Donavan admired the New Orleans style scene. The sweet tunes made the jazz club one of the most romantic spots in Dallas.

"So, do you like it?" Sarah asked.

"I'm just happy to be here with you," Donavan said. "I do like the traditional jazz sound and the vocalist. How about a cocktail? Your favorite is Cognac, right?"

"You know... I guess I forgot to tell you. I don't drink anymore," Sarah said, sitting nestled under Donavan.

"You! Not you. I remember back in the day you mixing your own version of trashcan punch. You'd mix Rum, Vodka, Everclear, Gin with orange juice, fruit punch, and pineapple juice. Man, we would get plenty wasted. And those jello-shots you'd make with Everclear... 190 proof."

"That seems like a lifetime ago. I couldn't even fathom doing that now."

"Do you drink at all?" Donavan said, surprised. "What else have I missed?"

"I've made God the head of my life," Sarah said.

"That's good. I'm going to church, also," Donavan responded.

"For me, it's not just about going to church; it's about living a life pleasing to God."

"Okay," Donavan responded while smiling at Sarah. "So, what's on the agenda for tomorrow?"

"I planned for us to attend my church in the morning, then there's the art festival in downtown Dallas."

"I didn't bring any church clothes."

"It's okay. My church is really laid back. The slacks and shirt you wore on the plane will be just fine. Or, you can wear what you have on right now."

"I've been in this suit all evening, and it's a little smokey in here. I'm accustomed to wearing a suit when I go to church. I wouldn't feel comfortable wearing slacks and a shirt."

"Donavan, it's not about what you're wearing; it's about your soul. Although my church is laid back and fairly casual, they have not strayed away from the truth of the Word of God."

Early the next morning, Donavan reluctantly attended church services with Sarah. To his surprise, Donavan was impressed with Pastor Fern's sermon.

"I really enjoyed your pastor's sermon and his message of how God desires a relationship with us. It was one of the best sermons I have heard in a long time."

"I'm glad you enjoyed it, especially since you didn't want to go," Sarah said. "I thought I'd cook brunch before we head to the art festival."

"So, what are we eating that's healthy? I sure hope it includes some meat."

"How about a vegetable omelette filled with a spinach, tomatoes, green onion, bell pepper, and mushrooms mixture...

sautéed in olive oil, topped with a low-fat mozzarella cheese and turkey sausage, served with a fresh medley of cantaloupe and melon?"

"I'll try it. I don't know about that turkey sausage, but I'll try it. I'm a beef man."

After brunch, Sarah and Donavan enjoyed the art festival until it was time for Donavan's departure.

"I've had a wonderful time with you this weekend. So are you serious about us or are you just pulling my leg? If so, how are we going to do this? What's your plan? What's our timeline? I'm willing to move to Dallas. I'll move mountains to get to you. Getting nervous yet? Guess I'm scaring you, huh?" Donavan said.

"I'm serious about building a relationship with the right person — a relationship that has the potential to develop into a life-long commitment. The right person will possess those essential qualities important to me — that is, someone who is Christ-centered, trustworthy, mentally and financially stable, caring, compassionate, and sacrificial. Someone who can love me with all his heart and soul. I think it's important that we get to know each other – good and bad habits, spending habits, and mood swings. For now, we've just scratched the surface. Sure, we have a history… from over 20 years ago. I've evolved. You've evolved. We need to make sure we've evolved in ways that promotes compatibility for a future life together. We will have to talk about the timelines and plans… your moving. You've got to find a job, sell your home. It's important that you understand that my life doesn't revolve around money and acquisitions — it's about care and concern for others. It's about living a Christ-centered life and helping others to recognize and experience the blessings of God. Yes, it's all scary. But, I'm ready to go out on a limb for the right person," Sarah admitted.

"I guess we both have some things to think about," Donavan said.

"We really do," Sarah reiterated.

"I want us to take a trip together... around the time of your birthday. Let me know when you can take off. I'll plan everything. I was thinking about Miami... Las Vegas... that's where your surprise is going to be. Let me know as quickly as possible," Donavan said.

"I'll check first thing Monday. And don't forget to check with your doctor about your cholesterol. Tell him he must have placed that 'all okay' comment on your report by mistake."

"I'm glad I shared the information with you. I was thinking everything with my health was great!"

The following months proved unsuccessful for Sarah and Donavan. Thoughts of a union were relinquished. No more telephone calls, emails, online photo exchanges, e-greeting cards, text messages or fresh cut roses. Sarah's fear of a long distance relationship — worry about issues of trust and fidelity and loneliness had come to pass. Sarah discovered that Donavan lived with his ex-wife. Once again, an avalanche of lies and secrets came descending down.

"Life goes on," Sarah said to herself as she sat weary eyed at her dining room table. "Thank you God for giving me the sense to move on and hold out."

Sarah's understanding that life was rife with failures and disappointments motivated her belief that God had someone tailor-made for her waiting in the wings. And while she was waiting, she understood God expected her to use the time wisely by doing works He would put before her. She continued to enjoy the freedom she had acquired to live spiritually, socially, emotionally, and physically balanced. She knew she would remain creative and innovative in the midst of life's uncertainties and adversities.

PART II

Deceptive Lifestyle Truths Revealed

Reflections of Deceptions

What an exhilarating feeling to finish running 26.2 miles. That's exactly what Suzanne felt on January 15, 2006 in Houston, Texas. After thirty-six weeks of training, she completed her fourth marathon in four hours, twenty-five minutes and sixteen seconds. As she crossed the finish line, a collection of emotions — joy, pride, pain, exhaustion, and relief — filled her. Nervous excitement jolted through her body. A scene she had acted out over and over in her thoughts had become a reality. Acknowledging the source of her power and strength, Suzanne lifted her head toward the clear blue sky and thanked God for answering her prayers.

"Babe... that smile you're wearing really looks great on you. You did it again! CONGRATULATIONS!" Jim shouted as he picked up Suzanne and turned her around, excited about her victorious finish. "Look at my wife, sporting that fit and fabulous label. You really came in strong."

"Thanks, baby. Finishing feels great! Deep down I didn't know if I would ever be part of this adventure again. The Lord blessed me to run the half marathon last year, but I never thought I'd ever run a full marathon again. But I did it! *Pomp and Circumstance* played in my head as I ran across the finish line," Suzanne said with a stream of tears flowing from her eyes. "For so long, I felt like a caged bird, but now I feel free to fly wherever I want to go."

"I'm so proud of you. You never gave up! You never tilted on the side of surrender. Even while experiencing uncertainty, adversity, and disappointment because of your health problems, you just kept going," Jim said, wiping the tears from Suzanne's eyes. He fought back his own tears of joy.

"It was by the grace of God that I finished. His power is what gave me the strength and endurance to complete the distance. And survive the HEAT! And I thank you for calming my pre-show jitters at the start of the run."

"You're welcome," Jim said.

"That last six miles was hard for me — I kept getting cramps and spasms in my legs," Suzanne said as she looked back at the trail of runners crossing the finish line. "But, seeing you at mile 20 gave me that burst of energy I needed to make it to the end."

"You ran well the entire time, even in the seventy-five degree temperature," Jim said.

"I hate you didn't run. I know you missed not running in the race with Trevor and the others."

"It was more important for me to capture every moment of your comeback. There will be plenty of other marathon races," Jim said.

"Thanks, baby. Seeing you at the various mile markers gave me the courage to continue on. And the volunteers, police and spectators were also wonderful. You could feel the compassion of everyone applauding and cheering us on. Crossing the finish line, I felt like I was waving to my own personal cheering squad. And the sight of you — my mom and dad — made my feat that more special."

"Your personal audience is waiting for you inside the convention center," Jim said, trying to shield Suzanne from the growing crowd of runners and volunteers. "They've got a serious breakfast buffet — eggs, biscuits, sausages, hash browns, fruit, and cookies. One of the ice cream companies is here. I saw a yogurt stand. You love yogurt."

"After 26.2 miles, I love it all. I've earned the right to eat everything in sight."

"Wait! Over there," Jim said, pointing to the merchandise tables for the marathon finishers. "Don't forget about your symbols of achievement — your medal, t-shirt and mug."

Jim ushered Suzanne through the crowd to the tables. "The tickets for your finisher items are on your bib. I got this bottle of water for you. Drink up!"

"Thanks, baby," Suzanne said, accepting the bottle of water. Suzanne became overwhelmed with emotion as the volunteer presented her with a medal, t-shirt and mug. "Jim, all I can do is thank God. All of the paralyzing aches and pains I've experienced over the past two-and-a-half years, I just never thought I'd see this day again. Before we go to meet the others, I just need a moment." Suzanne sat on the curb.

"Miracles do still happen," Jim said. "Two years ago, you were doubtful that you would ever walk without feeling pain. And you never imagined running another marathon. Nevertheless, you bounced back and fully recovered."

"I know, but you never doubted me. While I was picking myself apart, you were putting me back together," Suzanne replied.

"Never forget that I'll always be your defender. Whatever tries to tear you down, I'll always be the one to wage a war against those opposing forces," Jim said, squatting next to her.

Looking at the digital clock at the finish line that displayed four hours and forty-three minutes, Suzanne thought back. "For years, I thought I was doing the right things, eating healthy and all, but now I know that my secret encounters with unhealthy foods may have caused me to experience two-and-a-half years of health fallout," Suzanne said.

"We've always eaten better than any of our family and friends, Suzanne," Jim said. "When I met you, you exposed me to a style of eating I'd never considered. You taught me how to substitute the good for the bad. How to be creative with my family traditions. Because of you, my homemade chili has undergone a major transformation. No more high fatty meats or high sodium products. From high-fat ground beef to low-fat ground white chicken. Instead of the high sodium chili mix, I'm using fresh tomatoes and natural seasonings."

"I know. Your chili is the best. Still, I feel like I was a fraud. You never knew about my secret trips to Popeye's for their dirty rice, red beans and rice, Cajun fried chicken, and cinnamon apple turnover. Now, I'm wondering if the wear and tear on my body from years of running, mixed with my secret encounters with foods high in fat, cholesterol and sodium, and occasional drinking binges led to my health problems."

"Suzanne, today is your crystal ball. Savor it! Your doctors could never pinpoint any reason for your medical problems. I'm sure an occasional splurge at Popeye's wasn't the culprit. Your condition was more than likely caused by some genetic factor."

"All I think about are the things I had been telling others not to do. People at work. People at church. People I met by chance being out and about. Molly, the lady I met on the plane ride to San Diego."

"Suzanne, this is a time for celebrating the breakout powers of God. You've done an amazing thing."

"You're right. It's been over two years since the days of Popeye's, Sonic Drive-In, Rudy's Burger Hut, and Taco Bell. I'm glad you're not one to judge."

"I'm your husband. I would never judge you. You've made an amazing difference in my life and in the lives of others. It's only because of you that I started my quest for a healthier lifestyle. You're the one who taught me that looking good on the outside is fine, but what really matters is what's going on inside. Others, like Molly, are doing the same. She's even getting ready to run her first half marathon. Because of you!"

"I guess that's why I feel so much like a hypocrite. It's because of me that our dreams were placed on hold. While I was telling you and others what not to do, I was behind the scenes doing them. And that's why I can't help thinking that I caused both of us a lot of unnecessary grief," Suzanne said, placing her arm around Jim's shoulders. "I really do understand how hard it is for others to adopt a healthier lifestyle. The temptations that exist can be overwhelming. For a long time, I didn't know who I was. I had these feelings. These urges. And they caused me to seek consolation in food. Those creamy treats at Sonic filled periods of uncertainty in my life. That double decker cheesy taco and the 7-layer burrito at Taco Bell was my antidote for achieving peace against my internal struggles."

"Wow! I never thought of you eating the 7-layer burrito. That's a lot of sodium and fat. And what internal struggles?"

"Just things in my past."

"What things? We've been married for three-and-a-half years. You'd think I'd know about these feelings and urges," Jim said, looking puzzled at Suzanne.

"Let's table that discussion for another time. Yes, you're absolutely correct about the 7-layer burrito," Suzanne said, disappointed in herself. "After my marathons, especially the marathon in November 2002, we all ended up drinking an assortment of alcoholic beverages — Chocolate Martinis, Long Island Ice Teas, and Margaritas. I will always believe in my heart and soul that the excessive drinking after that marathon, along with the patchy periods of unhealthy eating, caused my health problems. The occasional original glazed donuts dripping with vanilla icing. Pork chops draped in a honey mustard barbecue sauce."

"The past is what it is... the past. You can't alter it. Past encounters and behaviors have come and gone. If you truly believe your part in a deceptive lifestyle led to your health problems, you'll be more faithful to doing the right things. Don't forget that God allows situations to happen in our lives to fulfill his perfect plan and his purpose for us. You never know how many people will be blessed by your testimony of what God has brought you through. A testimony of overcoming mistakes, setbacks, fears, deceptions, imperfections, and insecurities. Your look down memory lane should be one of hope, faith and perseverance. Yours is a reflection of how you weathered a storm and didn't give up in the midst of despair. You fought back in a way that only you could, and that was by eating the foods that could give velocity to rebuilding, regenerating, and retaining a healthy body."

"I love you," Suzanne said, hugging Jim. "I'm glad I married you."

"I know! Maybe we can make plans to start our family soon. Just thought I'd throw that in," Jim said, helping Suzanne up. "Let's go! Your mom and dad have probably gotten worried about us. They're waiting in the family reunion area."

Just as Suzanne and Jim were beginning to walk away, Trevor came through the crowd and embraced Suzanne.

"Congratulations, lady… you did it," Trevor said, excited. "I am so proud of you."

Trevor had been Suzanne's fitness consultant for years. She met him years ago while training for her first marathon.

"Thanks, Trevor. It is a great day for me. I especially thank you for helping me get back to this point. Your care and concern has really meant a lot to me."

It was over three years ago, November 2, 2002 in Chicago, that Jim and Suzanne experienced the same collection of emotions from their third marathon finish, knowing they wouldn't be racing for a while. After a few months of marriage, they decided to conceive a child. The fact that Jim and Suzanne were in their late thirties had cast a shadow of doubt on their ability to get pregnant immediately. Nevertheless, after reading tons of literature on increasing their chances of conception, the couple had thrown away any lingering worries about infertility. Healthy habits fueled the couple's belief that they would have a healthy offspring.

Deliriously happy and in love, Jim and Suzanne lived in an older community in Desoto, Texas. He was a cost estimator for Hensel Morton Construction Firm, and she was a claims adjuster for Union State Insurance Company. A picture of perfect health, Jim and Suzanne lived health-centered lives with great candor. Rather than trying to pursue the media's image of healthy bodies, professional athletes or skinny celebrities, Jim and Suzanne maintained a realistic definition of health. They followed a fitness program that improved and maintained their heart and lung functions; enhanced their muscular strength and flexibility; and kept their fat deposits at a low level. They enjoyed running, swimming, biking, and these activities safeguarded their health, allowing them to keep cholesterol and blood pressure levels low; manage stress; burn excess calories; preserve bone density; and sustain normal blood sugar levels. "The freedom to be fit without restriction" was their motto.

With a time of life that offered the perfect conditions for conception, Suzanne was blindsided by the calm before the storm. At the height of their ambitious pregnancy pursuit, her perfect health turned disastrous. Suzanne began to experience several illnesses. First, the discomfort of an uncontrollable cough, followed by an ongoing cycle of unmanageable skin breakouts, unrestrained swelling and stiffness — capped by paralyzing joint pain. Suzanne and Jim's dreams of having a baby were placed on hold indefinitely.

It was a hectic day at the office. Because of the recent winter storm mix, Suzanne was inundated with claims, deadlines, and consults. Just as she finished prioritizing her day, an unexpected visitor dropped in.

"Hi Suzanne," Jessica said, walking into Suzanne's office. Jessica was a long-time friend of Suzanne's whom she had met years ago in college. Jessica worked for the Union State Insurance Company two years ago, and recently returned as an Insurance Investigation Manager.

"Hi Jessica," Suzanne said, surprised to see Jessica. "Are you working here again?"

"Yes, I am!" Jessica said, as she sat in the chair beside Suzanne's desk. "I've been back for about two weeks. I've been busy in the field. I wanted to come by earlier to see you, but..."

"What made you come back?" Suzanne inquired.

"The money. They offered me a hefty salary to come back and lead the investigative team. After I heard about Bart's retirement, I decided to apply for the position. Luckily for me, I got it and a nice pay increase," Jessica said. "You look tired, Suzanne. Are you feeling okay?"

Trying to control her coughing, while listening to Jessica, Suzanne was visibly distressed. "If I could get rid of this cough, I'd probably feel a lot better."

"Do you need me to bring you something to eat? I'm going around the corner to Helm's Deli," Jessica offered. "Some soup or tea?"

"No, thank you. Jim made some homemade chili last night."

"Oh yeah, I heard that you recently married Jim," Jessica said with sarcasm. "So, how is married life?"

"It's great! We purchased a two-story starter house over on Trinity Drive in DeSoto. We're having a lot of fun fixing it up. We're giving it a custom look — installing crown molding, adding color, and embellishing the flooring," Suzanne said proudly. "We run together. Eat healthy together. We do everything together. He's my best friend and I love him."

"I'm glad married life is agreeing with you," Jessica replied. "And he cooks."

"Yes, he does. And he's good at it," Suzanne exclaimed.

"Is chili going to make you feel better?" Jessica questioned.

"I don't know if anything is going to help this cough," Suzanne answered.

"When was the last time you had your annual physical?" Jessica asked.

"I had one a few months prior to the marathon."

"Did the doctor reveal any problems?"

"My blood work indicated that I had low iron (mild anemia), but it wasn't anything to cause great alarm. The results of the other blood tests indicated I was in exceptional health."

"Low iron can develop into something serious. You probably need to start eating more foods that are high in iron, like beans, green leafy vegetables, and whole grains. You're a runner. You know that..." Suzanne said.

"I do know. Low iron has become a chronic state of condition for me. Each year my blood work portrays low iron stores, and each year my physician recommends iron supplements," Suzanne admitted. "I've always eaten a variety of foods rich in iron like soy milk, and grain choices like brown rice, whole wheat bread and oatmeal. Black-eyed peas. Vegetables like spinach, broccoli, and collard greens. Other foods like prunes, beef, lamb, clams, oysters, and turkey. I'm not a pill person, so I don't do the supplements. You know that, too, of course."

"I know you do the whole grains and soymilk. I know you try and eat a banana and orange a day. But prunes? And what about your trips to Popeye's, Sonic, Rudy's Burger Hut, and Taco Bell? Do you still eat the greasy food?"

"I think dried, pitted prunes taste pretty good," Suzanne said. "But, I do occasionally eat some of my favorites."

"Well, I hope you feel better soon," Jessica said, heading towards the door. "I've got a meeting in five minutes. I'll call and check on you later."

"Thanks for your concern. I'll be okay," Suzanne said. "Glad to see you back at Union." As Jessica exited the door, Suzanne breathed a sigh of relief. Shocked by Jessica's return to the company, thoughts of regret and repent revved up Suzanne's emotional engine. She thought as the door closed, *what is Jessica doing back here? There are tons of insurance companies in this area, and she had to come back to Union. What am I going to do?*

After nearly six weeks of unsuccessful resolution using over the counter medications, Suzanne scheduled an office visit with her physician. The coughing attacks and excessive discharge of mucus generated great concern. Unsure of the root cause, her physician used a combination of medications to treat symptoms associated with a cold, allergies, or respiratory tract illness.

"Good morning, baby," Jim said, walking into the bedroom. He had a bowl of cereal, glass of soymilk, and container of sliced cantaloupe for Suzanne.

Watching Jim as he placed the tray of food on her lap, Suzanne was moved by his thoughtfulness. "Good morning, sweetie. Breakfast in bed. I'm impressed."

"You had a rough night. I know you must be tired — the coughing and all. You didn't go to sleep until around two o'clock this morning," Jim said as he positioned the napkin and utensils. "I wish you could sleep in today."

"So do I, but...," Suzanne responded.

"I know," Jim added. "You have that meeting at nine o'clock this morning."

"You're right," Suzanne confirmed.

"That's why I wanted to do something special for you before I left for the airport."

"Thank you. Let me get up and wash my face and brush my teeth," Suzanne said, while carefully getting out of the bed with the tray. "What time does your flight arrive on Friday from Denver?"

"Around eight o'clock," Jim said. "I'm riding with the guys to the airport this morning. Our flight leaves at ten-thirty. Can you pick me up on Friday?"

"Yes, I can," Suzanne said. "I'm going to miss you."

"I'm going to miss you, too," Jim said, packing his garment bag.

"Do you need me to help you with anything?" Suzanne asked.

"I'm good. I hope you feel better soon," Jim said.

"I will. What kind of cereal do I have?" Suzanne asked.

"Your favorite, of course. The heart healthy, honey-toasted oat cereal," Jim responded.

"Great!" Suzanne shouted. "Don't forget to pack your running shoes. I'm sure you're going to run in Lake Hills Park."

"Thanks for reminding me," Jim said, walking towards the closet.

"I think I'll run today after work. I might see if Trevor has some free time," Suzanne said. "I haven't been able to run consistently since all this coughing started."

"Do you think that's wise?" Jim asked. "Just chill until the medicine kicks in. I'm sure Trevor would agree with me."

"I don't want to go too long without running," Suzanne said.

"Just take it easy. You're in tip-top shape," Jim said.

"You're probably right," Suzanne responded. "I do need to take it easy."

"Okay, I'm finished. I better get to the office before they leave me. I'll call you later. I love you," Jim said, stopping to hug and kiss Suzanne. "Eat your cereal."

"I love you, too. I'll see you on Friday evening at eight o'clock," Suzanne said.

Existing on a limited amount of sleep, Suzanne prepared for another hectic day at work. She had a large number of claims to process. Dealing with her medical discomforts, and the stress of having to conduct investigations, Suzanne began to question her ability to handle her daily responsibilities timely and accurately.

Jessica stopped by to check on Suzanne. "Hey, Suzanne. How are you feeling today?"

"Actually, I'm feeling better this morning. I had a terrible night last night. I went to see my doctor a few days ago, and the medications he prescribed should start to eliminate the terrible cough and discharge soon."

"I sure hope so," Jessica said. "I don't mean to get personal, but I forgot to ask you something the other day."

"What?" Suzanne asked.

"Are you and Jim planning to start your family anytime soon?"

"Probably so. We're really ready to make this baby. We were set and ready to go, and then, I started getting these coughing attacks. That can put a damper on the bedroom scene," Suzanne responded. "Of course, you know my quest for having a healthy baby started long before a marriage to Jim. Healthy tips from my physician has prompted me to implement habits like adding two tablespoons of wheat germ to my oatmeal and yogurt. He told me that wheat germ is a way to increase Folate," Suzanne said.

"I heard that Folate helps to reduce the risk of certain serious and common birth defects," Jessica said.

"Right. And wheat germ also provides a good percentage of Vitamin E, a powerful antioxidant that most researchers believe provides protection from age-related ailments such as heart disease and cancer. And you know I drink soymilk faithfully, eat plenty of dark green vegetables, and an array of colorful fruits."

"Running a marathon — 26.2 miles — can really take a lot out of you. It places a tremendous strain on your body. That's why I stopped running them," Jessica said. "Have you given yourself enough time to recuperate?"

"I'm fine. Jim and I will always run marathons. We're just taking a pause now to get ready for the baby," Suzanne said firmly.

"I just want to make sure you're ready to have a baby," Jessica replied. "Plus, you guys have only been married a few months."

"You knew my reason for getting married was to have a baby. That's why my healthy lifestyle is so important to me," Suzanne stressed.

"If you're ready, I'm there in your corner," Jessica said. "Maybe we can see a movie and have dinner sometime?"

"I'll see. I'm usually pretty busy doing stuff around the house with Jim," Suzanne replied.

"Fine. Just let me know when you have some free time," Jessica said.

"Really, Jessica, I don't know if it's a good idea for us to hang out," Suzanne said. "We've gone through a lot to get back to this point of communicating. And I don't want to risk letting memories… and emotions get in the way of us staying the course."

"Don't worry about me. I've got my feelings in check. Being away from you and the company the past couple of years has helped me get through some ugly feelings," Jessica said. "We're friends again and you're getting ready to have a child. I just thought it would be fun to hang out like old times."

"We'll see. I'll talk to you later. I've got a bunch of claims to review and process," Suzanne said.

"Okay. Let me know. I'll wait to hear from you," Jessica said, getting up.

It couldn't hurt to hang out… see a movie and have dinner. It's been over two years. Friends fall out and reestablish friendships all the time. Who am I fooling? It's more than a broken friendship. Pastor Wilcox says you must make a clean break from relationships that may tempt you and prevent you from being and receiving all that God has planned for you. He often says that history does repeat itself, Suzanne thought to herself. *Maybe I'll ask Trevor. He's knows everything about me.*

At the first sign of normalcy, Suzanne and Jim re-examined the idea of conception. Plagued by setbacks, a few weeks later, Suzanne began to experience unmanageable bouts of itching. To combat the chain reaction of itching and scratching, Suzanne tried a series of over-the-counter anti-itching creams and lotions. She bathed in lukewarm water with baking soda and oatmeal. After the repeated failed attempts of relief, she called her physician. Accustomed to once-a-year visits for annual checkups, Suzanne hated having to schedule another trip so soon.

Waking up to another morning of witnessing the suffering of his wife, Jim expressed his concern for her troubling disorder. "Honey, when's your doctor appointment?"

"I couldn't get an appointment until next Thursday," Suzanne responded. "I'm going to see Dr. Tamm because Dr. Conner doesn't have any appointments until next month."

"Next Thursday! You can't wait until next Thursday — that's a week away," Jim said. He was visibly disturbed about Suzanne having to wait. "I know the itching is making you miserable — you haven't had a good night's rest in a long time."

"It'll be okay — I'll get some Benadryl from the company doctor. It will help me until..." Suzanne said. "I'm just not that excited about seeing Dr. Tamm. He appears to be a good doctor, but he doesn't possess the knowledge and wisdom of Dr. Conner. Whenever I've seen him in the past, he seems to struggle with pinpointing the source of my problem and prescribing the right medication."

"See someone else. There are others doctors for you to see," Jim said, agitated with Suzanne's lack of urgency.

"Jim, let me handle this. I can wait," Suzanne said. "I know you're concerned, but I can wait a few more days."

A week of using anti-itch creams and Benadryl proved unsuccessful in alleviating Suzanne's irritating itch. The creams didn't reduce her problem; however, the Benadryl did make her drowsy enough so that she could sleep through the night. Persistent itching throughout the day caused Suzanne to become self-conscious about her urges to scratch. The subtle approaches to rub her itching arms, back, and stomach areas felt awkward. Wondering if anyone noticed her stealing moments to scratch her thighs underneath the conference room table worried Suzanne. Because her job required continuous contact with others — co-workers, claimants, witnesses, lawyers, and physicians — Suzanne often excused herself during meetings to go to the restroom to scratch the various parts of her body. She believed the mass scratching efforts would taper the itching long enough for her to conduct her business.

The morning of her scheduled doctor appointment arrived, and she knew her only chance for relief would have to come from Dr. Tamm.

"Suzanne, I took off this morning to go with you to the doctor," Jim said, walking into the kitchen.

"You didn't need to do that, Jim," she said as she finished washing dishes in the sink. "I'm sure he'll just give me some pills and the itching will be over."

"It's okay. I need to make sure of what he's going to do. I'll drive. I can drop you off at work afterwards."

"Jim, I don't want to wait an extra hour after work for you to pick me up."

"Baby, I've made arrangements to get off early."

"I love you. You are the best husband. Have I told you lately how blessed I am to have you in my life?"

"No, you haven't. But you just did."

They arrived at Dr. Tamm's office for her scheduled appointment. Suzanne sat quietly thinking about her conversation with Jessica. Jim read an outdated issue of *HealthMatters*. Forty minutes later, she and Jim were escorted into an examining room. Shortly thereafter, Dr. Tamm walked in.

Reading the information on Suzanne's medical chart, Dr. Tamm began to ask a series of questions. "What seems to be the problem?"

"I've been itching all over for about a month, but it's gotten worse over the last couple of weeks," Suzanne said.

"Looks like you had this same problem this time last year," he said, reading her medical history. "Where exactly do you itch?"

"Mainly on my hands, thighs, back, arms, and stomach," she said, touching the various areas of her body.

"Are you on any medications that we're not aware of?" Dr. Tamm asked. "Some medications can cause itching. Beyond an allergic reaction to a certain medication, someone who might also be taking prescription drugs, such as diuretics, can experience the effects of dry skin. Even beyond that, constant itching can sometimes be a sign of disease, such as kidney failure, diabetes, or even cancer."

"No, doctor, I'm not taking any medications," Suzanne responded. "Other than this problem, I'm one of the healthiest people I know, that is, next to my husband."

"What about the medications you were taking a couple of weeks ago for the coughing. The expectorant and decongestant," Jim reminded her. "Doctor Tamm, she's miserable. She itches all day and all night."

"I forgot about those medications," Suzanne said, giving Jim a curt look. "A few weeks ago, I had a terrible cough. Dr. Conner prescribed medications that helped to cure me. And you're right, I had this itching problem last year and that led me to try some home remedies before coming in to see you. Having dealt with this before, I've concentrated on increasing the moisture of my body by using bath oils and moisturizers daily. I know limited water intake can be a factor, so I drink plenty of water throughout the day. I generally drink a lot of water anyway because I exercise heavily. I know the importance of replacing what I lose through sweat, urine, and all that good stuff. I also apply cool compresses to my itchy areas, and I've tried an assortment of over-the-counter cortisone creams and lotions. This time, nothing is helping."

"Sounds like you're on the right track," Dr. Tamm responded.

"Doctor, she can't be on the right track... she's itching like a mad woman!" Jim shouted.

"Doctor Tamm, please excuse my husband. He's just concerned about me," Suzanne said apologetically.

"I understand," Dr. Tamm said.

"What about eczema? One of the ladies in my office has it and she experiences the uncontrollable bouts of itching," Suzanne inquired.

"You don't have eczema. Although the look of eczema differs from person to person, it is most often distinguished by dry, red, extremely itchy patches on the skin," Dr. Tamm stated. "Basically, when you itch, you rash. I'm going to prescribe you a topical that will soften and moisturize your skin. It is generally used as a lubricant to treat or ward off dry, itchy skin and minor skin irritations. Plus, I'm going to send you to the lab for some blood work. I need to see you back in a month. If you don't feel any relief over the next week, be sure to come back in."

Fallout-Treachery or Legacy

*A*fter a month of continual application of the medication Dr. Tamm prescribed, Suzanne felt minimal relief. Not only was she still itching, now she had red marks on her hands and thighs.

"Jim, come and look at these red marks!"

"What red marks?" Jim said, running into the bathroom.

"I don't know. They look like bloodclots. Look at my hands and thighs," Suzanne said, panicking. She began to examine her hands and thighs. "It looks horrible! Where did they come from?"

"Baby, whatever is happening to you appears to be getting worse," Jim exclaimed. "I think you should schedule an appointment to see Dr. Conner."

"Dr. Tamm wanted me to come back to see him, but... It's just so hard to get a timely appointment with Dr. Conner," Suzanne said, sounding disappointed.

"Just explain to Dr. Conner's nurse that you need to see him immediately. Explain your condition and that you need the next available appointment. You never know, someone might cancel.

I wouldn't waste time with Dr. Tamm. Go to the person you feel most comfortable with," Jim said, touching her hands. "Maybe you shouldn't go into work today. Can't you work from home?"

"We're having a team meeting today regarding the large number of claims we're still processing from that winter storm. It's mandatory that everyone is at work today," Suzanne said. "I'll call the doctor's office first thing this morning."

Suzanne was dedicated to her team and the company, but failed to recognize how the concerns of her itching disorder affected her ability to concentrate on her work. Having to work slower and repeat assignments delayed the processing of her claims. Over the past weeks, Suzanne had been counseled by her manager on her inability to deliver accurate and timely information. Suzanne knew it was in her best interest to go to work regardless of how miserable she felt.

Arriving home from work, Suzanne just wanted to submerge herself in a cold tub of water to alleviate the misery of itching and scratching. Walking in through the back door to the aroma of Jim's fish tacos temporarily eased Suzanne's discomfort. Jim's fish tacos were her favorite. His knack for rolling lightly seasoned fresh Tilapia fish, low-fat sour cream, mozzarella cheese, Picante sauce, mix greens and fresh tomatoes into a whole wheat tortilla was one of many of his creative approaches to healthier eating. Served with brown rice and fresh black beans, Jim never failed to amaze Suzanne with his clever ability to combine loads of nutrition.

"Hey, baby, I was able to get an appointment with Dr. Conner next week," Suzanne said, walking into the kitchen, extending her arms to embrace Jim. "My weeks of routine itching and scratching will surely come to an end after a visit with Dr. Conner."

"I certainly hope so, honey," Jim said, while holding her tightly. "It's been one thing after another. We need some answers. How was work today?"

"It was busy. How about yours?" Suzanne asked.

"Busy. Ever since Samuel quit, my workload has increased tremendously. I've got to track costs for the projects he was responsible for. Doesn't look like they're going to hire anyone to replace him anytime soon," Jim said, frustrated. "There's a rumor that the company might downsize. I don't know for sure, but that might be why Sam bolted."

"What about all of the projects?" Suzanne asked.

"Most of the projects are nearing completion. And I don't know if we have any new projects or contracts pending," Jim said.

"Hopefully, the rumor isn't true and they'll hire someone else soon," Suzanne said, trying to reassure Jim.

"I sure hope so. I am not going to drive myself crazy trying to stay on top of everything," Jim added.

"Do what you can during the allotted time, and don't worry about the rest," Suzanne said. "I see you're cooking our favorite."

"The grocery store had a sale on Tilapia, so I decided to make some fish tacos," Jim said.

"Great. What can I help you with?" Suzanne asked.

"I'm good. Just go and relax," Jim suggested.

"Okay. I'm going upstairs to get out of these clothes," Suzanne said. "I think I'll do some research on my medical ailments."

After another week of agonizing itching, Suzanne's trip to Dr. Conner arrived. Anticipating a breakthrough, she silently laid in bed praying for a healing.

"Honey, I'm sorry I can't go to the doctor with you this morning," Jim said, while entering the bedroom. "Mr. Perry, the construction manager, is coming down from New York for a meeting this morning. And I can't miss that meeting."

"That's okay, I'll be fine."

"Call me after your doctor's appointment. I love you," Jim said, leaving for work.

Suzanne loved her visits with Dr. Conner. He had been her physician for over ten years. Their bond grew as a consequence of their love and appreciation for running, particularly marathon running. More than a doctor, Dr. Conner was an avid runner. As a combination doctor and athlete, Suzanne believed he was better equipped to provide her with appropriate medical instructions and recommendations. She had confidence in his training because he kept current on the latest in medicine, he was attentive during his visits, he always gave professionally adequate time to her situation, and he was caring. He exhibited the common sense, knowledge, and confidence she looked for in a doctor. If he was unsure about something, he would admit to being at a loss; and she didn't have to worry about him referring her to a specialist.

"Good morning, Suzanne," Dr. Conner said, entering the room.

"Good morning, Dr. Conner."

"Looks like you've been having a difficult time lately."

"Yes, I have. After my last marathon, my health took a nose dive," Suzanne said, sitting on the examination table. "First, I had the cough, and now I have this uncontrollable itching and red marks on my hands and thighs."

"The blood tests Dr. Tamm ordered during your last visit to measure the levels of iron in your body revealed a deficiency," Dr. Conner said, reading through her medical information.

"Doctor, what exactly is iron? You always tell me that my iron is low and to take supplements. I try to eat foods that are high in iron routinely, but...," Suzanne said.

"Simply put, iron is a trace mineral needed for the transporting and storing of oxygen, functioning of metabolic actions, and producing of energy in cells. It's vital because your body needs iron to make hemoglobin, a substance in red blood cells that enables them to carry oxygen."

"Could it be a reason for my tiredness lately?" Suzanne asked.

"Characteristics that typically depict deficiency in iron are anemia, fatigue, rapid heartbeat, breathlessness, inability to concentrate, interrupted sleep, along with a lot of other things..."

"Dr. Conner, what is a trace mineral?" Suzanne asked.

"A trace mineral is a mineral needed by the body in a very small amount. Generally speaking, if you regularly eat a balanced diet made up of a variety of foods, you will receive the recommended amounts of trace minerals. Other trace minerals besides iron include zinc, manganese, copper, flouride, iodine, chromium, selenium, and molybdenum. Consider doing some research on the Internet so you'll have an idea of the nutritional role of other trace minerals. For instance, zinc plays an important role in body growth, development and maturation; in tissue restoration; and in resistance to disease," Dr. Conner responded.

"I've seen advertisements for chromium. The ads say chromium burns fat and lowers blood sugar. And that it builds muscle, lowers cholesterol, and reduces heart disease risk. Are the claims true?"

"Critics and proponents are always churning out theories... broadcasting reports about their clinical trials and studies. There is no concrete evidence that chromium could do any of these things in healthy individuals. In some instances, yes, and in others, maybe. More research is needed. Chromium is necessary for the functioning of the hormone insulin, among other things, and for the breakdown of protein, fat, and carbohydrates."

"I know a lot of my friends at the gym take chromium. I don't know about others, but my friends are trying to build muscle overnight."

"Additional chromium in the form of a supplement is not necessary for most people because the mineral is present in any healthy diet. Eating meat and whole-grain products, as well as fruits such as apples and bananas, or vegetables such as broccoli and potatoes, are reasonably good sources. An important exception that might lead to chromium deficiency is the consumption of highly processed, nutrient deficient foods. Something you don't have to worry about, since your consumption of processed foods is zero."

As Dr. Conner sat talking about Suzanne's healthy habits, she had visions of her trips to Popeye's, Sonic Drive-In, Rudy's Burger Hut, and Taco Bell.

"What do you think my iron deficiency is a result of?"

"I don't know. We need to run more tests. The fact that you're a marathon runner could be a potential cause for iron deficiency. The deficiency may result from increased red blood cell breakdown and increased iron losses in sweat. I also want to mention that thyroid hormones, which regulate metabolic processes, require iron for production. Iron is involved in the production of connective tissue and several brain neurotransmitters, and in the maintenance of a healthy immune system," Dr. Conner stated. "I know most of that sounds foreign to you, but the bottom line is that we're going to run some additional tests."

"At the beginning of this last training period, I required frequent breaks during my training runs. I just thought I was out of shape or getting older. That's why I pumped up my intake of foods high in iron," Suzanne said.

"Excessive running may take a toll on the immune system, especially if there's the presence of predisposed genetics or improper nutritional habits. It's important to understand that there are two different types of absorbable iron in food. You have the heme iron, which is typically found in red meat (beef tenderloin and chuck), seafood (canned tuna, Halibut, and clams) and poultry (chicken liver and turkey). Then you have the non-heme iron, which is typically found in breads (whole wheat), dried fruits (raisins and figs), breakfast cereals (Raisin Bran), vegetables (potato, baked with skin), and legumes (kidney beans)," Dr. Conner explained. "I'll get you a pamphlet on iron before you leave that discusses sources of iron in greater detail."

"I eat hot or cold cereal with a glass of soymilk every morning. Eight ounces of my brand of soymilk has thirty-five percent of iron. Plus, I try to be creative with other ways to incorporate iron. I've started adding clams to my spaghetti sauce," Suzanne said proudly.

"That's great! A good way to include a product high in Vitamin C to facilitate the absorption of iron is to induce combinations like fresh orange slices and oatmeal for breakfast. A homemade tuna salad sandwich served on a bed of romaine lettuce and sliced tomatoes and strips of green pepper for lunch. A serving of broccoli to accompany any dinner entrée, and a section of cantalope or a handful of strawberries for a snack or dessert," Dr. Conner stated.

"I pretty much do all of that," Suzanne said.

"Great!" Dr. Conner responded. "I'm going to prescribe a corticosteroid to treat the skin disorder, which is hives. It is a cream medication to reduce inflammation and relieve itching. Plus, I'm going to prescribe an antihistamine, an oral medication used to treat the symptoms caused by the release of histamine during an allergic reaction. Symptoms such as sneezing… runny nose… itching… swelling… tearing and redness of the eyes… and hives."

"What is histamine?" Suzanne asked.

"Histamine is a chemical found in some of the body's cells. It creates many of the indicators of allergies, such as itchy, watery eyes or sneezing," Dr. Conner responded. "Are you allergic to anything… food… dust… pollen?"

"Not that I'm aware of," Suzanne said hesitantly.

"When a person is allergic to a particular substance, such as a food or dust, the immune system wrongly believes that this usually harmless substance is actually harmful to the body. In an attempt to protect the body, the immune system starts a series of events that triggers some of the body's cells to release histamine and other chemicals into the bloodstream. The histamine then irritates a person's eyes, nose, throat, lungs, skin, or gastrointestinal tract, causing allergy symptoms. That's why we use antihistamine medications to help fight the symptoms."

"Thanks for the explanation and for being the wonderful doctor you are," Suzanne said, relieved. "I certainly hope it all works for me."

"As I mentioned earlier, I'm sending you for some more blood work," Dr. Conner said, patting her on the back. "If the medications don't show any signs of relief in a week, we'll probably need to refer you to an allergist. Just don't worry... we're going to get some answers."

"An allergist! I don't have any allergies," Suzanne said.

"We just need to rule out as much as possible in case the medications don't work," Dr. Conner said.

Departing the doctor's office, Suzanne noticed that she had missed two calls, one from Jim and one from Jessica.

"Let me call Jim before I get on the road," Suzanne said. "Hi, honey."

"Hey, baby. Where are you? How was your doctor's appointment?" Jim asked.

"I'm in the car and the appointment was good. Dr. Conner wants me to try some different medicines. We'll see how they work," Suzanne said. "I know you're busy, so I'll see you at home later. Are we running tonight?"

"Are you up to running?" Jim asked. "You probably need to minimize the stress on your body until Dr. Conner can figure things out."

"I'll be okay. Running will take my mind off the itching. And I don't have any red marks today," Suzanne said. "I'll see you at home later. I love you."

"I love you, too," Jim confirmed.

I guess I'll call Jessica. I'm hesitant because I don't want her to misinterpret our communications with one another, Suzanne thought to herself, while dialing Jessica's number. "Hey, Jessica."

"Hi! How did your doctor's appointment go?"

"It went okay. He ordered some more blood work. I guess I'll just have to wait to see what turns up."

"I have something for you. Are you coming back to work?"

"Yes, I am. What do you have?"

"It's a surprise. Call me when you get close to the building. I've got to go out on a site visit, so I can connect with you on my way out."

"I should be there in about thirty minutes. Why don't you just meet me in front of the parking garage?"

"See you then."

I guess I should get something to eat so I won't have to leave at lunch, Suzanne thought as she pulled out of the parking lot. *I think I'll go by Savory Café, since it's on the way.*

Savory Café was one of Suzanne's favorite restaurants. She loved the Southwestern cuisine. Her favorite item was their spinach and penne pasta dish — a mix of fresh spinach, whole-wheat pasta, red new potatoes, diced celery and carrots, roasted tomatoes, olives — lemon dressing and freshly grated parmesan cheese. *I'd better hurry so I don't miss Jessica.*

Turning into the parking garage, Suzanne called Jessica on her cell phone. "Hey, Jessica, I'm turning into the parking garage. Meet me at my parking space."

Moments later, Jessica appeared at Suzanne's car. "Hey Lady. I see you stopped by Savory Café. I could have gotten you something to eat. How are you feeling?"

"I'm feeling okay today. What's the big surprise?"

"I know you haven't been feeling well lately, and I wanted to do something special for you. One of Tyrone Park's stage plays will be in town on the 28th of next month — *Going from the Hood to the Palace.* I got us some tickets."

"Jessica, you should have checked with me first," Suzanne said, trying to sound polite about her disapproval. "My mother and I are supposed to be going to California next month to see my Aunt Faye. Plus, it's my one-year anniversary."

"I wanted to surprise you. I know you like Tyrone Park's plays. They're always hilarious," Jessica said. "When are you going to California? What day is your anniversary?"

"Next month is a busy month for me. I believe we leave on June 23rd for California, but I'm not exactly sure. My anniversary is on June 30th. I'll let you know. Plus, we need to talk. I'll call you."

"What's there to talk about? It's just a play!"

"Jessica, you should have discussed your intentions to purchase the tickets with me first. I want us to be friends. But, I don't want you to misinterpret the friendship. I love my husband and I'm devoted to him. He is first and foremost in my life. I don't make any decisions to do things without considering him."

"I apologize for wanting to do something spontaneous and nice for you. We were close friends at one point in our lives and I miss that closeness," Jessica said.

"Jessica, that's been a while ago," Suzanne said, interrupting.

"I know you love your husband. I know what's important to you. I care about you and will always care about you. I'm concerned about your health and I want to help you through whatever lies ahead."

"Jessica, I have a husband. He will take care of me. I've got to go. I've got to get to work," Suzanne said, walking away abruptly.

After a month of intermittent relief, mixed with the presence of red marks on her hands, thighs, arms and back, Suzanne contacted Dr. Conner's office to get a referral to see an allergist. As Dr. Conner had explained, the allergist performed a variety of allergy skin-tests, where he applied common allergens, like cat dander, to tiny pricks on her skin and waited to see if her skin reacted. The tests itched and burned a little, but they were not painful. Suzanne knew the pricks and sticks were necessary to give the doctor a better idea of her overall allergy profile. Afterwards, he prescribed several different allergy medicines. He stated that she needed to try a number of them, one at a time, to find out which one worked best for her condition.

Suzanne took the medications as directed for nearly a month; however, they provided minimal relief. With the onset of the summer season, Suzanne pondered plans to travel with her mom to California to see her Aunt Faye. An annual excursion that included a drive up the unforgettably picturesque coastline from San Diego to Los Angeles was now hampered as Suzanne sifted through her reasons to cancel.

Thoughts of the superior climate, superb beaches, and the wonderful collection of recreational and historic attractions was cheering, yet upsetting. How could she enjoy the things she loved so much in the present state of her health? The opportunity to run in Balboa Park. The chance to run on the Mission Beach boardwalk, parallel to the beach... stealing moments to look at the various specialty shops and restaurants. The break from eating farm-raised fish at their local restaurant to eating the fabulous Pacific red snapper at her favorite seafood restaurant in the world. Then there was the trip to Los Angeles and their usual stop and stay in Santa Monica. What an incredible opportunity for Suzanne to run the popular stretch of the 22-mile long beach in sunny Santa Monica before heading back home. Floating in a fog of uncertainty, Suzanne's time for making a decision was running out.

With plans to attend her twenty-year high school class reunion, Suzanne was overwhelmed by yet another planning dilemma. After twenty years of no communication with ex-classmates, Suzanne looked forward to traveling back home to get re-acquainted with everyone. The endless stream of conversations to catch up on where people lived, what types of careers they settled into, who was married and who was single, who had children and how many, filled Suzanne with a mixture of anxiety and calmness. Comforted by her physical appearance, Suzanne was quickly deflated by the fact that something was terribly wrong on the inside. She began to play "what if" scenarios in her mind — *What if the itching and scratching problem is not resolved by reunion time? What if they hadn't found a medication to at least contain it? What if people start thinking I'm contagious?*

Haunted by thoughts of her worsening condition, Suzanne settled on plans to enjoy a wonderful summer. She refused to allow her current health status to impede the upcoming events in her life.

Days later, Suzanne began to experience pain and swelling in her right hand. As the pain and swelling traveled to both hands, Suzanne's concerns intensified.

"Jim, wake up!" Suzanne cried out. "Look at my hands... they're swollen and very painful."

"You need to see Dr. Conner immediately," Jim responded, getting out of bed. "This is something new and it doesn't look good. Try some of my muscle rub to alleviate the pain. What about an ice pack? That might help to reduce the swelling."

Trying not to overreact, Suzanne massaged the pain in hopes that it would go away. "I'll call in the morning," she said. "Baby, why is all of this happening to me? Our first year of marriage has been nothing but turmoil."

"I married you for better or for worse. Don't you worry about our marriage; we are solid," Jim responded. "Let's focus on getting you better. God is going to give us the ammunition to restore your health. But, you've got to employ that tenacity and steadfast hope you're so famous for, until it happens."

"Thank you for erasing my simmering doubts," Suzanne said.

"I'm excited about our one-year anniversary. I do have something special planned," Jim said.

"What?" Suzanne asked.

"You'll have to wait and see."

The following morning, Suzanne was able to get an appointment to see Dr. Conner. While waiting for the doctor, she began to raise the question, *Why? Why am I, of all people, experiencing these things? Lord, I'm trying to release my doubts, fears, and frustrations. I know you have a health breakthrough laying in wait for me, but how much longer must I endure these attacks on my body?*

Entering the examination room, Dr. Conner exhibited a look of concern. "Good morning, Suzanne and Jim."

"Good morning, Dr. Conner," Suzanne and Jim both responded.

"So, what's going on?" Dr. Conner asked.

"I'm now experiencing severe pain and swelling in my hands," Suzanne explained. "What's causing all of this? I'm healthy! These sorts of things don't happen to healthy people, do they?"

"Suzanne, you can do everything right and still face health concerns. A healthy lifestyle reduces your risk of disease and illness. However, there's no foolproof scenario that prevents disease and illness," Dr. Conner explained. "The ailments you're experiencing could be the result of a number of things. Because you have no known history of allergies and your trip to the allergist proved non-conclusive — I just don't know. Your last set of blood work revealed high levels of protein in your urine."

"What's the reason for that, doctor?" Jim asked.

"The reason is usually associated with a kidney problem. Or, it could be any number of other reasons... high blood pressure... acute allergic reaction... lupus," Dr. Conner said. "I need to run some more specialized tests and see what turns up."

"What about my red marks? They come and go. I read that foods may be a cause, but I can't pinpoint any triggers," Suzanne said.

"The red marks are known as Urticaria. Uticaria are hives that are usually an allergic reaction to food or medicine. Hives are a common reaction, especially in people with other allergies like hay fever."

"I don't have allergies!" Suzanne shouted.

"I know. They also develop because of infection or illness related to emotional stress, extreme cold or sun exposure, excessive perspiration, all of which could pertain to you — that is, because you participate in a sport that places stress on your body, places you in extreme weather conditions, and causes excessive perspiration," he said. "Meanwhile, I'm going to prescribe a different set of medications."

"Doctor, all of these medications are adding up. Not to mention the co-pays. First, Dr. Tamm prescribed a set of medicines, then you, then the allergist — now today it's something different," Suzanne said with frustration. "This going around in circles is becoming taxing on my pocketbook. Plus, it seems like you and the other doctors are prescribing allergy medicines, and I don't have allergies. What's really going on? It seems like a lot of trial and error. Do you at least have some samples?"

"Unfortunately, I don't have any samples of what I'm getting ready to prescribe you. Believe me, I understand your frustration. It's frustrating for me not to be able to pinpoint the cause of your health problems. And for now, it is trial and error," Dr. Conner said apologetically.

"In two weeks, I'll be traveling to California with my mother, and the way I feel right now I'm thinking I should cancel my trip," Suzanne said, seeking reassurance that everything would be okay.

"Let's see how you react to the new medicines," Dr. Conner stated.

"What is lupus, Dr. Conner?" Suzanne asked. "A lady at my job has lupus and said she started out experiencing some of the same problems I'm having. I've performed some research of my own. Can you tell me in simplistic terms what it is?"

"Simply put, lupus is a disease in which the immune system malfunctions and turns on itself. Your immune system is a defense zone of different types of cells that protect you against the invasion of infections caused by bacteria and virus. Our immune cells are exterminators and therefore must be able to tell the difference between harmful bacteria and virus cells and your own good cells," Dr. Conner explained. "Visualize going into battle against an enemy defense team wearing the same uniform as your own troops. In a case of lupus, you unavoidably kill troopers on your own side by accident. Consequently, lupus is referred to as an autoimmune disease. This means that the immune system can no longer tell the difference between the enemy and itself, so it tries to attack some of your own good cells."

"What causes lupus?" Jim asked.

"There is no known cause or causes of lupus, except that there are environmental and genetic factors involved. Those who study the disease believe there is a genetic predisposition to the disease. However, there is once again no known gene thought to cause the illness. Environmental considerations like infections, antibiotics, ultraviolet light, extreme stress, certain drugs, and hormones are thought to play a critical role in triggering lupus. Lupus is often associated with women, because it occurs more frequently among adult females than males. For reasons unknown, the disease typically impacts individuals of African, American Indian, and Asian descent more frequently. Some theorize that hormones may be a reason for the progression of the disease. However, the exact reason for the greater frequency of lupus in women, and the repeated increase in symptoms, is unknown," Dr. Conner explained further.

"Are the symptoms of lupus comparable to what Suzanne has been experiencing?" Jim asked. "Could Suzanne have done something to cause lupus-like symptoms?"

"There are a number of things that could be causing Suzanne's condition," Dr. Conner stated. "As far as lupus, the symptoms mimic those of so many other illnesses — achy joints, swollen joints, severe muscle weakness and tiredness, frequent fevers, hair loss, pain in the chest when breathing deeply, anemia, or sun or light sensitivity."

"She has suffered an enormous amount of stress at work, and then there's the marathon training she has participated in throughout the years. The constant stress on her body from routine running on hard surfaces, outside in various weather conditions, and then there's the chronic anemia," Jim stated.

"Dr. Conner, we need to go through an elimination process. How can we determine if I have lupus or not?" Suzanne asked.

"Unfortunately, there is currently no single laboratory test that can determine whether a person has lupus or not. The best we can do is run a battery of laboratory and specialized tests," Dr. Conner stated. "I don't want to fast forward ahead to thinking about lupus. For now, we need to see if the new medications work to alleviate your problems."

"Okay, doctor," Suzanne said.

After much contemplation, Suzanne decided to travel with her mom to California. Jim was concerned about her traveling under unfavorable health conditions, but he respected Suzanne's decision. Suzanne, an only child, often felt torn between her husband and her parents. For years, before her involvement with and marriage to Jim, Suzanne and her parent's lives had been interchangeable. Although they lived in different cities, they were never separated. Since her marriage, Suzanne often felt a sense of obligation to both her husband and her parents. Before Jim, Suzanne's parents occupied every part of her life. Even after nearly one year of marriage, Jim was often stressed by their close involvement.

"Why don't you cancel the trip with your mom?"

"Jim, you know my mom has been looking forward to this trip for quite some time," Suzanne said. "You know my aunt is very ill, and I need to travel with my mom to see her. She can't very well go to California alone, and I can't disappoint her by canceling the trip."

"Why can't your dad go with her?"

"You know my dad doesn't travel."

"If your mom knew about your illness, she wouldn't expect you to go on this trip."

"Jim, I want to go. I think the change of climate might do me some good. Plus, you are welcome to come with us," Suzanne said. "I would love to experience the beaches and hot trendy spots with you."

"You know I can't go with all these construction projects I've got going," Jim said. "I don't know why you insist on going. All that airport madness — lugging baggage, security checks, standing in long waiting lines, flight delays, cramped seating, and hopping on and off shuttle buses will surely exacerbate your condition."

"Jim, it's settled! I am going," Suzanne said. "Don't forget about my class reunion. It's the first weekend in August. Please don't schedule anything for that weekend."

Passing the Baton through the Storm

A week later, Suzanne traveled to Houston. She went earlier than planned so she could spend some time with her father before leaving for California. The medication Dr. Conner prescribed provided some minor relief, but her symptoms were still present. To ensure an ailment-free trip, Suzanne decided to visit the company doctor to get a cortisone injection a day before leaving for Houston. She remembered that an injection two years ago helped her get through a bout of itching during the winter months. *Dr. Blake knows my history. She wouldn't give me something harmful. I just need to make sure I have a wonderful trip. No itching. No scratching. No hives. No pain. I don't have time to consult with Dr. Conner. It's not like I'm taking the kind of steroids athletes use to get bigger muscles. The corticosteroid will help to contain my swelling, redness, itching, pain,* Suzanne thought, trying to rationalize the cortisone injection.

Suzanne began to read her running and fitness magazine as she waited for take off. With all that had been going on, she was four months behind with her reading. *I sure hope I don't get a talker next to me.* Suzanne was a friendly, outgoing individual, and often a magnet for those needing a listening ear.

Moments later, a woman asked, "Is this seat taken?" Suzanne graciously made the lady welcome to sit next to her.

As they sat, preparing for the plane to depart, Suzanne could feel the lady glaring down at her reading material. Noticing the lady's attempts to view the contents of her magazine, she felt compelled to initiate a conversation with her.

"Hi, where are you traveling to?" Suzanne asked.

"I'm going to Arizona for a church convention," the lady said. "What are you reading? The cover looks interesting. Is it a health magazine?"

"I guess you could consider it a health magazine for runners. I'm a runner, and this particular magazine provides me with a variety of training tips, the latest research reports from health professionals, and motivational stories that help keep me committed to living a healthier lifestyle."

"Wow, a runner! I wish I could run or just even get motivated to do some sort of exercise," the lady responded. "I ran track back in high school. Needless to say — that was minus twenty years ago and 75 pounds ago. Over the last year, I've been participating in a weight loss program, but I can't seem to incorporate the exercise piece. I've lost quite a bit of weight, but I still have a long way to go."

"With the right program and motivation, you could be a runner, also. A commitment to exercise and healthy eating habits are the minimum requirements," Suzanne explained.

"That's exactly what I need. The right program," the lady responded.

"What sort of food do you eat?" Suzanne asked.

"For the past few months, I've routinely eaten a grapefruit and two eggs for breakfast, soup and crackers for lunch, and a piece of meat like a steak or chicken with a salad for dinner. Sometimes I'll have one of the meal replacement bars or drinks for breakfast or lunch."

"You may not be consuming enough calories," Suzanne said. "However, it does sound like you're taking in a lot of cholesterol between the eggs and steak, and probably a lot of sodium between the soup and crackers."

"I don't want to eat a lot of calories. That's my method for losing the weight," the lady replied. "I hadn't thought about cholesterol and sodium."

"My fitness consultant, Trevor, says when you don't get enough calories, your body will go into a starvation mode. In order to lose weight, it is necessary to reduce the amount of calories you consume. But not eating enough calories can have damaging effects. Your body needs a certain amount of calories to live, plus a little more to support your daily activity level. Trevor says the moment you start restricting caloric intake, your body recruits lean muscle mass for fuel... to keep you living."

"What's wrong with that?"

"The last thing you want is to lose muscle mass. Have you ever seen someone who's lost a lot of weight? Their skin sags. Although the scale shows that magical number they were aiming for — they look thin, but they're actually fatter. They have more fat than muscle. Because fat weighs less than muscle you don't need as many calories. And that's okay if they can eat less calories for the rest of their existence on earth. Unfortunately, it never works out that way. Sacrificing... resisting those temptations... eating less... eventually comes to an end. And when it does, they go back to their familiar style of eating."

Suzanne continued to explain to the lady how the weight returns in the form of fat. "It becomes more difficult to lose the weight because they probably have a lot more to get rid of. Always remember muscle burns fat. If there's no muscle or limited muscle, you can't burn fat. Burning fat is what creates a lean... tone body."

"I guess that's why most health articles encourage exercise," the lady responded.

"Absolutely. One of the reasons for that is so you can lose unwanted pounds and build muscle mass," Suzanne confirmed.

"I'm just eating the grapefruit, egg, soups and salads until I lose all the weight I'm aiming for."

"Like I said, eating less activates your body's starvation mode. Your body expects a certain level of food every day... and when that doesn't happen, it conserves energy by slowing down your metabolism. In return, your body is taught to be more efficient at storing fat for those times it doesn't receive what it expects. When you resume that familiar style of eating, the food you eat will more than likely get stored as fat... and the weight will return. If you're not careful, a cycle of food restriction and food over consumption can cause a series of health problems."

"I saw an ad for a weight loss program last week," the lady said. "Basically, you purchase all of your meals from the company... breakfasts, lunches and dinners... and desserts. All for approximately $10 a day. Since I don't like to cook... and I'm getting tired of the same meals everyday... I thought it would be ideal. Plus, you don't have to worry about counting CARBS, points or calories. I only wish I could afford the program. There's no way I could shell out $300 a month."

"Three hundred bucks is a lot," Suzanne replied. "In order to become healthier, some adjustments are necessary. Cooking is one of those adjustments. You can develop your own repertoire of healthy, easy-to-make dishes that can be eaten in one or two settings. Healthy, nutritious and tasty foods like a turkey loaf, new potatoes with rosemary, and steamed asparagus are easy to prepare. Most of the pre-packaged, ready-to-eat meals are full of chemicals... preservatives... and sodium. We're all oblivious to the unhealthy levels of chemicals we're consuming everyday. Our quick and convenient lifestyle has us inhaling unhealthy levels. Start looking at the ingredients on the packaging... start researching those ingredients to see what they are. Sorry... guess I got on my soapbox for a moment."

"I know you're right," the lady said. "I do need to make an effort to cook more. I've never thought about chemicals in foods. I just know what I like to eat. I buy the fully-cooked chicken breast to eat with my salads. I guess I could cook my own chicken."

"The chicken you cook would not have the levels of chemicals and sodium that are in the pre-packaged... pre-seasoned... fully-cooked... or frozen, ready-to-eat versions. Just remember that even the packaged fresh chicken purchased out of the grocery store's meat department's refrigerated cases have chemicals... unless the company states that their chicken is 100% all natural, meaning they were raised without use of hormones and steroids, and do not contain any artificial flavoring, coloring, chemical preservative, or synthetic ingredient, and has been minimally processed. And let me tell you, there aren't too many of those companies out there," Suzanne said.

"I need to start thinking about these things," the lady said.

"You have to eat in order to lose weight. So try and eat four to six small meals a day, and that will be a good way to keep your metabolism going... burning fat. And you have to exercise. Only exercise can build muscle mass."

"How did you get started with the running?"

"Actually, I've been a runner for over ten years. I remember years ago watching episodes of *Baywatch* every Saturday night, wishing for a lean, soft, sculptured body like the girls running on the beach. One day, I decided to join one of the local fitness clubs. My first encounter with the fitness consultant and the machines was disastrous. First, I was placed on a stairclimber. I couldn't last five minutes. Then I was placed on a stationary bike. Once again, I couldn't last ten minutes. I remember thinking that I'd never get the hang of exercising long enough to make a difference. I contemplated over and over just giving up. But, I went everyday, and over a period of time my stamina improved. I remember walking on the treadmill and observing the younger ladies next to me running effortless with ease and confidence. With a craving to do the same, I began to execute a combination of walking and running. Over a period of time, I was able to do more running than walking. In 1999, I ran my first marathon. My fitness consultant, Trevor, who at that time was my running coach in a program I joined, helped me train for about six months."

"That's awesome! Were you fat at the time you started exercising? I'm sorry, were you larger back then?" the lady asked.

"I wasn't a large size, but I was a little chunky. As a result, I wasn't happy, and I think it showed externally through my lack of self-confidence and relationships with others. I was basically a recluse. I didn't go out. Like I said, my weekends were pretty much spent watching sitcoms and drama shows. And believe me I had a lot of spare time. I even felt uncomfortable getting on airplanes. The tight seating areas reminded me of how oversized I was. The times that I did decide to venture out, I did everything by myself. I often went to the movies alone," Suzanne said.

"There's nothing wrong with going to the movies alone," the lady interjected.

"I know. But, I did it because I was unhappy with myself and didn't feel deserving of the company of others," Suzanne shared. "At the time, I had a job that required me to do a lot of traveling. I had an opportunity to visit some exciting cities, but I never felt comfortable venturing out to explore the activities, attractions and events... or the shopping districts, restaurants or nightlife. All because I didn't feel worthy. So I would stay in the hotel room after transacting my daily business, order room service and watch the pay-per-view movies."

"You look great! How did you get out of your rut?" the lady asked.

"I didn't like the way I looked, so I decided to do something about it. Plus, I didn't want to end up like the multitude of my family members — who died untimely deaths from diabetes, heart disease, and cancer. I decided to raise my bar and live a better, healthier life. The gym was my first step toward doing just that."

"Before I started eating the grapefruits, soups and salads, I was solely a fast food eater," the lady said. "How did you get into marathon running?"

"I had a supervisor who ran daily and was inspired by his enthusiasm. I listened to him talk about running outdoors, breathing God's fresh air and enjoying the sunshine, rain, sleet, and snow — along with the scenery, the people and the varying terrain. He was my first introduction to running. More amazing for me, he had run a marathon race — 26.2 miles. It was then that I moved from the inside, running on a treadmill, to the outside, running the track. I traded the confinement of running inside for the freedom of running outside."

"How were you able to travel and eat healthy?"

"Traveling made eating healthier a little challenging. I mainly focused on eating establishments that offered healthy choices — steamed vegetables and fresh fruits, wheat bread, etc., eliminating the butter and condiments high in all the wrong stuff. I always asked the hotel concierge about the nearest cafeteria or deli."

"What were your initial steps for becoming a runner? Did you walk and run everyday, every other day — did you go fast or slow? I'm just asking because it's something I've been thinking about, but I don't know how to go about getting started. Even more than that, I guess I'm just scared."

"Through the years, I've gone through a lot of trial and error. If I had to give any one particular piece of advice, it would be to first get a good pair of shoes. Proper footwear protects the body from injury. For years, I ran in the wrong type of footwear that caused a series of unpleasant injuries," Suzanne said.

"What kind of running shoes should I get?"

"The type of running shoes varies for everyone. Once you get to the running stage, it's important to understand that you need a shoe specific to running. When inappropriate shoes are utilized for running, the result can be a plague of leg and foot problems. The best way to ensure you get a running shoe that fits properly is to go to a specialty running store. The staff is generally experts at recommending running shoes. They will conduct an assessment of your feet, such as measurement of length and width of each foot... and observe your walking and running style. After the assessment, they will recommend two to three pairs of running shoes for you to try. Based on the fit and comfort, you make the selection. It's a good idea to take the shoes you've utilized in the past so they can review your wear pattern. Additionally, the right pair of socks is critical to prevent running ailments, such as blisters. Cotton socks are not recommended at all."

"Are running shoes very expensive?"

"Prices will vary. I see so many people walking and running in the wrong shoes... old tennis shoes, fashionable shoes, and recreational sports footwear. Women especially like to exercise in cute shoes that match their workout outfits. In the long run, they pay for it and have to take an extended break from exercising. If you're serious about getting started the right way, check out the running stores in your area that can guide you on selecting the correct walking and/or running shoe for your foot type — flat, high arched, or normal. The right shoe will offer the right motion control, cushion, flexibility and stability for your foot type."

"What do you mean by motion control?"

"Because I have flat feet, my feet tend to roll inward when I run. To control the inward motion, I need a motion control running shoe. The motion control shoe prevents my feet from rolling inward. It's kind of like having a corrective shoe. The early years of running in the wrong footwear caused me to experience a series of common injuries like plantar fascitis, shin splints, and knee pain."

"I didn't realize the importance of correct running shoes."

"For right now, you should concentrate on developing a structured walking program to help you lose some more weight. With running, each time your foot strikes the ground you are applying a large percentage of your body weight in force to each leg and your spine. If you start out trying to run, your excessive body weight on the joints, tendons and ligaments can make you more susceptible to injury."

Suzanne encouraged the lady to focus on establishing a daily walking program for at least one month. "One month of consistent walking, coupled with sound eating habits, will generate a weight loss of eight to ten pounds. Your body will be better conditioned. At that point, it will be safe to initiate a mixture of walking and running, for example four minutes of walking with two minutes of running."

She recommended starting out on a treadmill since it provided a soft surface. "Exercising on pavement can be extremely taxing on the body. The key is to start slowly."

Suzanne gave the lady some of the basic tips that helped her in beginning. Her tips included exercising at least three to five days each week. Warming up for five to ten minutes before her main aerobic activity. Maintaining her exercise intensity for thirty to forty-five minutes. Suzanne stressed the importance of gradually decreasing the intensity of her workout and stretching to cool down during the last five to ten minutes.

"In order to generate weight loss, you should progressively increase your minutes to sixty (five days per week)," Suzanne suggested. "First and foremost, visit your physician for a check-up before starting any exercise program."

"I did have a physical last month, and my doctor encouraged me to exercise. I think I will join a gym in my neighborhood. I received an advertisement on my door last week. The monthly cost of the gym in my neighborhood is $19 per month. And, no contract! Is that a good rate?"

"That's good. If you decide on a personal trainer to help you develop a personalized plan, there will be an additional cost. Trevor, the guy I've mentioned, owns a fitness facility, Faith-Based Fitness Solutions over on Maple Lane in Dallas. I could give you his contact information. He can also develop a solid walking program for you," Suzanne suggested. "As far as using the fitness equipment, I would advise you to invest in a few sessions to make sure you're knowledgeable about the equipment and how to gain the most benefit. And most fitness facilities will surely have aerobic and kickboxing classes."

"Maybe aerobics, but not kickboxing. I mainly want to start off on the treadmill. Are there any special considerations for the treadmill?"

"Whether you walk outside or on a treadmill, you should walk at a pace that increases your heart rate. You can't walk at a casual pace and expect to burn calories. You have to walk at a quick pace or a higher incline. Another thing… don't hold onto the rails. Holding onto the rails prevents you from maximizing your legs to do the work. Also, don't stand too close to the front of the treadmill. You will shorten your stride. Stand back and aim for a comfortable, normal stride."

While they were talking, the flight attendant approached with her cart of refreshments.

"Would you like peanuts or pretzels?" the flight attendant asked the lady.

"I'll take the pretzels," the lady stated.

"What would you like to drink?" the flight attendant asked the lady.

"A diet soda will be fine," the lady responded.

"Would you like peanuts or pretzels?" the flight attendant asked Suzanne.

"None for me. I'll just take a cup of ice, thank you," Suzanne said.

"So, I guess you don't eat peanuts or pretzels for some health reason," the lady asked.

"I've just gotten in the habit of traveling with my own healthy snacks and beverages," Suzanne responded as she retrieved a granola bar, apple and bottle of water. "The peanuts and pretzels are too salty for me. Their beverage choices are soda, fruit juices, or coffee — I don't drink caffeinated or diet drinks, and the fruit juices are too sugary and high in calories. My mother and I will be in California in a day or so, and I'd rather save my excess caloric intake for my favorites, like Key Lime pie."

"You are disciplined with your eating," the lady replied.

"Eating healthier is probably the hardest hurdle to overcome. Everyday we're bombarded with the food industry's attack on our weakness for food. They're always coming up with something. I always love to see what the pizza companies are going to come up with next. My favorite is the company that has the pull-apart crust with thirty cheese-filled bites. Each one of the cheese bites is seasoned with the flavor of garlic butter. Being the researcher that I am, I looked on the company's website for the nutritional value of the pepperoni version they advertised. One slice is 420 calories, 19 total fat grams, 10 of those grams are saturated fat... 55 milligrams of cholesterol, 1170 grams of sodium, and 42 grams of carbohydrates. Back in the day, I would have eaten at least three slices... more than likely four slices. Eating three slices was enormous, and that doesn't even consider the other foods I had eaten that day."

"I saw an advertisement last night for a new lasagna pizza... I'm sure it contains a lot of unhealthy levels of this and that," the lady said.

"Now that's pretty innovative," Suzanne replied.

"It's a lot to absorb and figure out. What to eat? What not to eat?"

"You might consider seeking the services of a registered dietitian or nutritionist. They can give you specific guidance on how to incorporate healthier eating habits," Suzanne suggested.

"What do you think about weight training?"

"Weight training can definitely help you lose weight. The higher your ratio of muscle to fat, the faster your metabolism will be and the more calories you'll burn 24 hours a day. Strong muscles developed under the right conditions are important, because you'll develop the power to do more. Daily life activities are easier — moving a large planter, lifting your bike into the car or onto a bike rack, repositioning a large television, moving furniture — plus, you'll be less likely to get injured during exercise. Routine weight training also helps to prevent osteoporosis, the loss of bone mass that inevitably comes with age and makes you more susceptible to broken bones."

"You're like a walking fitness encyclopedia. I'm glad we had an opportunity to sit next to one another. By the way, what is your name?"

"My name is Suzanne, and yours?"

"My name is Molly."

"Maybe we can exchange email addresses so I can periodically contact you for fitness tips, and to let you know how my exercising is progressing," Molly said. "I am going to start doing something. You have motivated me. I don't know why, but there's that fear of exercising. Not getting results quick enough. Worrying about what others think. Making excuses about finding the time.

Finding somewhere to exercise where no one will see me. No one to exercise with. I just need to stop making excuses, get started and stick with it."

"There's a host of information I can share with you regarding nutrition, water intake, safety tips, and injury prevention. You might also consider running a half marathon or full marathon one day."

"Let me get started with walking and we'll see about the other."

"I recommend that you contact Trevor. He will be happy to give you some tips. He can get you into a structured walk and run program that will guide you on how to build your endurance through progressively increased intensity. He'll ensure you reach your fitness goals," Suzanne said.

"It couldn't hurt to get his name and telephone number," Molly admitted.

"I can also give you the names of walk/run programs in the area that meet each week. They have coaches equipped to provide instruction on proper form and technique, injury prevention, resistance and flexibility. Best of all, you will receive valuable information on eating healthy, meal preparation, and sports nutrition."

"It all sounds wonderful. Please write down the information," Molly said, handing Suzanne a piece of paper.

"Meanwhile, I don't mind sending you tips to help you along the way. My motto is… 'The freedom to be fit without restriction'. I'll also put the name of a running store on here… Luke's Locker. It's over off Mapleville Lane, not too far from Trevor's fitness facility."

"Thanks… I like that motto. I'd appreciate any information you send."

"What sort of convention are you attending?" Suzanne asked.

"It's a national Baptist convention."

"What goes on there?"

"All sort of things. I'm overseer of the Sunday School and Baptist Training Union at my church, so I mainly attend for the christian leadership seminars and workshops. The classes are designed to help church leaders and individuals take their ministry and relationship with God to the next level. The schedule of events will include teaching and preaching all day, drill team competitions, and a musical concert on one of the nights. It's pretty awesome!"

"It sounds awesome."

"Are you and your husband members of a church?"

"Yes… we attend Bethany Baptist Church."

"Are you active in ministry?"

"No. We're Sunday Service saints. We've thought about getting involved, but…"

"You should really consider doing so. There's a lot of work to be done in the church. Involvement in ministry is a great way to become fully connected to the church. You'll never get a sense of belonging if you're not involved with other believers… your church family. Also, it's a great way to use your gifts and talents to give back to the community. You never know, there might be a need for you to share your fitness tips."

"I'll see. Right now is not a good time."

"There's no time like the present."

"My life is so shaky right now. I've been dealing with sporadic medical concerns for the past few months."

"Sounds like you need to reach in and grab a hold of your spiritual life preserver," Molly said.

"Have you ever felt like the demons of your past were buried alive? And were just waiting to resurface," Suzanne asked.

"We all have the demons of our past lying in wait. It's up to us to keep them buried," Molly said, confused about the direction of conversation.

"I have a friend. She was involved with someone a few years ago. She ended the relationship because of her struggles with the type of lifestyle she was involved in. The person went away, but now they're back. She wants to be friends with the person, but she doesn't think she can suppress the feelings she once had for the person. The feelings she thought had gone away," Suzanne said.

"It's like being a babe in your Christian living. You have to remove yourself from those things that will divert you from being the person God has designed for you to be. If your friend can't be a friend to the person without experiencing those old feelings, then she should sever all ties until she's strong enough to do so. And that might take years. Most importantly, her only source for relinquishing those thoughts and feelings is through prayer. She has to ask God to deliver her from those things that can arrest her mind, body and soul. She'll never be all HE has designed for her until she lets go of what's holding her captive," Molly said.

"For so long, I've been simultaneously trapped by my past and tormented in my present. The stress of living two lives... two lies... is starting to tear me apart inside. The fear of exposure is overwhelming... the betrayal, hurt and pain my husband... parents... friends... co-workers... and church members would experience if they knew the other side. I love my husband, Jim, with all my heart and soul, but the internal struggles are waging a war inside of me," Suzanne said. "I know you probably figured out that the friend was me. And please don't misunderstand me; I have not been unfaithful to my husband."

"I understand. Suzanne, I don't want to get all preachy and sanctimonious with you. Lord knows I'm fighting my own internal battles — my addiction to unhealthy eating — an addiction that has controlled my very existence. But, the fact that you're even considering your feelings for this other person is trouble. It doesn't sound like you've really let go. I don't know how quickly the transition from the relationship to your marriage occurred, but it doesn't sound like you gave yourself enough time to heal or to feel the sadness and pain associated with ending a relationship," Molly said. "I'll be praying that you dispel those demons that have you trapped in the past and tormented in the future. I encourage you to pray for the strength to break those chains of secret desires... secret feelings... and secret thoughts so they won't yank you into a web of deception. There has to be something greater in front of you... a relationship with God, a future with your husband free of deception. An internal peace that will allow you to break the chains and not get yanked back in. For me, I know a continued unhealthy lifestyle will eventually catch up with me. And with that… the possibility of a life saddled with disease, illness, and unable to be all God has orchestrated for me to be."

"We've shared a lot for two people who just met. I feel like a weight has been lifted off my shoulders. Just being able to say the things I've been thinking… the things I've kept bottled inside… saying them out loud has freed me to believe in a future with no more lies. No more secrets. And no more pain."

"I don't think it was by coincidence… I believe that it was by divine appointment that we were placed in this seating arrangement together. I'll also be praying for restoration for your body and the strength to break those chains."

"Sounds like we're starting our descent."

The flight attendant confirmed the aircraft's descent, and began the announcement of the standard protocol for picking up trash, placing seats in their upright positions, securing tray tables, and issuing final instructions for those with ending and connecting flights.

"When we first began talking, I wanted to credit myself for taking control of my life. But now, I know the true credit belongs to God for giving me the power to change," Suzanne said. "After talking with you today, I believe that God will give me the power to defeat the demons that keep me anchored in deception, fear, regret, shame and selfishness. I'm tired of being ocean floor bound. I'm ready to be air bound."

Suzanne departed the plane to meet and greet her mother and father, and Molly stayed behind to continue her flight to Arizona.

"Hi Mom and Dad," Suzanne said, moving with excitement toward her parents.

"Hi, sweetie, it's good to see you," Suzanne's mother said as she embraced her.

"Give your father a hug. Your mother may never let you go," her father said.

"Are you hungry?" her mother asked.

"Actually, I am," Suzanne responded. "I need to get my luggage. I believe it's on carrousel C. And I need to call Jim and let him know I made it."

"Okay. We'll wait over by the pay telephones."

While waiting for her luggage to arrive, Suzanne telephoned Jim. "Hi, honey, I made it."

"How are you feeling?" Jim asked.

"I'm feeling fine. I forgot to tell you about my wonderful idea," Suzanne said, waiting for Jim's response.

"What?" Jim asked.

"I got a cortisone shot from Dr. Blake before I left work," Suzanne answered.

"Suzanne, you should have told me. You didn't forget," Jim said, irritated.

"I had a wonderful flight. No itching. No pain. The hives are somewhat visible, but no itching. I talked with a lady the entire flight about running. How's everything at work?"

"We're really busy," Jim responded. "I'm glad you had a good flight. What are you and your parents getting ready to do?"

"We're going to get something to eat."

"Call me later. I love you."

"I will. I love you."

"How's Jim doing?" Suzanne's dad asked, walking toward her to assist with the luggage.

"He's okay," Suzanne responded. "He wanted to come on the trip, but he has a lot of projects going."

Suzanne and her parents went to one of the local restaurants. Suzanne enjoyed talking to her parents in person. Because of the long distance and her hectic work schedule, she rarely got a chance to see them. Whenever they saw one another, Suzanne and her mom caught up on life's happenings while partaking in their favorite adventure of shopping. She and her dad's catch-up time generally occurred in front of the television while watching some sporting event.

A day of visiting quickly came to an end. Suzanne and her mom were off to California to check on Aunt Faye in her assisted living facility. The opportunity to vacation in the area was a bonus.

After enjoying a three-hour nap on the plane, they arrived safely at the San Diego Airport. Walking through the terminal, the first order of business was to get their bags, take the shuttle bus to the rental company to pick up their car, and check into the hotel. After checking into the hotel, they would go and take Aunt Faye out to dinner.

During the meal, Suzanne excused herself to call Jim. She knew he'd worry about how she was feeling.

"Hi, honey," Suzanne said.

"Hi. Did you have a good flight?" Jim asked. "How are you feeling?"

"I think all the movement has aggravated something. I'm starting to itch again and I have the hives," Suzanne admitted. "I had planned on running, but I guess that's not going to happen."

"How long is the cortisone shot supposed to last," Jim asked. "What about your hands? Are they hurting?"

"I thought the shot would last for at least three to four days… at least until the new medicines kicked in," Suzanne said. "My hands are not hurting, but they are a little swollen."

"If it gets too bad, go to the emergency room," Jim said. "And Suzanne, do not do any running."

"I'll be okay," Suzanne said.

The next few days proved to be well worth the discomforts of itching and hives. The superb climate and beaches were magnificent. Rather than running, she enjoyed walks with her mom through Balboa Park, the Mission Beach boardwalk, and the shopping districts. Their favorite seafood restaurant was still as gorgeous as ever. Their usual drive up the coast to Los Angeles was breathtaking. Towards the end of the trip, Suzanne was unable to hide the increased discomforts of her itching and hives, and was forced to tell her mother about her health problems over the past months. Suzanne's mother shared her experiences with a similar situation when she was in her thirties. At the time, she remembered her doctor suggesting that she had lupus. Her mother shared how she dismissed the doctor's suggestions... incorporated a better eating plan, and eventually the ailments vanished.

"I wasn't going to let some doctor tell me I had a disease. I worked hard at implementing the things I had control over to help me to get better. Above all, I relied on God to pull me through a difficult period in my life. I was inspired as I listened to the testimonies of others and saw how God's goodness pulled them through various situations and illnesses. I kept Him as my focal point."

On the flight back from Los Angeles, Suzanne realized that she needed to be more assertive with her doctors. She knew she needed to follow the footsteps of her mother, and rely on God's healing powers.

"Hi, baby," Suzanne said, embracing Jim.

"I missed you. I'm glad you're back home," Jim said, putting her luggage in the trunk. "That was the longest four days. Oh yeah, I need to give you your anniversary gift a little early."

"Our anniversary isn't until Sunday," Suzanne said, getting inside the car.

"I know, but I've got a surprise for you," Jim said.

"I like surprises," Suzanne said.

"Well, you'll have to wait until we get home," Jim said. "And it's paper. I bet you thought I wouldn't remember or know about the paper."

Before Suzanne could get settled in the house, Jim presented her with a box. Suzanne opened the box and to her amazement were two tickets to see Tyrone Park's *Going from the Hood to the Palace* on June 28th, the same day Jessica had purchased tickets for. Suzanne knew she needed to sever all roads to rekindling a friendship with Jessica, and now she had the perfect opportunity to do so.

The Eye of the Storm

*B*ack home, Suzanne called Dr. Conner's office to schedule an office visit. Informed that he was on a summer vacation, Suzanne decided to wait for his return, rather than see someone else. Meanwhile, she and Jim conducted their own research on the Internet, searching for more answers. As Dr. Conner previously stated, her health disturbances mimicked a variety of health conditions. Sorting through the vast amounts of information became discouraging. Feeling some relief from the medications, Suzanne assured Jim that it was okay to wait for Dr. Conner's return.

A few weeks later, the time for Suzanne's class reunion arrived. She had been communicating back and forth with Dan, one of her ex-classmates, through email. He was a part of the planning committee. Monthly emails to Dan had generated enthusiasm for seeing the other members of their class. For weeks, Suzanne told Jim about the history of their class, her best friends in high school, scandals, etc. She looked forward to the Friday night social gathering and the event lineup for the weekend.

Jim and Suzanne left town as scheduled and arrived at the class reunion's Friday night social. After the introductions of friends and spouses, the blending of memories started. Discussions surrounding favorite and worse teachers, and how both groups encouraged, motivated, and shaped their lives enlisted participation from all assembled in the room of seventy ex-classmates. The highlight for Suzanne came when her best friend from high school entered the room. Having no communication since their sophomore year in college, nearly eighteen years earlier, the two embraced and carried on a conversation as though no time had lapsed. The various cluster of special friends reminisced until the early morning hours.

"Jim, are you having a good time?" Suzanne asked while preparing for the Saturday morning brunch.

"A marvelous time," Jim said, trying to imitate one of Suzanne's classmates.

The remainder of the weekend proved to be well worth the journey — discussions about the old times, good times, and the adventures of sneaking off campus to drink alcohol. The special tributes to deceased teachers and classmates at the Saturday night banquet were inspiring. Classmates and their spouses and guests had fun renewing old acquaintances, making new ones and seeing the evolution of the school after twenty years. The rekindling of friendships and fond memories brought forth vows from all in attendance to keep in touch until the next reunion.

A few days after the special and memorable event, Suzanne's life was altered dramatically without warning. She awoke to a body paralyzed with pain, swelling and stiffness, and was unable to get out of bed. She yelled out to Jim, "I can't move my body! Everything hurts when I move!" Curled up into a fetal position, Suzanne tried to minimize the pain.

"I'm going to call your doctor!" Jim said, picking up the phone. "What's the number?"

"No, Jim! I have a doctor's appointment on Monday morning. Just give me a few of the anti-inflammatory pills," Suzanne said, pointing to the dresser. "I'll just stay in bed until Monday."

"What hurts?"

"It's my entire body! It's indescribable!"

"Is it your joints, bones, or muscles?"

"I don't know. I can't move."

"You can't stay like this for three days. You need to go to the emergency room. They can run test and stabilize your condition until Monday."

"Jim, they won't give me anything to take. I'm under the care of a physician. It'll be a waste of time. Going to the emergency room will be more stressful for me… long hours in a waiting room… grumpy patients… I'll be okay."

"Okay. Either you're going to let me help you put on your robe and house shoes, and take you to the emergency room, or, I'm going to call an ambulance," Jim said, demanding Suzanne's cooperation. "Which is it going to be?"

"Help me put on some clothes."

A combination of pain, stiffness, and swelling saturated Suzanne's body. The trip to the emergency room proved to be unsuccessful. After waiting for five hours, unsure about when she would be seen by a physician, Suzanne demanded that Jim take her home.

The next few days, Jim tried to make Suzanne as comfortable as possible with soup, cold compressions — but nothing eased the truckload of troubles she described.

The morning of her doctor's appointment, Suzanne recruited every fiber in her body to manage the pain while getting dressed.

"Baby, what can I help you with?" Jim asked.

"If you could run me some bath water and help me into the bathtub… I'd appreciate it," Suzanne said, drained of energy.

"What do you want to wear, so I can get your clothes ready?'"

"Just pick me out something easy to get in and out of."

Jim became disheartened watching the physical deterioration of his wife. She was unable to get out of bed, lift her legs in and out of the bathtub, and dress herself without assistance.

An endless stream of health ailments began. Routine doctor visits produced a lot of confusion. Dr. Conner's diagnosis of Suzanne's health woes was inconclusive. Because of her severe pain, Dr. Conner referred her for a bone scan to obtain a view of her entire skeleton to detect injuries, infections, bone cancer, or disease. It would hopefully help him to evaluate the unexplained bone pain. Suzanne was a little apprehensive about the procedure because of the injection of a radioactive substance. After reassurance that the substance was safe, she agreed.

Dead-end conclusions from the battery of blood tests revealed no medical reason for Suzanne's present condition. On the advice of a colleague who specialized in rheumatology, Dr. Conner ordered a different set of blood tests. Suzanne was directed to return in three days for her test results. During her visit, Dr. Conner reviewed the latest blood work with Suzanne. The blood work indicated a high level of inflammation flowing inside her body. Dr. Conner couldn't pinpoint the cause and sought further consultation from his colleague on the readings of the blood tests.

Each time, the blood tests revealed that her number of red blood cells were low. Dr. Conner explained that a low number of red blood cells indicated the presence of chronic inflammation causing her body to react with pain, swelling, warmth and redness. The routine test Dr. Conner ordered to measure the inflammation in her body was called a "sed rate." Once again, the results revealed that the "sed rate" was high, indicative of a great amount of inflammation.

"Dr. Conner, all of the tests appear to be inconclusive," Suzanne stated. "Why doesn't the test reveal the source of my pain, swelling, nights sweats, hurting hands and red welts?"

"You are truly a medical mystery, Suzanne," Dr. Conner said. "We need to do two things. First, my nurse will schedule you an appointment with a dermatologist to have a skin biopsy done on the hives, and secondly, we need to get an X-ray of your hands and knees."

"What is a skin biopsy for?"

"The skin biopsy helps to determine whether or not you have a connective tissue disease."

"What is a connective tissue disease?"

"Connective tissue disease is a chronic inflammatory autoimmune disease, involving a disorder of the body's connective tissues — tendons, cartilage, ligaments, bones, muscles, and other parts of the body such as skin and internal organs. We've talked before about autoimmune diseases like lupus. A connective tissue disease may be or evolve into an autoimmune disorder, like lupus, scleroderma, polymyositis, vasculitis, rheumatoid arthritis, sjogren's syndrome, and fibromyalgia. The skin biopsy will help us to analyze the hives and determine the presence of disease," Dr. Conner stated. "And the X-ray can help determine any bone abnormalities. My nurse will schedule you an appointment with Dr. Eichon, a very good dermatologist."

The visit with Dr. Eichon resulted in another dead end. The skin biopsy did not reveal a connective tissue disease. A mixture of piercing pain, seizing stiffness and swelling, and horrifying hives launched an assault on the life Suzanne had enjoyed for so many years. Weakness and fatigue made daily life activities difficult to the point that twisting the plastic cap off a bottle of water was a struggle. For Suzanne, the worse part was her inability to run. Frequent doctor visits continuously showed that Suzanne's blood tests were all borderline... that something was going on with her autoimmune system, but Dr. Conner couldn't identify the cause. After weeks of drawing a blank, Dr. Conner referred Suzanne to the rheumatologist.

"Hey, baby, how did you make out at your doctor's appointment?" Jim asked, entering the living room.

"Dr. Conner set up an appointment with a renowned rheumatologist. He's supposed to be the best in his field. My appointment is next Wednesday," Suzanne said, trying to fold some clothes.

"Honey, let me fold those," Jim said, reaching for the clothes. "He should have referred you to a specialist some time ago. All these doctors worry about is saving the insurance companies money. You probably could be on the road to recovery had he referred you to someone weeks ago. It's about time he admitted defeat," Jim said. "I just hope you're not going to have to pay dearly for it with prolonged sickness."

"Jim, he's just as worried about all of this as we are," Suzanne said, defending Dr. Conner.

"I'm going with you," Jim said. "The office is so crazy right now, but I'm still taking you."

"What about the talks of downsizing? You haven't mentioned anything about it in a while," Suzanne said, sounding disturbed.

"Suzanne, I don't want you thinking about my job. You have enough on your mind," Jim said.

"Jim, I want to be kept in the loop. Now what's going on?" Suzanne asked.

"Since we didn't get that major construction project with Mim's Computers, I really don't know..." Jim paused.

"What about all of the other projects? The projects you've been handling since Sam left," Suzanne questioned.

"They're all coming to an end. I'm thinking I'd better start looking around at other opportunities. What would you like for dinner tonight?" Jim said, trying to change the subject.

"Whatever you decide is fine with me. Don't worry! Everything will be okay. We have some money saved. So whatever happens... You're good at what you do. We are prepared."

"Thanks, baby, for your support. I love you."

"I love you," Suzanne said, embracing him. "What did I do to deserve you?"

"I feel the same way," Jim said, kissing Suzanne. "What about our chicken macaroni casserole? I can put that together quickly. Do we have some whole wheat elbow pasta and shredded chicken breast?"

"I believe we do."

Another week of managing ailments had Suzanne doubting her chances of ever having a baby. Jim tried to stump out any doubts of restoration, reminding Suzanne to focus on her faith.

"Jim, maybe we should accept the fact that we may never be in a position to conceive."

"Baby, you must remain positive. Now that you're finally being referred to a specialist, he can figure out what's happening inside your body. I know the rheumatologist will sort it all out. If you don't believe, then God can't heal you. Don't let this temporary setback drain the life out of our plans for a wonderful future," Jim said. "I'm going to take a shower so we can leave on time."

"I need to get rid of this defeated mentality. I definitely don't want to bring you down. I know you're worried about your job."

"I can handle the stress on my job. My primary focus is getting your health back on track," Jim said, hugging Suzanne. "Be sure to get the directions to the rheumatologist's office."

"Okay," Suzanne said, looking for her curling iron. "What exactly are they saying around your company?"

"No one knows anything. It's real quiet. I know they have some other projects pending. They're just waiting. I might need you to update my resume."

"Okay. I'll update it this weekend for you. See if you can get a copy of your job description."

"I'll get one from Human Resources tomorrow."

Driving to the doctor's office, Suzanne talked non-stop about getting back to running. Jim tried to shift the conversation to exercises that would cause less stress on her joints. From the time they awoke, he had noticed that she exhibited more mobility, but it was a far cry from normal.

"Baby, now is not the time to be thinking about running. You need to focus on performing low-impact exercises. I spoke with Trevor the other day and he stated that you should be concentrating on exercises that provide range-of-motion, like stretching. As you know, stretching helps to maintain normal joint movement and relieve stiffness. It also helps to improve your flexibility. You can also do some mild strengthening exercises to help keep your muscle strength in tack, like lifting some light weights. Strong muscles will help support and protect your joints affected by the lupus-like symptoms."

"Jim, I do not have lupus," Suzanne shouted. "And I sure hope you didn't tell Trevor I had lupus."

"No, I didn't. Anyway, I said lupus-like symptoms," Jim emphasized. "Low-impact aerobic activities, like bicycling and water aerobics will help you to maintain your cardiovascular fitness. I'm sure the doctor will back me up on this."

Suzanne wasn't interested in Jim's research, nor his recommendations. All she wanted to do was run. She was hopeful that the rheumatologist would help her transition back to a healthy state.

"Good morning. I have an appointment with Dr. Fletcher," Suzanne said as she and Jim stood at the receptionist's window.

"If you would, please sign in," the receptionist replied. "I'll need to make a copy of your insurance card and driver's license. Here's some paperwork we'll need for you to complete. Are you familiar with the HIPPA privacy rules?"

"Yes, I am familiar with HIPPA. Here are my cards," Suzanne said, handing her insurance card and driver's license to the lady through the window.

"Thank you," the lady said. "I'll make a copy and return them when you return with your paperwork."

"What's the paperwork?" Jim inquired, looking at the forms in Suzanne's hand. "Do you need me to write for you?"

"Yes, if you would please."

"Sure," Jim said, taking the paperwork.

"Thanks."

"The first two forms require your signature and initials... medical disclosure... payment responsibilities," Jim said while flipping through the papers. "Okay... this is the questionnaire. Have you experienced any of the following over the last month... morning stiffness, joint pain, trouble sleeping, red/burning of eyes, fever, cough, unexpected hair loss, depression, genital/vaginal discharge, joint swelling, generalized weakness, weight loss, difficulty swallowing, sun sensitivity, unexpected bleeding or bruising, color changes in hands when cold, weight gain, hearing loss, fatigue, numbness, genital sores/ulcers, muscle weakness, changes in vision, shortness of breath, nausea, skin rash, and chest pain?"

"You know just as well as I do."

"Okay. At this moment, are you able to dress yourself, including tying shoelaces and doing buttons?"

"Barely."

"The responses are without any difficulty, with some difficulty, with much difficulty, or unable to do."

"With much difficulty."

"Are you able to get in and out of bed?"

"With much difficulty."

"Are you able to lift a full cup or glass to your mouth?"

"With much difficulty."

"Are you able to walk outdoors on flat ground?"

"With much difficulty."

"Are you able to wash and dry your entire body?"

"With much difficulty."

"Are you able to bend down to pick up clothing from the floor?"

"With much difficulty."

"Are you able to turn faucets/taps on and off?"

"With much difficulty."

"Are you able to get in and out of a car?"

"With much difficulty."

"Considering all the ways that your arthritis affects you, rate how you are doing on the following scale by placing a vertical mark through the line… very well or very poor…"

"I don't know that I have arthritis," Suzanne said, thinking about the question. "Place a mark next to very poor."

"This other side is for the doctor. Sign here and here," Jim said, handing Suzanne the pen and papers. "I'll take the forms back to the lady."

"Thanks, Jim."

Moments later, the nurse came out and escorted Suzanne and Jim to an examination room. The nurse checked her vital signs prior to Dr. Fletcher's arrival.

"Good morning," Dr. Fletcher said as he entered the room.

"Good morning," Suzanne and Jim both replied.

"So, tell me what's going on with you," Dr. Fletcher inquired.

"Well, for the past couple of months, I've been getting worse in terms of pain in my body… swelling and stiffness of my legs and hands…. red breakouts on my legs, thighs, back, and arms, along with fevers and sore throats," Suzanne stated.

"When do you experience the pain? In the morning? Late in the day?" Dr. Fletcher asked. "And how long does the pain last?"

"All day. From the time I get up in the morning," Suzanne said.

"When did all of this start happening to you?" Dr. Fletcher asked.

"I've been experiencing some sort of discomfort all year. As far as the pain — probably for the past couple of months. The itching and hives started the first part of the year," Suzanne responded. "Night sweats, fevers, and sore throats are recent and have been sporadic."

"What about the hives? Are they present all day, every day?" Dr. Fletcher questioned.

"The hives come and go," Suzanne said.

"Is there a family history of arthritis or rheumatic disease?" Dr. Fletcher asked.

"My father has arthritis in his knees, but I think that's from his work as a truck driver for many years — loading and unloading trucks," Suzanne said.

"What medications are you taking?" Dr. Fletcher asked.

"Dr. Fletcher, over the past few months there have been so many medicines. I brought the pill bottles with all the names," Suzanne responded. Jim handed him the bag of prescriptions.

"It mostly appears to be allergy-related medications," Dr. Fletcher said.

"I've never had allergies, so I can't understand why I'm taking allergy medicines for hives, pain, and swelling," Suzanne said.

After a series of questions regarding her ailments, Dr. Fletcher informed Suzanne that he was going to test her for autoimmune disorders like rheumatoid arthritis and lupus. He explained how the immune system operated as the body's natural defense against foreign invaders. Further explanation revealed the process of what happens when autoantibodies are created to protect against what the body mistakenly believes are foreign invaders. The first group of blood tests, rheumatoid factor measured whether a certain amount of abnormal antibody was in her blood. The antinuclear antibody test (ANA) was necessary to help detect a group of autoantibodies that are found in most people with lupus.

"Do you think I have lupus or some other autoimmune disease?" Suzanne asked.

"I don't know. We need to conduct the specialized blood work," Dr. Fletcher stated. "I'll need to see you back next week to review your results."

"Dr. Fletcher, I've read quite a bit of information trying to figure out what's causing the ailments I'm experiencing. My symptoms have led me to research more and more information about lupus, rheumatoid arthritis, and the other autoimmune disorders," Suzanne said.

"Suzanne, I will find whatever is causing you to experience the pain, swelling, stiffness and everything else that's going on with you. I've written a lot of those articles you're speaking about. I'm considered the authority in this field," Dr. Fletcher stated.

"Can you prescribe any medication to help alleviate the pain?" Suzanne asked.

"I don't want to prescribe any additional medications right now because we don't know what we're dealing with," Dr. Fletcher responded. "I'll see you back in a week."

"Dr. Fletcher, I have some sort of fluid or swelling located on the back of my knee," Suzanne said. "See how it's bulging out back here."

"Let me take a look," Dr. Fletcher responded, lifting up her leg and feeling the back. "You have a Baker's Cyst."

"What's that?" Suzanne asked.

"The cyst usually occurs because of some inflammatory problem like arthritis. I can drain the fluid from the knee joint today using a needle. It's a simple process where I will inject cortisone into your knee to reduce the volume of fluid being produced. It's not a foolproof solution; there's a chance that the cyst will return."

"What do you think, Jim?" Suzanne asked.

"I think you should wait and think about it," Jim responded.

"It's really a simple process. I do them all the time," Dr. Fletcher said, trying to reassure them.

"I think I'll wait," Suzanne said hesitantly.

"Let me know if you change your mind. Be sure you're not trying to perform any activities like squatting, kneeling, heavy lifting, climbing, and/or running," Dr. Fletcher said.

"When do you think I'll be able to run?" Suzanne responded.

"Now is not the time to be thinking about running. We're going to focus on developing a treatment plan to stop your condition from worsening."

On the way home, Jim verbalized his suspicions about whether Dr. Fletcher would recommend the right course of action.

"Your Dr. Fletcher appears to be arrogant with a God-like mentality," Jim said. "I don't like people like that."

"He came highly recommended by Dr. Conner," Suzanne said. "We'll see how the visit goes next week."

"If he's not quick at drawing some conclusions, we will find someone else. You're not going to waste time with him, like you've done with Dr. Conner," Jim said.

"Not now, Jim! Besides, I don't think I've wasted time with Dr. Conner. He felt he needed to exhaust all of his options for resolving my problems before referring me to a specialist," Suzanne said. "Please, just keep your opinions to yourself."

"I'll do just that. By the way, the old group is getting together to run the Black Top half marathon next Saturday. I'm thinking about going out to run with them. I know you're not feeling up to going to the event, but do you mind if I go and run?" Jim asked.

"If I'm feeling better, I'll go. Maybe I can ride my bike alongside you during the run."

"I really don't think riding your bike is a good idea. Dr. Fletcher told you to avoid activities like squatting, kneeling, heavy lifting, climbing, and running. I'm sure bending your knees in a circular motion falls in the scheme of things. You don't want to make things worse than they already are."

"I think I'll be okay," Suzanne said. "You haven't told anyone about my condition, have you? I don't want anyone to know. I don't want anyone feeling sorry for me. And I don't want to answer a bunch of questions about my condition. I'll take a lot of anti-inflammatory medication until the day of the run."

"The only person aware of your situation is Trevor. And you told him," Jim stated. "I haven't told anyone. Our running partners have missed you at the lake. I've just said you've been busy at work. That you've taken a temporary hiatus from running until things slow down."

As the days progressed, Suzanne continued to take the medications given by her doctors, along with the over-the-counter anti-inflammatory medicines. The day of the run, Suzanne felt good. She didn't have any pain, swelling, or stiffness. And the hives had disappeared. She was convinced that she could ride her bike for 13.1 miles without any problems.

"Are you sure about riding your bike around the race course?" Jim asked.

"I'll be okay. Riding a bike is much easier than running," Suzanne said.

"I don't know, Suzanne, there are quite a few hills along the course. Going up hills on a bike isn't as easy as you think. You're carrying your body weight plus the weight of the bike."

"I think I can manage it," Suzanne confirmed.

Although she wasn't participating as a runner, Suzanne was excited about the half marathon. It was her first trip back to White Rock Lake since her health problems began. As she waited nearby for Jim to return with his race packet, Suzanne reminisced about her six o'clock Saturday morning runs around the lake. A standing appointment she kept for nearly six years. This would be the first time she'd ever circled White Rock Lake and the scenic tree-lined Forest Hill neighborhood by bike.

As Suzanne began to walk near the shore of the lake, Jessica walked up behind her. "Hey, Suzanne. It's been a while. I haven't seen you around the workplace. Are you feeling better? Did the doctors ever figure anything out about your health problems?"

"I've been doing better. I'm going to ride alongside Jim during the race today," Suzanne said, looking around. "Are you running in the race today?"

"Yes, I am. I don't mind doing the half marathons, but not the full ones. I've called you a couple times. I guess I expected you to have the courtesy to call back at some point," Jessica said, irritated. "I didn't want to stop by your office, especially after receiving your message about you not going to the play and your reason. I wasted a hundred and fifty dollars."

"Jessica, I think we need to postpone this conversation. Jim will be back in a few…"

"Are you afraid he'll overhear something you don't want him to know about? Afraid he'll find out about your past?"

"Not here, Jessica," Suzanne said.

"When is there ever a good time?" Jessica responded. "I don't know why I thought we could be friends."

"You know, a friendship is not possible for us at this time. I'm focused on my life with Jim and starting a family with him. Before I met Jim, you were a part of that life. And although our friendship has always been important to me, and I would like to rekindle it, I know it's not possible to do so right now. My life is different now. God saw fit to bless me with a wonderful husband, and I don't want any unnatural thoughts or feelings to jeopardize my marriage."

"Unnatural! Ain't that a… All of a sudden it's unnatural. A few visits to church and now it's unnatural. It wasn't unnatural when I freed you from the confines of your mental instability. It wasn't unnatural when you used me as your emotional first-aid. Whatever, have a happy life with your HUSBAND!" Jessica said, running off abruptly to join the starting lineup.

Suzanne felt a cloud of relief. The tone in Jessica's voice and the disgust in her eyes were enough to let Suzanne know the relationship had reached a point of no return. She had prayed to God for a way out. And she knew her prayers had been answered.

Thank you, Lord, and forgive me for doing things that weren't pleasing to you. Now Lord, I'm asking and believing that you will heal my body. I don't want to be cellmates with sickness anymore. Free me from the load of guilt, shamefulness and deceit.

The beginning of the race started out fast and flat. As the mileage increased, the run progressed into the nearby neighborhood. The terrain changed from flat to hilly. Suzanne seldom rode her bike and quickly discovered the challenge of riding up and down hills for several miles. By mile nine, Suzanne was exhausted and welcomed the final 4.1 miles to the finish. Proud of his pace, Suzanne rode alongside Jim, cheering him on to an impressive one hour and forty-five minute finish. At the end, Suzanne began to notice a series of hives consuming her body.

"Jim, the hives are back! We need to leave before anyone notices my legs and arms," Suzanne said.

"Okay, baby. I'll catch up with Brent and the others later," Jim said, taking a hold of Suzanne's bike. "Let's go."

"Thanks, Jim. I guess it wasn't such a good idea to ride my bike today. I guess the stress I exposed my body to was too much," Suzanne said. "Please don't say I told you so."

"Baby, you're going to be fine. Don't worry! I'm going to ride those doctors until they figure out what's going on with you," Jim said, trying to reassure Suzanne. "I think we've been patient long enough."

CHAPTER 11

Surviving the Aftermath

The following weeks, Suzanne's life was filled with a series of doctor visits, blood tests, urine tests, joint fluid tests, skin biopsies, and X-rays. She was under the care of her general practitioner, Dr. Conner... a rheumatologist, Dr. Fletcher... a hematologist, Dr. Elder... and her third dermatologist, Dr. Rainer. Thoughts of never returning to a state of normalcy prompted Suzanne to keep a journal of her thoughts.

She began by writing, *Well, it looks like I really messed myself up riding my bike during the half marathon. The hives came back with a vengeance — big blotches of red spots. It was so scary. I guess it was the inflammation doing its thing. That Sunday night both my knees were saturated with excruciating pain, making it difficult for me to walk. It's a good thing I already had an appointment with Dr. Fletcher Monday morning. That Monday, Dr. Fletcher advised against draining the fluid out of the leg, since he would have to inject cortisone (steroid). He said the cortisone would still be in my system at the time of my visit with Dr. Rainer, the new dermatologist. The injection would prevent the hives from being present. That meant I couldn't have the fluid drained, and I had to endure the pain and swelling another week. My hands are hurting so bad as I write. Just one thing after another. Lord, why is all of this happening to me? Is this my punishment?*

Jim walked into the living room as Suzanne was completing her journal entry. "Baby, your mother has been calling you… and so has Molly. I think you need to call your mom and let her know what's going on. I'm guessing Molly wants some fitness tips."

Suzanne avoided her parents' telephone calls for days. She dreaded having to endure the question and answer sessions about her physical and mental well-being. "You're right," Suzanne responded. "Could you hand me the telephone?"

"Hi, Mom! How's everything going with you and dad?" Suzanne asked.

"Everything is fine with us. Your dad and I have been worried about you," she said. "What's going on with you?"

"We've been going back and forth to doctors trying to figure out what's causing my health problems. Dr. Conner says it's a medical mystery to go from such a healthy state to an unhealthy state. Next week I'm scheduled to visit the hematologist and dermatologist. Hopefully, the hematologist can give me a diagnosis on the source of my anemia and treat it. I'll be visiting a third dermatologist. My rheumatologist says this particular doctor works with patients with autoimmune disorders. He wants another biopsy of my hives," Suzanne explained.

Consoling words of faith from her mother ignited hope. In spite of tests that revealed plummeting red blood cells, resulting in increased fatigue and weakness, Suzanne's feelings of doubt and defeat began to subside.

Suzanne's examination with Dr. Elder, the hematologist, revealed that her red blood count had fallen drastically. In response to the abnormal blood test, Dr. Elder performed a bone marrow biopsy to diagnose or rule out leukemia or bone marrow cancer, and to determine if she had a specific blood disorder. The test was also used to diagnose or rule out infection or any other cause for her low red blood count. The results of a bone marrow biopsy confirmed that Suzanne had a severe case of anemia, which led to the start of Procrit injections. The injections were necessary to stimulate Suzanne's bone marrow to make red blood cells. Amid her doctor's inability to connect the dots, Suzanne continued to believe that she would one day emerge from the pit of pain and suffering. She began to visualize a healed body, crossing another finish line, and birthing a baby.

"Suzanne, what time is your injection today?" Jim asked as they laid in bed listening to the morning news. "I can go with you, if your appointment is this morning."

"It's at ten o'clock this morning," Suzanne responded. "Don't worry about me. I'm going into work for a couple of hours, leave and go to the doctor's office, and go back to work."

"Okay," Jim responded.

"You know... each week while getting my injections, I see the cancer patients receiving their chemo treatments. They are hooked up to machines, with medicines going into their veins — medicines that cause tiredness, sickness, and baldheadedness. Nevertheless, the patients take it all in stride while reading magazines, listening to their CD or MP3 players, or watching the personal T.V. attached to their recliners. The scene lets me know how blessed I am and that my situation could be a whole lot worse."

"How long do you need to take the injections?" Jim asked.

"I don't know... I think for at least another twelve to eighteen weeks. The blood count is inching up slowly... but it's improving," Suzanne replied.

"Does the hematologist know what's causing the low red blood cell count?" Jim asked.

"He doesn't know. He says it could have something to do with the inflammation in my body. He asked me about what the rheumatologist thinks... And then about what the dermatologist thinks... You would think they'd communicate with one another, but they're asking me about what the other one thinks. It's just a horrible situation," Suzanne said with frustration. "Normally the PROCRIT helps treat anemia associated with cancer, chronic kidney disease, HIV, or some type of surgery. But since none of those things apply to me, it must have something to do with the inflammation.

But no one knows what's causing the inflammation. I'm scheduled to see Dr. Fletcher again tomorrow... maybe he'll have some answers," Suzanne said.

"I'm going with you tomorrow. If Dr. Fletcher doesn't have any answers for you, he'll definitely have some for me," Jim said, while getting out of the bed. "Let's meet after work at Sam's Cafeteria. I can get off early today."

"I don't know, Jim, the days simply wear me out," Suzanne said. "Can't you just get something from Sam's after work and bring it home?"

"I'll get the food to go and meet you at home," Jim said, accommodating.

"Great!"

Back at work, Suzanne noticed an email from Molly. Embarrassed that she hadn't contacted her first, Suzanne opened it. Molly started out by thanking Suzanne for her advice. She stated how the information about the walking and running shoes was invaluable. She talked about the mishaps she experienced by not taking her advice about the shoes initially. How she had started her walking program in some of her recreational shoes and experienced some problems with her knees. But now she was on track. She went on to say how her nutritional habits had improved, and that she was striving to eat more servings of fruit, vegetables, and whole grain products. She talked about cooking more. She had started watching *B's Cooking Show* on late-night cable T.V. She was learning how to modify traditional recipes with simple, flavorful and healthy substitutions. Her favorite being garlic spinach mashed potatoes. She talked about how she reduced the caloric value by using low-fat products, like low-fat milk and low-fat sour cream.

Molly's email continued on and on about how she had transformed her unhealthy habits. "I now understand better what a healthier style of eating consists of... nutrition for my body and portion control. And I'm watching out for the chemicals...

preservatives... and sodium you mentioned. The revelation is really amazing when you start evaluating the volume of chemicals in virtually everything we eat... packaged products... T.V. dinners... the meat we buy." Molly went on to talk about her exercise regime. She had contacted Trevor, and he had her performing a combination of walking and running for 45 minutes, five days a week. "My goal is to lose an additional 60 pounds. I'm thinking I just might do that half marathon you mentioned. Also, Trevor is starting to introduce me to some strength training exercises. I've been praying for you. Let me know how things are going with you."

Reading the email made Suzanne proud of Molly's accomplishments and Trevor's contributions. Instead of trying to say everything she needed to say in an email, she decided to telephone Molly.

"Hi, Molly... it's Suzanne. How's everything going?"

"Hi, Suzanne! This is a surprise. It's good to hear from you."

"Sounds like you're headed in the right direction with your healthy eating and fitness program. I'm glad you contacted Trevor."

"Girl, everything is going great! Trevor is great! And he's a devout Christian," Molly said. "When you mentioned his name on the plane, I thought it sounded familiar. He's on Heaven 79.5 on Saturday mornings."

"I forgot to mention it," Suzanne said.

"Anyway, I'm all about serving the Lord, relaxing and enjoying life, and treating myself to an occasional facial or massage. I'm even experiencing the rejuvenation that a yoga class with stretching and meditation can offer," Molly confirmed.

"Great!"

"Trevor has helped me a lot with my caloric intake," Molly said.

"How's the strength training going?"

"I'm learning how to concentrate on proper form and technique, how to move through the full range of motion, and how to warm-up and stretch properly," Molly said.

"That's good. He will eventually train you on how to integrate new exercises into your program every four to six weeks," Suzanne responded. "One good thing about Trevor is that his goal is to train you on how to be independent with living a healthier lifestyle. A fitness consultant is someone you hire for their expertise and to help get you on track with developing better health and fitness habits. Once you get that, you should be able to go it alone. But, it's a good idea to go back periodically for maintenance check-ups."

"Great!" Molly said. "That's what I need to hear. Thanks so much, Suzanne, for taking the time to call me."

"Let me know when you're ready to get started on that half marathon."

"I'm thinking about it," Molly said. "So, what's up with you?"

"As far as me, my doctors are still in a state of confusion as far as my health is concerned. It's okay, though. I know God is going to heal my body."

"I'm praying for you. What about the other?"

"That relationship I mentioned to you on the plane is over. God worked it out for me. Sometimes I experience these urges to call her, but I don't. I want to send her a card apologizing for the abrupt way I ended it, but I know I can't. I want to call her up and ask that we work towards being friends, but I know it's not possible. I am so grateful for God's intervention. I often wonder if I should disclose the truth about my past to Jim, but I can't risk the backlash. Continue to pray for me."

"It's up to you to stay the course. God has moved your stumbling block... your stronghold," Molly said. "As far as Jim, you must pray for guidance on how to handle disclosure. Sometimes secrets are better left untold. It's better if they die with us. However, if someone else knows the secret, there's always the risk of disclosure, and you'll always be in fear of its release. And if that someone is a disgruntled someone, the manner in which the disclosure is released can be devastating for all associated parties."

"I'll pray about it," Suzanne agreed. "I've got to go to a doctor's appointment, but keep me updated on your progress and I'll email you soon. It was good chatting with you. And thank you for your encouragement, concern, and friendship."

Driving to the hematologist, Suzanne was weak and tired. She decided that after her injection she would go home for the remainder of the day, and prepare for her visit with Dr. Fletcher. She wanted Dr. Fletcher to provide her with his strategy for restoration. Suzanne was out to win the fight against the conglomeration of illnesses.

The following day, Suzanne's visit with Dr. Fletcher produced a definite plan of treatment to combat her problems. Since her skin and joint symptoms mimicked the systemic form of lupus, he designed a treatment plan comprised of a corticosteroid (Prednisone) to minimize the symptoms, reduce inflammation, and restore normal bodily functions. An explanation of the side effects caused concern, but Suzanne was willing to take the risks associated with the drug.

"Dr. Fletcher, how long will I need to take the steroid medication?" Suzanne asked. "The side effects do cause me to have some concern… weight gain, a round face, acne, easy bruising, "thinning" of the bones (osteoporosis), high blood pressure, cataracts, onset of diabetes, increased risk of infection, stomach ulcers, hyperactivity, and an increase of appetite."

"I don't know. We'll have to wait and see how your body responds," Dr. Fletcher said. "The main thing to remember is to not let the increased appetite control you."

"I don't think I'll have a problem with that, doctor. I eat really healthy and know how to maintain appropriate portion sizes," Suzanne responded.

"That's good; however with the steroids, people tend to gravitate towards unhealthy foods, like donuts, candy, and soda," Dr. Fletcher said. "So, just be careful not to gain any unwanted pounds. I'll see you back in about seven weeks."

The next morning, Suzanne awoke believing in her healing. She began to write in her journal, *Dear Lord, I do understand that I must go through what I'm going through for your purpose and plan. And I do know that whatever the outcome, I will be a better person because of it. Yesterday, I started two new major things in my life — my 40-day spiritual journey and the Prednisone. I'm excited about my spiritual journey and going deeper to where I need to be spiritually. I'm not excited about taking the Prednisone because I don't know the effects of the medication on my body. I pray that you guide Dr. Fletcher in his experimental solution for my situation. I will remain positive and trust you, Lord.*

The ongoing parade of doctor visits with Dr. Conner, Dr. Fletcher, Dr. Elder, and Dr. Rainer continued. Follow-up blood work, tests, and bone exams seemed never to cease, but at least Suzanne was feeling better. The itching, pain, swelling, and stiffness had faded away over the period of eight weeks, and the hives only appeared on occasion. Her red blood count reached normal levels, eliminating the need for the Procrit injections. The Prednisone was effective in reducing many of the ailments Suzanne had experienced. To further move her toward a state of reduced side effects, Dr. Fletcher prescribed a medication typically given to lupus patients. It was an antimalarial medication (hydroxychloroquine - Plaquenil), a much milder medication than the Prednisone, which would hopefully prove effective in Suzanne's full recovery. The side effects of the Plaquenil were rare, and consisted of occasional diarrhea or rashes. Suzanne was happy and hopeful that she was on a path to restoration. Dr. Fletcher's strategy included weaning Suzanne off the Prednisone and stabilizing her on the Plaquenil.

"Dr. Fletcher, I feel like I'm almost back to normal. When can I begin exercising?" Suzanne asked.

"I don't see any reason why you can't start walking," Dr. Fletcher said. "Just take it easy. It's been over eight months since you've exercised consistently."

"What about having a baby?"

"Your baby plans should be postponed for a while. We need to see how you react to the new medication."

The approval to exercise was the best news Suzanne had received, and she couldn't wait to share it with Jim.

"Hi, honey, I'm home," Suzanne exclaimed. "Guess what?"

"What?" Jim asked.

"Dr. Fletcher says I can start back exercising. I think I'm going to contact Trevor. Although I feel comfortable with starting back up, he'll make sure I do so in a progressive manner."

"I'm so glad you're feeling better!" Jim shouted, embracing Suzanne. "What about a baby? Did you ask him about the possibilities of conception? When we could start?"

"Dr. Fletcher said we'll have to hold off on having a baby. He just wants me to focus on a full recovery. He started me on a new medication to start weaning me off of the steroids," Suzanne stated. "Sounds like I will probably be on this drug for a while. The main thing is that it doesn't have the negative side effects like the steroid medication."

Other than an occasional flare up here and there, the next few months were blissful. Suzanne enjoyed the ability to maintain a steady running schedule mixed with resistance training at the gym. Each time Suzanne visited with Dr. Fletcher, they both marveled at her improvement. He applauded her determination to be proactive in contributing to the restoration of her health. Each week she drew closer to reducing her dependence of the steroids. Noticeably, she did have a round face, acne, and an increased appetite. Self-conscious about her 20-pound weight gain, she was eager to rid her body of the steroids.

"Good news! We hired a new guy to take Sam's place. He's smart and will be able to hit the ground running. And now that you're back on track with your health, I was thinking about us taking a vacation. You've always enjoyed the white sandy beaches. What about Cancun? Would you like to go to Cancun?" Jim asked. "Can you take a vacation at this time?"

"Can I take a vacation? That sounds wonderful," Suzanne said, jumping up to hug Jim.

"Great, go ahead and request the time off, and I'll schedule the trip around the third week in September."

"Jim, I've been thinking. Since I'm back to normal — I know the medication has a great deal to do with it, but I was thinking about training for the half marathon in January. I'm up to six miles. What do you think?"

"Don't ask me; it's about what Dr. Fletcher thinks," Jim said. "Have you consulted with him about it?"

"No, I haven't. I've just started to think about it the past couple of days."

"I think you need to consult with him. You're not out of the woods yet. They still don't know what happened with your body and why."

"Okay, I will," Suzanne said. "I'm scheduled to see him again in October."

Jim and Suzanne escaped to paradise. A fan of the outdoors, Suzanne positioned herself on the shores of the beach while soaking up the sun. But by the third day, the agonizing itch resurfaced.

"Jim, I don't feel so good. I think I'm coming down with a cold. I've got a sore throat and a slight fever. The hotel room is so cold."

"Do you want me to see if the hotel has a doctor?"

"No. I brought some of my itching cream. I'll see if it helps," Suzanne said. "I think I can bear it for the last two days."

Despite her setback toward the end of the trip, Suzanne and Jim had a fantastic vacation. Arriving back to the States, Suzanne contacted Dr. Fletcher. After speaking with his nurse, Kitty, she was advised to increase her dosage of the steroids. Adhering to Kitty's recommendation, Suzanne recovered from the itching and cold symptoms.

Suzanne's visit with Dr. Fletcher a couple of weeks later revealed that her sensitivity to the sun and exposure to extreme temperatures possibly caused the flare-up. One week away from discontinuing the steroids, Suzanne's usage was prolonged an additional two weeks. At first disappointed, Suzanne knew by paying attention to the conditions around her, the end was near. And best of all, she was given the green light to train for her half marathon.

The weeks leading up to the half marathon were not without incident. She experienced the occasional flare-ups. Then came the unexpected.

"Jim, come look! My hair!"

"What about it?"

"Look in the bowl. It's filled with my hair. It's breaking off! I can't stop it," Suzanne shouted.

"Could it be the medication?"

"I don't know. I guess it could be the new medication or even the steroids."

"Did you read the side effects of the new medication?"

"Yes, I did. Here's the information from the pharmacist — abdominal cramps, abnormal eye pigmentation, acne, anemia, bleaching of hair... diminished reflexes, dizziness, emotional changes, excessive coloring of the skin... headache, hearing loss, heart problems, hives, irritability, itching, light flashes and streaks... loss of hair, muscle paralysis, ringing in the ears, skin eruptions, skin inflammation and scaling, skin rash, and on...," Suzanne read.

"Wow, that's a lot!" Jim stated. "I thought you said the new medication wasn't as bad as the steroids. That's sure a lot of bad trying to salvage some good."

"I guess they consider high blood pressure, onset of diabetes, increased risk of infection, stomach ulcers... worse. I just can't lose my hair," Suzanne said. "My hair is my glory. Everyone compliments me on my hair."

"Check with the doctor and just see," Jim said. "What about your stylist? Maybe she can treat your hair with something to keep it from falling out. What about the dermatologist?"

As the weeks progressed, Suzanne suffered tremendous hair loss. She changed stylists over and over, searching for one with advanced knowledge of treating hair loss. Name brand shampoos, conditioners and hair treatments were useless in restoring her hair. This setback took an emotional toll on Suzanne because of her inability to conceal the obvious. For months, she had been able to mask the true state of her physical condition, but the hair loss was visible for all to see. *I guess I could buy a wig? How would I explain wearing a wig? Everyone is accustomed to seeing my hair perfect most days. I'm sure they're noticing how thin my hair is now. Beatrice is always talking about her brand of hair products. Maybe I'll ask her the name of the product line at work tomorrow,* Suzanne thought to herself.

Days later, on the advice Beatrice, Suzanne purchased the entire line of KeraCare hair products — shampoos, conditioners and styling products — known for hair restoration. After several weeks, the product line proved effective in curtailing her hair loss.

Through it all, Suzanne remained steadfast to reach her goal. Aside from the training, she resumed a normal life. She dedicated her life to Christ and committed herself to leading a life pleasing God and serving others. She and Jim evolved to more than Sunday service saints. They became involved in ministry and used their gifts and talents to serve in the church and the community.

Other than Jim and Trevor, no one knew that Suzanne was running again. January 16, 2005 was a day of new beginnings — the day of Suzanne's half marathon. Seated at the nerve center of the 13.1 miles chase were consistency, determination, discipline, and progression. It wasn't until the start of the race that Suzanne returned to her spot with the old running group. Unsure of her stance, the group quickly realized that she was in a ready, set, go position. Moved by her return, they all approached the starting line as a team reunited with all of its partners. The firing of the starting gun earmarked Suzanne's escape from the storms in her life.

Running alongside his wife, Jim was proud that she hadn't given in to a defeated mentality. A two-hour and ten-minute finish time signaled that Suzanne was back on track. The sight of her family and friends witnessing the miracle made her feat that much more special.

A year later, on January 15, 2006, God's power took Suzanne to another level. Amid a conglomeration of psychological and physical challenges, setbacks and obstacles — Suzanne completed her fourth marathon. As she crossed the finish line, she lifted her head toward the clear blue sky and thanked God for planting the seeds of hope inside her heart. She remained faithful in believing that God's power obliterated any situation. It was his power that freed her to move toward restoration, knowing that the circumstances surrounding her medical mystery and past was a part of his plan.

Lord, I give you all the praise for blessing me to be able to run 26.2 miles today. I never thought I'd ever see this day, but I know with you by my side all things are possible. Thank you, Lord, for restoring my body beyond the capacity I knew before my illness. Thank you, Lord, for the strength to twist another water bottle cap. Thank you, Lord, for the ability to walk without pain. Thank you, Lord, for deliverance from sinful thoughts, feelings and actions. Thank you, Lord, for deliverance from brokenness. Thank you, Lord, for loving me in spite of me. Thank you,

Lord, for not giving up on me when I gave up on myself. Thank you, Lord, for your patience and for not passing me by. Thank you, Lord, for the ministry of Molly. Thank you, Lord, for Trevor's encouragement. Thank you, Lord, for looking beyond my faults and seeing my needs. Thank you, Lord, for giving me a husband who stuck by my side through sickness and in health. Thank you, Lord, for another chance to make the right choices. Thank you, Lord, in advance for the gift of childbirth. Thank you, Lord, for the gift of service. Thank you, Lord, for allowing me to be a testimony of your goodness, grace and mercy. Thank you, Lord, for your SACRIFICE and SALVATION.

PART III

Surviving the End of Marital Bliss

CHAPTER 12

Picking Apart the Layers of the Masquerade

*L*istening to the harmonic sounds of birds chirping outside his office window, Todd canvassed his memory for answers. How had he failed to see the approach of his life's biggest upset? It was one year ago when he experienced the best and worst day of his life — a day of both victory and loss. For fifteen years, Todd and Joan Holder had lived in Forest Groves Landing, a beautiful rolling subdivision in north Dallas, with their three children. Todd was a successful software engineer, and Joan, a pharmaceutical sales representative.

After months of agonizing over the thoughts of operating his own software development company, Todd dismissed his fears and pursued his dream. Having the support of Joan, Todd used a portion of their savings and 401k to match funding he borrowed from their bank. A day after receiving good news about the financial backing for the business venture, he was later ambushed with the sobering truth that his wife, Joan, didn't love him. Confessing her love for another man, Joan admitted to Todd that she could no longer portray the happily married and devoted wife. With suitcases and boxes loaded in her car, she told him, "My attorney is finalizing the divorce papers. Expect to be served in a few days.

I'm sure you'll agree with the terms of the settlement. I want nothing from you but my freedom." Her final words were 'take care of the kids'. The tone in her voice depicted no opportunity for reconciliation. A marriage that ended after seventeen years had assassinated Todd's dream of *until death do we part*. He knew without hesitation that his life with Joan was like being sucked into the vortex of a cross-current. Shattered in spirit, Todd was thrust into the arena of single parenthood, responsible for Trey, Trinity, and Tarrynn... seven, twelve, and fifteen years old.

Todd continued to ponder the forces that had resulted in the destruction of his marriage. Reflections of the past unveiled the thick cloud that concealed a faulty perception of a healthy and happy marriage. Picking apart the layers of the masquerade, Todd sifted through the emotional debris that had smothered the life out of his marriage. Was it his disconnect that had caused him to ignore the visible signs of a marriage on the road to devastation? A relationship empty of laughter? A bond absent of nice gestures? A connection detonated by nasty fights? A union severed by self-ishness? A partnership lacking physical attraction and intimacy? He realized that his passive personality and apathetic attitude had annihilated his marriage, prompting Joan's decision to leave her husband and kids behind.

To cope with feelings of betrayal, anger and emptiness, Todd threw himself into his software development company, SDC Technologies. Compensating for his loss, he worked non-stop at promoting and growing his company... 12-hours, six days a week. Successful with creating a striving business, Todd still grieved internally over the termination of his marriage — a grief filled with social isolation and loneliness. Witnessing his lingering seclusion, Luke stepped in to offer Todd solutions on how to pull himself together. Luke, owned a financial consulting firm in Las Colinas and had been Todd's friend and financial advisor for over ten years.

"Todd, it's time to let go. Joan is not coming back. You can't continue to contaminate your mind with anger, resentment, guilt, and pain. This lingering pity-party has got to stop," Luke said, while adding sweetener to his tea. "And you can't continue to work day and night. The business is doing well. Your clients are happy.

You've got potential customers beating down your door. And because of your drive, creativity, and commitment to creating a successful business, you're going to see a profit your first year," Luke said, trying to generate some excitement. "That's amazing. You need to start thinking about hiring some additional staff."

"It's all because of you and your business savvy that I've done this well my first year in business," Todd said with extreme gratitude.

"No, it's because of your energy and creativity," Luke said. "It's time for you to step back and slow down. You're going to have a heart attack or something if you keep going at this pace. You never sleep. You never allow yourself any down time. If I lived fifteen minutes away from my office, I'd go home sometimes for lunch or somewhere just to get away for a moment. Learn how to chill, Todd. You've got to stop using your company as an escape. Most importantly, you never see or spend time with your children."

"I know, Luke. It's just so hard. I never want to go home. There are too many reminders… the photographs of our family on the walls and tables… the smell of her favorite perfume that still lingers… the beautiful floral pieces she arranged on our tables… the scent of her favorite candles in our bedroom and bathroom. I still love Joan. I know if I had another chance I could make it right," Todd said, punching the keys on his computer. "How could she flush the promises we made… the dreams we had down the toilet? How could it be so easy for her to erase the memories we created, the marriage we built, the family we birthed, and…?"

"I know, it's been quite a year!" Luke interjected. "She has gone on with her life. I heard she's engaged to be married. Why are you refusing to move on? You've got all of these options in front of you telling you which way to go, but you won't budge. You've got plenty of paths to take, but you just sit there… stuck in the mud of torment, loneliness, anger, brokenness, hopelessness, and disenchantment."

"I am stuck alright… stuck on a highway called misery," Todd admitted.

"Todd... life is going to have you navigating through some curves. And with the curves of life, you never know what's coming up next. Will it be that unexpected diagnosis that leaves you distraught? Will it be the unexpected death of a loved one that leaves you lonely? Will it be that unexpected telephone call from the police station telling you that your kid is in jail for smoking marijuana? Will it be that notification from your employer that your employment will end in thirty days that leaves you in a state of panic? Will it be that unexpected moment of disclosure when your spouse tells you she wants out, that she loves another, a disclosure that leaves you hurt and hopeless? In order to survive the curves, you must have faith that God will pilot and protect your path through whatever lies ahead. Faith is the key variable in the equation of life's uncertainties."

"The kids told me that Joan is getting married in a couple of months. Earlier, I was thinking about the day she told me she wanted out of our marriage. I never knew she was so unhappy with our life. The mean and hurtful things she said to me were heartbreaking. How she was bored. How she conned me into marriage... leading me to believe we were soul mates... all the while she was targeting a sole provider. How she never wanted kids. How she had found someone fun and exciting. How she endured unfulfilling sex with me for years — that I was inadequate. Now she had someone who was spontaneous and creative in the bedroom. And larger. Someone who had made her dreams a reality. A successful businessman with a lot of money. Someone who could set her up in a larger home. Then she went on to talk about those trips... the national convention trips... the sales trips — all were cover-ups to be with her new man, Chuck."

"She told you his name?"

"Yes, she did. It was her moment of truth. The only time it appears she had been truthful during our seventeen years. She went on to talk about the late-night outings with Leslie and Simone — all cover-ups. She even told me about taking our son with her to Chuck's 6,000 square foot home. It was a sea of confessions that ended with 'take care of the kids'. I realized that I never knew her at all. After all was said and done, I remember walking up the stairs to our bedroom, going inside the closet, reaching for a box on the top shelf, walking back to the bed with the box, sitting on the bed, opening the box, and embracing the pistol inside. I loaded the pistol, placed my finger on the trigger, and aimed it at the right side of my head. I was ready to shoot when Trey began to call my name from the bottom of the stairs."

"I'm so sorry, Todd. To think that you considered ending your life is hard for me to comprehend. I'm glad you didn't take the easy way out. Cowards take the easy way out. I'm glad that God's divine intervention placed Trey in the house at just the right moment."

"Rejected and abandoned... the impulse to pull the trigger was so right and relevant at the time. But, you're right... I'm also glad Trey entered the house at the right moment and diverted me from death."

"It's time to move on! You've been living underground far too long... suffocated by grief... isolated from social interactions. Jump out of that pit of despair! Life is too short! You're letting it pass you by. Spend time with your kids. Get involved in some activities where you can meet new and positive people. I ride with a cycling club on Saturday mornings. We're getting ready to participate in a city-to-city 150-mile ride next month. With the right training, you could do the same with us on the next long-distance ride at the end of the year."

"It sounds great... but 150 miles? I could never ride for a 150 miles. I probably couldn't ride 20 miles."

"You don't start off at 150 miles. Over a period of weeks, you train with others in the club to build your endurance in preparation for the distance. The club offers different group training levels. You would start off at the beginning training level. A new group will be starting in three weeks — you should consider joining. And I believe the next group will be training for the year-end 150-mile ride."

"Man, I've gained so much weight over the years. That's probably another reason why Joan left me. I know she wasn't attracted to me anymore. Before she left, we hadn't been intimate in months. I guess she could no longer fake enjoying unfulfilling sex, but maybe that's because she was having sex with Chuck."

Dismissing Todd's comments about Joan, Luke redirected the conversation. "The great part about cycling is that it's easy on the body. The bicycle supports your body weight so you don't have to. Plus, there's no impact on the body from pedaling."

"It sounds like a good program. But I don't know. I'd probably be the largest guy out there trying to ride a bike. I'm not ready to show this body to the world. That's the best part about my business… I can shield myself from the world… conduct my work in the office or over the phone," Todd said, sounding relieved. "And it doesn't hurt having you as my financial advisor sending those high-dollar deals my way."

"Don't think about your size. Think about the camaraderie with others and the scenic rides. You'll be improving your health by getting fit, taking off the pounds you've packed on. It's really a lot of fun," Luke said, trying hard to convince Todd. "Best of all, we're doing the ride for charity! Although my initial intent was to get in shape and improve my health… my focus shifted when I heard others talking about the families that the ride benefits. That's the real reason I do the rides. I get to experience the satisfaction of knowing that I have played a part in the fight against cancer. By gaining the financial support of others like you, I'm helping with the initiative to fund vital research, education, and patient care. Thousands of lives will be saved."

"Joan would always participate in the 5K and 10K charity walks. She always wanted me to go, but… my mid section has gotten so far out of control. I might feel better if I looked better. I look like something's growing inside my stomach."

"When's the last time you had a physical?" Luke asked, looking in his briefcase for some paperwork for Todd to sign.

"It's been a few years."

"Before you get started, I recommend that you get a physical," Luke suggested. "It's important to visit your physician and follow his or her recommendations before engaging in any type of exercise activity. A physical exam beforehand can detect a hidden medical problem and prevent a life-threatening situation."

"There's nothing wrong me…. just a little extra body weight. Anyway… give me the information about how to sign up for the cycling group. I'll think about it."

"Before the program starts, we can go by Mike's Bike Shop to purchase your bike and cycling gear," Luke said. "Here's the paperwork I need for you to sign. This will be a lucrative contract for you."

A few days later, Todd contacted Rocky's Cycling Club to enroll in their upcoming training program. Rather than signing up for the beginner program, he selected the intermediate program. He figured if Luke was riding 150 miles, then he could, also. *If I sign-up for the more advanced program, there's the added bonus of looking good faster when Joan comes over next time to pick up the kids. This intermediate class should get me in shape faster. I should have joined Joan when she asked me to exercise with her. She's always been committed to exercising,* Todd thought to himself. *I wonder if Chuck exercises.*

Excited about his enrollment in the training program, Todd drove by Luke's office to tell him the good news. Todd was grateful to Luke and credited him for helping to grow his business, raise capital, execute strategies, and achieve success his first year in business. Now he was helping him in other ways.

"Hey Luke, I enrolled in the cycling training program today," Todd said, entering the office. "Any fresh coffee brewing?"

"It's all gone," Luke said. "I'll put on a fresh pot. You're going to have fun riding with the group. We should go by Mike's Bike Shop this weekend to get your bike and cycling gear. Did you get your physical yet?"

"No, I didn't. I completed the registration form attesting that I'm healthy… releasing the club from liability. Rather than the beginner group, I signed up for the intermediate group. Are you in the intermediate group?" Todd inquired.

"Since I've been in the program awhile, I'm in their advance level group. However, I started with the beginner group. It's important to begin at a level that allows you to increase your mileage and endurance at a safe and progressive pace. With this exercising business, you can't aim too high. If you do, you're likely to crash and come tumbling down. A lot of times when people make a decision to start exercising, they go in with a preconceived notion to lose a lot of weight in a short period of time. Often for a class or family reunion. A wedding. A cruise. A black tie affair. The holidays. The summer swimsuit season. They'll start off exercising everyday... doing grueling activities to burn the excess body fat. They go in with a drive-thru mentality, wanting the perfect body quick, fast, and in a hurry. Because they can't keep up the quick, aggressive, grueling style of exercising, they eventually fall off."

"I don't know about other people, but I do want the perfect body fast. By any means necessary... aggressive or whatever the case may be. You've planted the seed that I can create some seismic health changes, and now I'm going to fertilize it."

"In most instances, our daily lifestyles won't allow us to remain aggressive for very long. You've got to be level headed about your approach. As a beginner, you must proceed with caution. Even if you don't fall off, the possibility of getting injured is greater because you didn't prepare your body. Either way, you're subject to leave the game of exercise, never to return. That's why I started with a structured program. They start you off with a few days of riding, and over a period of time, you progress to a level that prepares you for your goal. And it's fun and enjoyable. Like I said, if an exercise program is too aggressive at the beginning, you'll probably dread doing it and will eventually stop. The goal is to get you involved in a sport that you will enjoy for the rest of your life. Not just for the moment to lose body fat. People have got to start thinking about exercise more in terms of a habit — something they consider just like eating and working. Just like there's no thought about whether you're going to eat or go to work, there shouldn't be a thought about whether you're going to exercise. It's just automatically a part of your daily routine. Your body requires exercise, just like it does food."

"You said a mouthfull, didn't you?"

"Be sure to get your physical before the program starts."

"Riding a bike is simple. After I get the rust off, I should be in the advanced group in no time," Todd said with confidence, admiring the collection of photos on the walls. "You have quite a few pictures on your wall."

"They are pictures of the different training groups — my training partners."

"Who's this pretty lady?" Todd inquired, pointing at the picture of young, well-defined woman with long dark brown hair. "She has a body like Joan."

"Her name is Alexandria. She's in the group. And she's married with children."

"So sorry to hear that. Nevertheless, if that's what I get to look forward to — pretty ladies — I'm more excited than ever. I might meet the next Mrs... The only thing is next time my heart will be sequestered from love."

"Take it slow, buddy. Let's stay on point. Anyway, they say the second time around is better than the first," Luke said, looking around for a couple of clean coffee mugs. "Just remember, it isn't about the beginner group or the more experienced group; it's about consistency and building your endurance to go farther and faster in a progressive manner. I'm riding about 110 miles for my long-distance ride, averaging around 12-15 mph (miles per hour). I didn't progress to that distance and mph overnight. My endurance building started over six months ago, riding varied distances 5-6 days per week. I average around 10-12 mph. I also mix in yoga, pilates and strength training. The extras like yoga and pilates are similar to filling in the blanks — covering those areas that are missed when training on the bike. Yoga, pilates, and strength training help to increase your overall health. I remember that you were a swimmer a few years ago. You might consider resuming your swimming to complement your cycling. You'll learn more about crosstraining as you get deeper into the training program."

"What is yoga… and pilates?"

"I'm sure there are many definitions for yoga, but from what I've learned in the short months I've been doing it, yoga is a form of exercise based on the belief that the body and breath are intimately connected with the mind. For me, the yoga poses stretch my leg and hip muscles and joints, as well as my back, shoulders, and arms. Stretching improves flexibility, which can reduce your risk of injuring yourself. Although it can be quite intense at times, yoga is extremely enjoyable and relaxing. Recently, I started a pilates class, which helps my cycling by strengthening my "core" and increasing my sense of balance."

"What is pilates? And what do you mean by your core?"

"Pilates is a total conditioning program that works your body from the inside out by focusing on core muscles — mainly those muscles in the stomach and back. It's also a mind-body exercise, which, like yoga, stresses proper breathing while you do very precise body movements," Luke responded, while getting up to perform one of the moves he had learned.

"Luke… we're men… we're naturally strong… it all sounds like something for women — the whole mind-body connection thing," Todd said, observing Luke. "What are you doing? Looks like it should hurt."

"Hand me that yoga mat in the corner, please. I'm going to show you a Cobra pose. The Cobra opens your chest and strengthens your core body while stretching the spine and stimulating your kidneys and nervous system. You lie on your stomach with your chin on the floor… your palms flat on the floor under your shoulders. Your legs should be together."

"Looks like you pull up on your kneecaps."

"You're right… all while gripping your thighs and buttocks and pressing your pelvis down into the floor."

"Okay, Luke. I think I've seen enough," Todd said.

"At least consider coming to one of the classes with me," Luke said, getting up. "It's really okay. I'm still learning my pilates moves. Yoga and pilates are for both men and women. My yoga class is about 35 percent male. A lot of the pro-athletes are doing it to improve their flexibility and sports performance. As I stated, yoga is all about associations between the body and the breath... the muscles and the skeletal structure... between your body and your emotions... your psyche and your body... yourself and those around you. It gives men authorization to stop and pay attention to the voices inside and connect with the reality of their lives."

"I should have been doing yoga years ago. The voices inside my head would have let me know Joan was cheating on me," Todd said, deflated. "Luke, I'm impressed. You're pretty knowledgeable about exercising. With you helping me, I'll be slimmer by the next time I see Joan. I need to get rid of this extra belly," Todd admitted, while rubbing on his stomach.

"First of all, you should be exercising for you. Joan has moved on, and now it's time for you to do the same. The cycling program will be a great start for you," Luke said. "Let's plan on going to the bike store tomorrow — I'll come and pick you up around ten o'clock in the morning."

The next day, Luke arrived early at Todd's home. As he began to ring the doorbell, the disturbing sounds of amplified voices resonated through the door. Luke stood outside, waiting for the right opportunity to proceed forward. In a matter of moments, Tarrynn, Todd's eldest daughter, exited the front door in a rush. Moving quickly to catch her, Todd noticed Luke.

"Hey Luke, I didn't know you were here," Todd said, startled.

"I was just going to ring the doorbell," Luke said, watching Tarrynn move swiftly down the street. "Is everything okay?"

"Yes... Tarrynn and I are just having a difference of opinion," Todd said, going back inside the house. "I forgot about us going to the bike store this morning. Give me a moment to get ready."

"If this is not a good day, it's okay," Luke said, trailing behind him, closing the door.

"No… everything's okay. Let me put on a different pair of shorts and get my shades," Todd said, going up the stairs. "You know how we do. Make yourself at home. Go and get something to drink in the kitchen."

"I'm okay. I'll just wait in the family room," Luke said, looking around at the disorder in Todd's house. "Looks like you guys need to clean up. Where's Trey and Trinity?"

"They're with some of their friends," Todd said, shouting from his bedroom. "I plan on calling a cleaning service to come next week."

"The kids can't clean up?" Luke asked, surveying the room.

"I can't get them to do anything," Todd responded.

As they drove away, Luke began to inquire about the disconcerting scene he witnessed. "Looks like you and Tarrynn are having some serious problems."

"Everything's okay. She's sixteen now and thinks she's an adult. We're trying to come to terms with our differences. She insists on coming and going as she pleases, all times of the day and night. I guess she's the typical sixteen-year-old," Todd said, adjusting his seatbelt. "Turn your radio on 103.5 — they're doing the top 25 hip hop sounds."

"I don't know about today's typical sixteen-year-old, but we didn't come and go as we pleased. We didn't go anywhere without parental permission. And we definitely completed our chores before we thought about going anywhere," Luke stated firmly. "Sorry man, I keep my radio station on gospel or talk radio. I haven't listened to hip hop in ages. I believe Trevor MacElroy is on Heaven 79.5 this morning."

"Who is Trevor MacElroy?" Todd asked.

"He's a church member of mine. We both attend Grove Missionary Baptist Church," Luke said.

"Why is he on the radio?" Todd asked.

"He's a fitness consultant. He talks about health and fitness on Saturday mornings. He's one of the reasons I got into cycling. He encourages the listeners to expose themselves to a variety of fitness activities. Not to get stuck on one thing," Luke said, increasing the volume on the radio. "I think we've missed him. Along with the cycling adventure, you should consider contacting him to get an official fitness consultation. He has a fitness facility over off Maple Lane. He also conducts fitness sessions at our church."

"Okay. We'll see," Todd responded. "So, what about that bike? What kind of bike should I buy for long-distance cycling? I know I need a bike that will prepare me for the city-to-city 150-mile ride. I hear a lot about those mountain bikes."

"There are many different types of bikes on the market... road bikes, mountain bikes, and hybrid bikes."

"What's a hybrid bike?"

"It's a mix between road and mountain bike. For the type of long-distance riding we're going to do, you'll be looking at road bikes."

After twenty minutes of driving and idle conversation, Luke and Todd arrived at Mike's Bike Shop. Luke preferred this store because of Mike's knowledge of cycling and cycling equipment. Mike built a reputation for being a friendly resource in the cycling community. He was great at helping beginners prepare for their cycling adventures.

"Wow! They've got tons of bikes to choose from. How will I ever make a decision?" Todd said, looking through the store window.

"Hi, Mike, this is my friend Todd. He's just getting started as a cyclist. We're going to get him ready for the end-of-the-year city-to-city 150-mile ride," Luke said.

"Great! Let's see about fitting you for your first long-distance bike," Mike responded, extending his hand to shake Todd's.

"We will need to measure you to make sure we sell you the right sized frame."

"Measure me!" Todd responded, rubbing his head. "Not this waistline!"

"Not that kind of measuring, Todd. One of the most important factors to consider before buying a bike is frame size. It is absolutely vital to your safety, comfort and enjoyment. An ill-fitting bicycle is a bad start, and will lead to all sorts of problems in the end," Mike said.

"Mike will start you off with a good quality bike with at least 12 speeds," Luke said. "Buying a bike can be overwhelming. It helps to understand all the components, such as axle, gears, brakes, bearing, frame materials, and bearing materials."

After spending over forty-five minutes with Mike, Todd became knowledgeable about how a bike ride is determined by the frame. Mike explained that different brands of bikes have a different geometry and a different ride and fit. After the frame, there was the evaluation of the bike's wheels, suspension, and drivetrain components. He adjusted the seat to make sure Todd was positioned just right. Todd road tested several bikes before determining what felt good to him. And then there were the accessories he needed for fun, safe rides. Mike recommended an under-seat bag so he could place necessities like a couple of tubes and items to perform a flat repair on the road. He also recommended a portable high pressure pump, bike lock, bike rack, water bottles, helmet, and padded cycling shorts.

"Thanks, Luke, for taking me to Mike's. I can't tell you how excited I am about starting the training program. Because of you, I'm on my way to pedaling off the pounds," Todd said, loading the bike into Luke's truck.

"I'm just glad you're willing to give it a try. In order to be successful with exercising, you have to find an activity you like to do and one that you get enjoyment from. Otherwise, it requires effort to get motivated each time, and sooner or later, you will be tempted to fall off the wagon."

"I know. You keep saying that... 'fall off.'"

"You just need to understand that it takes commitment and dedication to go the distance. Personally, I get really bored in gyms. I like to be outdoors. That's why cycling has worked so well for me. I can enjoy an early morning sunrise or an evening sunset, the changing of the trees and flowers during the seasons. It's amazing what you miss riding around in a car. I think you'll find that there is more to life than making money and shedding some weight."

"All I really want to do is edit out the memories of my marital masquerade. If the cycling program can do that, I will be eternally grateful."

CHAPTER 13

Sorting Through Life's Priorities

*T*hree weeks later on a breezy cool morning, Todd met the training group at White Rock Lake for the beginning of many rides to follow. Todd was not a fan of the outdoors, but the beauty and tranquility of the lake mesmerized him. The sight of people fishing, walking, running, biking, and sailing early on a Saturday morning exposed him to another side of life.

"Hey! Good morning, Todd. Are you excited yet?" Luke said, walking with his bike towards Todd.

"Good morning. Everyone's talking about the 150-mile ride you guys completed last weekend. Sounds like it was nice."

"It was pretty awesome. The weather was great. I'm still recovering. I'll do a short ride today. I wanted to come out and support you on your first day. And also thank you again for the monetary donation."

"You're welcome. The program administrators and coaches put a lot in riding a bike," Todd said, sounding frustrated. On his first day, the cycling coach directed the group to a handout in their packet regarding cycling etiquette and traffic rules.

"Look at this handout. There are quite a few rules and regulations. *Communicate with your fellow riders at all times. Obey all traffic laws, signs and signals. Use signals to indicate turns and point out hazards to others. Give warnings to your fellow riders. Ride leaders call out right turns, left turns and stops, in addition to signaling. Announce turns before the intersections to give riders a chance to position themselves among the pack prior to turning.* This is a lot of information!"

"It's not that bad — they want to make sure everyone is aware of all the safety precautions while riding," Luke said reassuringly.

"Just look at this. *Try to avoid sudden stops or turns except for emergencies and move to the left or the right correctly.* **That's common sense.** *Slower moving traffic stays to the right and faster traffic to the left.* **That's common sense. Same concept as driving a car.** *Pass slower moving vehicles on the left and announce your intention to do so. Announce passes on the right. Call and point out the road hazards like potholes, excess gravel or sand, glass, parked cars, stray animals, and bumps on the road. Wear protective safety equipment: helmet, glasses, and gloves,*" Todd recited word by word.

"I know, Todd, but it's important. Be sure to watch for traffic from the rear. It pays to be extremely cautious around cars and intersections, because it can get dangerous around here. Always make eye contact with drivers. And by all means, when stopping for a flat tire or adjustment, always move clear off the road, then only if conditions permit should you move back onto the road. Always yield to traffic in the roadway and ride single file. It is illegal out here to ride more than two abreast. And don't follow too closely behind riders."

After a couple of months, Todd was on the road to resurrecting his life with an activity that proved to be successful in boosting his social, emotional, and physical well-being. With all of the extras Luke suggested, he was noticing his improved strength, stamina, and aerobic fitness, and best of all, he had reduced a stockpile of excess weight. Unfortunately, Todd's devotion to cycling had become parallel to his devotion to his business.

While Luke witnessed Todd at the lake and his camaraderie with the other team members — he began to question the well-being of Todd's kids.

"Hey Todd, thought I'd stop by and see if you wanted to go to lunch."

"Sure, but I have a conference call in ten minutes. It will last about twenty minutes."

"I'll just wait around and send some emails from my laptop," Luke said as he reached for his computer bag to move to an empty office.

After about forty minutes, they were on their way to Jake's Café. Jake's Café offered a large assortment of cold and hot sandwiches, salads, and plates, fostering a fresh, healthy alternative to fast food.

While scanning the menu, Luke was overwhelmed by Todd's discussion about his cycling schedule. It became difficult for him to sit and listen to Todd rave about his healthier lifestyle changes and the training group, with no mention of his kids.

"How are the kids doing?" Luke asked, placing the menu on the table.

"They're fine," Todd responded. "What are you eating today?"

"I don't know yet. Did you and Tarrynn ever work things out?"

"We're doing okay."

"Do they ever see Joan?"

"Every so often — she hasn't come to pick them up in a few months," Todd answered, looking puzzled.

"Did she get married yet?" Luke asked.

"I don't think so," Todd responded quickly. "I think I'll have the albacore tuna with pecans. This is a great restaurant. They have grilled turkey burgers and look... the caption on top of the menu... *Jake's hamburgers are all natural, hormone free, ground chuck.* I've got to tell the group about this place. They're all afraid to eat a hamburger because of the antibiotics, growth stimulants, pesticides, and hormones. Hamburgers have been the hardest food for me to give up. There's nothing like a thick, juicy hamburger. Look here, they've got a burger called the Grass-Fed Texas Buffalo Burger. I guess that's why it's $8.50. That grass must be pretty expensive."

Luke ordered the grilled chicken breast with brown rice and steamed vegetables. Todd got the albacore tuna with pecans and a side salad with Balsamic vinaigrette dressing on the side. Both ordered the fresh-squeezed lemonade.

After placing their orders, Luke resumed his inquiry. "I know the business is keeping you on the go and now the cycling, but what about the kids?" Luke said. "It doesn't seem like you're making any time for them."

"They're okay. I appreciate your concern, but I don't need you scolding me about not making time for my kids," Todd snapped. "Let's change the subject. How's the portfolio looking for my company?"

"I didn't mean to come off abrupt, but... And I don't want you to misinterpret my concern and think I'm scolding you."

"It's okay, man. Just remember that I don't pay you to dole out parental advice. How's the portfolio looking?" Todd said, cutting Luke's attempt for further discussion short.

The insinuations expressed by Luke, that Todd was a passive parent who never spent quality time with his children, left Todd questioning his viewpoint on parenting. Work always came first. He never took time out to provide the daily nurturing, guidance, attention, and affection his kids were starving for. And as a result, the kids reacted in a way that generated inappropriate actions. Todd ignored the signs alerting him his kids were hurting and out of control. Letters from the school about disruptive behavior and reports of failing grades sat on Todd's desk. He had always been solid on his thoughts about his role. *I provide housing, clothing, transportation and food*, Todd thought, sitting at his desk. *It's the wife's*

job to attend to the children. It's my job to make a lot of money so that my family is well taken care of. Maybe Luke is right. Maybe I do need to play a more active role in their lives. But how? All they ever need from me is money. I really do need to contact their teachers. For fifteen years I've never had to deal with teachers, schools, grades... that was Joan's job.

Amid his quest for reinventing himself, Todd's household was a battleground. His inability to transcend his personal feelings of despair, anger and failure had led to chronic turmoil between himself and his kids. Jolted by Luke's comments, Todd began to recognize that his attention to his own personal pain had caused him to be negligent in establishing emotional stability and security for his kids. Todd had overlooked the impact of the divorce on the kids. Filled with blame, anger and resentment, Trey, Trinity and Tarrynn's behaviors were radical remnants of a painful breakup. Still mourning the abandonment by their mother, the once friendly, cheery and well-behaved kids were now unfriendly, unhappy and unruly. A family engulfed in chaos, Todd realized how a year of his isolated behavior affected the actions and attitudes of his children. It was time to save his kids from self-destruction.

Mentally and physically absent from the lives of his kids, Todd had also separated himself from his extended family. After avoiding his parents' telephone calls for nearly a year, Todd mustered up the courage to call them in hopes of receiving words of support, advice and direction. He needed their help with figuring out how to achieve a normal, productive life with the kids in spite of their hurts and disappointments.

"Hi Mom," Todd said, imitating a demeanor high in spirit.

"It's good to hear from you, son," his mother replied. She was uncertain about the true well-being of her son. "How's everything with you and the kids? We've been calling you, but can't seem to get in contact with you. Anytime we call your office, your secretary says you're in a meeting. And we never get any straight answers out of the kids, that is, when your answering machine at home doesn't come on."

"Everything is okay, Mom. I've been busy trying to develop my company. Seems like I live at the office," Todd stated, followed by a long pause. "No, mom, actually everything is so messed up," Todd revealed in a tone that had turned to panic.

"What's wrong? Are the kids okay?" she asked, fearful.

"Joan dismantled our life and I don't know how to put it back together again," he said in anguish. "I hate her for destroying our family."

"Son, hate is a strong word. She's the mother of your children," his mother said. "Sure, she betrayed you and the kids and committed a selfish act, but you've got to move past it for the sake of your children."

"I know, mom. It's been over a year. It's been so hard to move on, but I think I'm starting to do so. I joined a cycling group a couple of months ago and it's helping me to escape the pain. I've met some new friends. I wish you could see my new bike; it's pretty awesome. I'm planning to ride in a city-to-city 150-mile ride in a few months. And my business is doing well," he said. As he talked, his tone flipped from panic to relief.

"Son, I'm glad you're starting to move on, but you've got to stop thinking about yourself and start thinking about your kids," she said. "Where are the kids right now?"

"They're somewhere — I don't know exactly where — I just got home. They constantly bicker and fight. I do whatever I can to escape the war zone. The teachers keep calling and sending letters about their disruptive behaviors — and now the neighbors..." he said with a defeated voice. "I've got a summons here to appear in Truancy Court. Trinity has been skipping school."

"Son, let me and your father help you," his mother said. "I want you to bring the children out to the country. We haven't seen you guys in a long time. Pack your bags and plan on spending the weekend with us. Are you and the kids attending church?"

"No, mom, I haven't had the time to find a church. I didn't want to go back to the church we attended together as a family," Todd said. "Joan is still a member there. I believe she's remarried. She hasn't called the kids in months. I guess she's still on her honeymoon."

"I want you and the kids to come out here. If you leave this afternoon, you can be here before dark. Stop thinking about Joan and start thinking about your family. Be sure to have the kids pack some church clothes," his mother insisted before hanging up the telephone.

Todd hung up the telephone dreading the ordeal of convincing the kids to go with him to their grandparents' for the weekend. "I've got to stop thinking about me and focus on the kids," Todd said to himself while contemplating his approach.

Wondering if the kids had come home while he was on the telephone, he yelled out, "Trey, Trinity, Tarrynn — are you home?" Receiving no response, he searched the house, going up and down the stairs from room to room. *Where are they?* Todd thought anxiously to himself.

The kids had become accustomed to surviving without parental supervision. Tarrynn had taken on the role of caretaker — ensuring that they had food in the house and that the younger kids were fed. Todd always made sure he gave her money for food, clothes, school and routine necessities. After the departure of her mother, Tarrynn became quite skilled at ordering take-out — pizza and Chinese from the neighborhood establishments. A few times a week, she drove to the grocery store for their favorite treats.

As Todd picked up the telephone, Tarrynn walked through the front door. "Where have you been?" Todd asked.

"I've been down the street at Treese's house. Why?" Tarrynn questioned.

"What's that smell on you? It smells like marijuana. Come here! Have you been smoking marijuana?"

"Nope."

"We don't smoke dope in this house."

"I told you I haven't been smoking. My friend Leslie had some weed. She was smoking it, but not me. I guess being in the room with her... it got into my clothes."

"Did you know your sister has been skipping school? I've received a letter to appear in Truancy Court."

"No, I didn't know. Contrary to what you believe… she's not my kid to watch over."

"You know I depend on you to take care of the household, and your sister and brother. You know I need to work long hours to keep the company going."

"Yep! Long hours and riding that new bike."

"Your grandmother invited us out to the country for the weekend. Where are your sister and brother?" Todd responded, ignoring Tarrynn's comment.

"They're down the street," Tarrynn responded rudely. "Why did she invite us?"

"Don't speak to me in that tone," Todd demanded. "She and your grandpa want to see you guys. Trinity and Trey are down the street where?"

"I don't know. Down the street. Probably Bobby and Samatha's houses."

"Well, find them. I want them home," Todd said. He was becoming angry.

"You need to find them. They're your kids," she replied in a fiery manner.

"You're right. You all are my kids and there are going to be some changes around here — from now on, no one leaves this house without letting me know the who, what, when, why, and where of their comings and goings. Do you understand?" he demanded. "Now where down the street?"

"Bobby lives in the red brick house on the corner, and Samatha lives in the brown brick two doors down. What's the deal? You never care about us and where we're at," Tarrynn said, walking abruptly up the stairs.

Todd knew their situation had to change if the family was going to survive the collision course they were traveling. He had to rebuild their infrastructure. He had to figure out how to gain traction with his kids. He had allowed them too much latitude to live their lives as they saw fit. Recognizing his duty to intervene and gain control, Todd left the house in search of Trey and Trinity.

Tarrynn resented the fact she had lost two parents, one by choice and the other by circumstance. Because of the divorce, she had been forced from adolescence into adulthood. Unable to participate in and attend school activities, she was saddled with overseeing the daily obligations of their household. Mocked by the kids at school because of her weight and outdated clothing and hairstyle, Tarrynn hated her life. To console herself, she secretly sought the affections of an older boy she had met on the Internet. Deceived by his acts of kindness, Tarrynn did not realize that his primary goal was to lure her into a mesh of drug use and sexual manipulation.

Trinity, now 13 years of age, was riddled with blame. The day before Joan left, she asked Trinity to clean her room. After failing at several attempts, her mother just gave up. The next day while they were at school, Joan packed her bags and loaded her car to leave their lives forever. Trinity had never forgiven herself for her actions. In a quest for approval, she performed mischievous acts with a gang of girls at her school — skipping school to drink wine coolers, hanging out with older boys, and taking dares to shoplift in stores at the mall.

Trey, now eight years old, probably suffered the most. He had clung to his mother as a child, and had cried to be with her at all times. Unaware of the situation, he had not understood the secret travels to Uncle Chuck's house with his mother. Still, after one year, he was angry with her for leaving him for another man.

Todd obliviously contributed to the magnitude of distress in his family. More than disruptive behaviors and poor grades, the kids were using sex, drugs, and unhealthy relationships as a way to suffocate their sorrows. His lack of involvement, support, and guidance perpetuated the frenzy of erratic acts and behaviors.

"We're home," Todd yelled out. He had informed Trinity and Trey about their invite to their grandparents. As expected, they weren't excited about going. Because of a school in-service day, the kids had two days off merged with the weekend. They were on their second day off and had big plans for the upcoming weekend.

"Hey kids, we're going to our grandparents' for the weekend," Tarrynn said with sarcasm, coming down the stairs.

"Why are we going out there?" Trey asked.

"They haven't seen you kids in a while," Todd replied. "Go and pack some clothes so we can leave by two o'clock. Also, your grandparents want to show you off at church, so pack some church clothes."

An hour later, with bags in tow, the kids were ready for the ride. Todd tried to generate conversation during their drive. The kids weren't comfortable with their father, since they rarely spent time with him. Even before their mother left, his work had taken him away most evenings and weekends. Now, with the recently added cycling adventure, they rarely saw him at home.

"I've been receiving reports from your teachers about your grades and classroom behavior. They aren't looking good. Tarrynn looks like you might be going to summer school to retake Geometry and English. And Trinity, what about this court date? You skipping school?" Todd said, waiting for a response.

After an unsuccessful attempt to connect with the kids on the three-hour journey, they finally arrived at the home of Todd's parents. His parents live on twenty acres in Longview, Texas, a place noted for its rural splendor. Before reaching the end of the driveway, his parents came out to greet him and the kids with intense enthusiasm. Grandma Holder couldn't help but notice how much the girls had grown. She was a retired teacher. A very health conscious lady, she was appalled by the physical appearance of her granddaughters.

"Hi kids, come and give your grandmother a big hug," she said, holding out her arms. "I haven't seen you in such a long time."

Each of the children greeted their grandmother and grandfather. Todd's parents were the only grandparents they had living. Joan's parents died when she was a child.

"Hey Trey… you're going to be taller than me in a couple of months. Come on inside the house and tell your grandparents about your lives in the city. How's school? What kind of activities are you participating in?" she asked inquisitively.

They visited and reminisced for about an hour, looking at old pictures of the kids when they were younger.

"I know you kids are probably starved. I cooked up a lot of good food for us to eat. We have baked chicken, mixed vegetables and mashed potatoes," Grandma Holder said, trying to generate some excitement. "For dessert, we're having frozen fruit yogurt cups."

The kids displayed looks of disappointment. Their favorite foods included hamburgers and fries, pizza and Chinese food. They hadn't eaten a home cooked meal since their mom left. Even then, Joan only cooked on occasion. She would warm up pre-cooked meals, or mix packaged mashed potatoes, rice and pasta dishes, or microwave frozen lasagna or pizza.

While eating, their grandfather inquired further about school, friends, and outside activities. He was particularly interested in Tarrynn and her plans for college. Grandpa Holder was a retired school administrator.

"Have you started taking the practice exams for those college entrance tests?" Grandpa Holder asked.

"I haven't decided on whether or not I'm going to college," Tarrynn replied.

"If you don't go to college, then what are your plans for the future?" Grandpa Holder asked.

"I don't know yet," Tarrynn responded.

"Tarrynn has got to take Geometry and English again," Trinity said, laughing.

"Shut up!" Tarrynn yelled out. "At least I go to school."

"Okay, girls! What's the problem with English? I was an English teacher for thirty years," Grandma Holder said, waiting for a response. "Good English skills are in your DNA."

"I don't like to read for one thing…" Tarrynn replied.

Todd sat quietly listening to the exchange.

"Kids, go with your grandpa into the family room. He went out earlier and rented some movies for you guys to watch this weekend," Grandma Holder said, motioning for some alone time with Todd.

While cleaning the kitchen and dining room, Todd's mother probed him about the current state of his family. She expressed her concern for the children and his lack of parental involvement and responsibility.

"Sounds like the children have been raising themselves, Todd. Your parental neglect has facilitated their feelings of anger and hostility. The girls are twice the size they should be. And I know that has significant ramifications. Because of their internal feelings, they are probably doing whatever is necessary to protect themselves from further disappointment and disapproval," she said with a scolding speech.

"I know, Mom. I'm a failure as a parent," Todd said with disappointment.

"You're not a failure, Todd. You just need to get your priorities in order before it's too late. The children need for you to assume your full-time role as a father. Your role is not just about providing a home, clothes, transportation, and food. It's about being a loving, nurturing, committed, and supportive father."

After catching up and allowing Todd and the kids an opportunity to get settled, Grandpa Holder escorted the kids to their rooms for a good night's sleep.

Stepping Up and Taking Charge

*T*he next morning, Todd awoke before everyone. He decided to go downstairs to look at the collection of childhood photographs. While bending over to pick up a photo album, he noticed a health magazine with the heading "Pre-teen Obesity: The Downfall of the Next Generation." Intrigued by the caption, he decided to read the article. The article discussed an alarming increase in the number of overweight kids. It also stated that children are developing chronic conditions like adult onset diabetes, heart disease (high blood pressure and high cholesterol), orthopedic disorders and respiratory disease.

After reading the article, Todd thought about how he had improved his eating habits, but had neglected to transfer those same habits to his kids. *Am I contributing to the slow death of my kids? The information in this article suggests that my kids' lifestyle habits might result in death or long-term suffering, as a result of overindulgence in high fat, high cholesterol, high sodium, high sugar, high carbohydrates, high calorie foods like hamburgers and fries, chicken nuggets, fried foods, cookies, donuts, candies, and sodas. I've cut out these foods to enhance the longevity and quality of my life, but according to this article, it's important for my kids, also. If I don't get my kids on track, I'm a detriment to their ability to live long, healthy lives.*

"Good morning, son," Todd's mother said, tiptoeing into the room. "What are you reading?"

"Actually, it is one of your health magazines," Todd said. "There are several articles about overweight and obese kids."

"It's really serious. That's why I'm so worried about the girls," she said with a consoling tone. "They're too large for their ages. It's my opinion that girls suffer so much more when they're overweight or obese. They are more likely to be subject to ridicule and discrimination. They tend to avoid public encounters. They often go to one of two extremes. That is, they prefer to be alone and withdrawn, or they try desperately to be accepted by others. And please don't misinterpret what I'm saying... I'm not saying they need to be thin to the point that their bones are visible. I'm saying they need to be following healthier habits — eating healthy foods, participating in exercise, getting plenty of rest, and drinking a sufficient amount of water."

"I know, mom."

"They should be eating foods with nutrients like vitamins, minerals and antioxidants, which help us all to stay healthy — foods that are going to protect their cells from disease and illness. The sooner parents understand the concept of healthier habits, the better off our kids will be. Parents allow too much of the wrong foods into their kids' lives. When I went to our school's football and basketball games, I often remember the procession of parents and kids traveling back and forth to the concession stand with hot dogs drowning in cheese, onions, chili, mustard, and/or relish and pickles... or nachos swimming in cheese, chili and the occasional beans, sour cream, and/or jalapenos... or... chicken fingers, french fries and hush puppies basket... or chili cheese fries with a hot dog or hamburger... all flushed down with a super-sized soda. And that's just one segment of the day. The consumption of high caloric, artery clogging foods at football, basketball, or soccer games doesn't even take into consideration that probable breakfast trip to McDonald's for pancakes, hash browns, and sausage...

or the lunch or dinner at Taco Bell for a burrito supreme. The habits that you're allowing can cause generations of health problems."

"It's all troubling, Mom," Todd said, slumped over at the desk.

"Son, your father and I are here to support you," she said. "Why don't you go and see if the kids are up? I'm going to go ahead and get breakfast started. Your father and I typically eat around nine o'clock most mornings."

Todd folded the corner of the page in the magazine to mark his stopping point. He took a deep breath, anticipating a fresh start with the kids. Walking up the stairs, he heard the sounds of running water in a sink, the flushing of a toilet, and the gurgling of mouthwash. He was relieved to hear signs of movement.

"Hey, guys, your grandma is getting ready to cook breakfast," Todd said, making his presence known from the hallway. "Come downstairs after you finish getting dressed."

The only acknowledgement came from Trey. Back downstairs, Todd offered to help his mother.

"What's for breakfast?"

"I think we're going to have French toast, with some of your father's venison sausage and a medley of fruit."

"I can't believe you're going to cook French toast," Todd said. "That's fattening, isn't it?"

"The one thing you should understand — with kids, you've got to be creative with making foods healthier plus tasty. Although my French toast has been altered from the traditional style to contain healthier products, the kids will not notice the difference. I've prepared the French toast with eggs that are high in Vitamin E, contain Omega-3 fatty acids, and have less than 25% of saturated fat; soy milk that contains a number of vitamins and minerals; and whole grain bread, nutmeg, ground cinnamon, cooked in olive oil, then topped with a low calorie, sugar-free syrup. As far as the venison sausage, it contains far less fat than the sausage from the local grocer, and it has no preservatives. The medley of fruit consists of banana, cantaloupe, and strawberries. It is packed with nutritional benefits."

"I've really gotten into the health stuff since joining the cycling group," Todd said. "One week we received a handout stating that the Omega-3 fatty acids that exist in fish have the good fat to help prevent the formation of bad fat in your blood. What is it exactly?"

"Omega-3 fatty acids are a form of polyunsaturated fats, one of four basic types of fat that the body receives from food. You're probably more familiar with the fats most commonly referred to… cholesterol, saturated fat and monounsaturated fat. Omega-3 is critical for good health. The only way you can get it is through food. It has been published that Omega 3 helps to protect us from health threats. Research has shown that it boosts our immune system. And you know the immune system fights off foreign invaders that try to enter our bodies. There are also claims that Omega-3 lowers cholesterol, reduces blood pressure, improves autoimmune diseases like rheumatoid arthritis and lupus, improves insulin sensitivity, and eases menstrual pain."

"What foods does it exist in?"

"It is more abundant in Atlantic salmon and other fatty, cold-water fish like sardines, Atlantic halibut, bluefish, tuna, and Atlantic mackerel… venison and buffalo are both good sources. Other sources include canola oil, broccoli, cantaloupe, kidney beans, spinach, grape leaves, Chinese cabbage, cauliflower, and walnuts… and my Omega-3 enriched eggs."

"I heard something about mercury and fish on the news the other day. What's that all about?"

"I remember hearing a recommendation the other day that fish consumption should be limited to two to three servings weekly because so many fish are polluted with mercury and other contaminants. The fish I've mentioned have relatively low levels of mercury. Fish with high levels include shark, swordfish, tilefish, and king mackerel… red snapper also has a high level. As long as you stay away from the fish with high levels of mercury, and eat fish in moderation, you'll be okay," his mother stated, while she stacked the French toast on a platter. "Todd, your children must become your priority. They have a radar detector inside of them that signals their priority level in your life. Right now, they know that priority level is low. They need a nurturing and supportive father. A father who cares about what they eat. A father who cares about their whereabouts. A father who's excited about spending time with them. A father who's front and center for the important moments in their lives. Believe me, if you don't make some necessary changes, your life will be full of regrets when you realize what you missed out on. Plus, a supportive and nurturing parent helps to keep a kid from going down the wrong path."

"I know you're right, Mom. I think Tarrynn is smoking marijuana."

"Why would you think that?"

"When she came in yesterday afternoon, she smelled like it."

"Did you ask her about it?"

"Yes... she said her friend was smoking it."

"Do you believe her?"

"I don't know, Mom. I've been out of touch for so long. I don't know what to believe."

"When you were growing up, I wanted more than anything to trust you. But kids will be kids. I was a kid once. And there were a lot of acts I hid from my parents. I always kept those memories in the back of my mind while raising you and your sisters. My goal was to establish a foundation of right and wrong for my children. I wanted my children to know and understand bad choices and their consequences. You can do everything you deem possible to shape the mental, physical, social, emotional, and spiritual foundation for your child. But, no parent ever knows if and when outside influences will infiltrate and crack the foundation. My best bet was to implement a strategy of distraction... involvement in church activities... involvement in extra-curricular activities. We spent quality time with you and your sisters. You all didn't come and go as you pleased. Your whereabouts were tracked and monitored. We had discussions with you all about drugs, drug dealers, gangs, and sexual relations. We had discussions about your futures. We supported your dreams and created every opportunity for them to become a reality. We set boundaries... and when you all deviated from those boundaries, there were consequences. Disciplinary actions. Above all, I prayed for my children."

Just as their grandma was finishing up, the kids dragged into the kitchen with Grandpa Holder leading the way.

"Kids, help your grandma set the table," Grandpa Holder said. "The dishes are in the top cabinet. Trey, look in the drawer near the sink and give me some knives, forks, and spoons, please."

One by one, the kids carried out their grandparents' instructions. They weren't accustomed to eating from real dinnerware, having grown accustom to cardboard boxes and plastic containers.

Seated at the table, Grandpa Holder began to bless the food. "Bow your heads." Everyone sat quietly, waiting for Grandpa Holder to proceed. "Lord, thank you for this day. Thank you for family. Thank you for the food we're about to eat for the nourishment and strengthening of our bodies. We thank you for the hands that prepared the food. Amen."

Todd watched for the kids' reaction to the food. As usual, his mother was right. They didn't notice that the French toast was made from whole grain bread or that it was topped with sugar-free syrup. Trinity mentioned that the sausage tasted differently, but she liked it. After finishing their breakfast, Grandma Holder directed the kids to clear the table and wash the dishes. After everything was put back in its proper place, Grandma Holder prompted her husband to take the children into the pasture to explore country living.

"Grandpa, take the fishing gear and show the children some country fun," Grandma Holder said.

The gleam in his mother's eyes as she watched the kids trot off with their grandpa triggered a peaceful emotion inside Todd. Visions of her singing and reading to him as a child warmed his heart. She had that natural instinct when it came to caring for him. She knew when he was hungry, tired, not feeling well. And when he was troubled and needed to be held. Todd wanted to have those same instincts toward his kids. And most of all, he wanted to create an environment for his kids to have the best chance of becoming happy, healthy, and morally upright citizens.

Todd stayed behind to visit with his mother. "That was a great prayer Dad said at the breakfast table."

"It's important that children learn about giving thanks to our Father in Heaven for the gifts of the earth that sustain us everyday. Praying should be a common practice for you and the kids."

"I've never thought much about it."

"I don't know why. You grew up in a home that prayed."

"You're right…"

"Son, can you help your father out? He hasn't been feeling that well. This would be a perfect opportunity for you to help me get the garage in order. I would like to get my car inside, if at all possible."

"Sure, Mom," Todd responded as he embraced his mother. "Is it anything serious with Dad?"

"No, he's just been working hard around here lately. The daily chores can become overwhelming. I'm sure he's worn himself out. He won't admit it, though."

"Mom, I just want to thank you for being a wonderful mother and person," Todd said sincerely.

"Thank you, Son," she said. "Now that the kids won't experience the benefits of a two-parent family, it is important that you don't allow them to become victims of circumstance. It is important that you understand your role as a father. Number one, a father loves and protects his children. The best way to do that is to get involved in their lives. Teach your kids about empathy. Be an example to your son on how to be a man and how to connect with women. He will be a husband and father one day, so teach him how to take care of a family. Love your daughters. Teach them how to interact with men. You are their first encounter with a man, and it's your responsibility to lay the foundation for how they should expect a man to treat them. They should see themselves as queens of femininity, and deserving of someone who will treat them with respect, courtesy, and dignity."

"What about the fact that Joan is virtually non-existent in their lives?"

"It is something to think about. We should never make the mistake of thinking that all mothers are created equal. There are mothers in the home that are non-existent."

"Seriously."

"Yes, Son," she responded. "Sure, a mother's emotional bond begins in the womb. She helps her kids to develop a sense of right and wrong, capacities for intimacy, compassion, and confidence. While Joan is on a hiatus, it's going to be up to you to perform the dual role. It's going to be up to you to be available and devoted to your children. You must teach them how to adapt to life's pursuits, challenges, and uncertainties with compassion and confidence."

"You're absolutely right."

"Sounds like it's time for you to find a church home for you and the kids. Involvement in a church community is invaluable. For Trey, now is the time when the most basic beliefs about God, His way of life, and His Word can be easily understood. For Trinity, now is the time when maturity and principles begin to develop and affect her life. Finding a church that's dedicated to providing information, guidance, encouragement, and opportunities that can assist you in shaping her pathway in life is essential. She should be striving to implement God's way into her life. Tarrynn is on the verge of adulthood, a crucial time when life-altering, character-forming behaviors are created. A church dedicated to encouraging and facilitating the development of young adults can make a tremendous difference in her future."

"I know, Mom, kids are molded by example and by their own experiences."

"Throughout the year, our church educational ministry sponsors a variety of programs that allow children, youths and young adults to participate in worship services and in the life of the church," she said. "Are you leaving tomorrow?"

"Yes, I need the extra day to get ready for a business meeting."

"Well, before you and the kids leave, I want you all to attend church with your father and me," she said. "Did you and the kids bring church clothes like I asked?"

"I did and I told them to pack some. Hopefully, they did," Todd said, looking around at the clutter in the garage. "Mom, it's going to take me a while to move everything out and put it back in order. You go inside and get some rest."

"I can help, son. I'll move out the light stuff."

"Dad has accumulated a lot through the years. He's had this compressor since I was a boy," Todd said as he worked to move the heavy piece of equipment along the wall. "It's a wonder dad can find anything."

"You're right. He can't ever find what he's looking for when he needs something. That's why he has so many cans of motor oil, and bags and bags of fertilizer, insect killer, and plant food. There's no order. It's a cycle of wasting money."

During the intermittent conversations with his mother, Todd worked diligently for three hours to organize the garage. Arranging chainsaws, weed eaters, edgers, riding lawn mowers, manual lawn mowers, tall ladders, short ladders, water hoses, car products, and gas cans. Discarding inoperable appliances, outdated paint cans, and broken furniture pieces.

"Mom, it's like dad has two of everything."

"Just wasteful!"

"Why doesn't he put some of this stuff in the barn?"

"The barn is filled with more old furniture, televisions, farming tools, and equipment. Just junk. Plywood, bicycles, and Christmas decorations."

"I think you should be able to fit your car inside now."

"Okay. Looks like your dad and kids are headed down the road. I hope they had a good time," she said. "They didn't stay gone that long."

Todd headed outside the garage to greet his father and the kids. His mother followed behind him. "How was your tour of the pasture?" Todd asked. "You guys didn't stay gone that long."

"It was great," Trey responded. "Seeing Grandpa's dog chasing the cows was funny. Plus, we saw squirrels and a turtle in the pond. Tarrynn started feeling sick."

"We started fishing… we didn't catch any," Trinity added.

"The fish weren't biting today," Grandpa Holder said.

"What's wrong, Tarrynn?" Grandma Holder asked. "Is something hurting you?"

"My stomach started hurting. I think it was the sausage we ate this morning," Tarrynn said, staring at her father.

"I don't think it was the sausage. Everyone else seems to be okay. Let me get you some medication to soothe your stomach. Come on upstairs with me," Grandma Holder said, hugging and holding Tarrynn.

"Dad, I'm hungry," Trey stated.

"Kids, we're going to give grandma a break from cooking — we're eating out this evening," Todd said. "I'll make us some sandwiches to tie us over until later on."

"Todd, you know your mom bought enough groceries for an army this weekend," Grandpa Holder responded quickly after thinking about the money spent making sure the refrigerator and pantry were well stocked with healthy foods and snacks.

"I know. It's okay. You and mom will be well stocked for the upcoming week. I know she's going to cook tomorrow," Todd said. He really wanted to reward his mother for her support and advice. "Come on, kids, let's go into the kitchen and make some sandwiches."

"What kind of sandwiches are we making?" Trey asked.

"Let's see what Grandma bought," Todd said, roaming through the refrigerator. "Great! She has some of that fine deli meat — Mesquite Wood Smoked Skinless Breast of Turkey. And whole grain bread. Honey mustard. Fresh spinach and tomatoes."

"What about potato chips? We can't eat a sandwich without chips," Trinity asked.

"Let's look in the pantry. I know Mom has chips," Todd said, opening the pantry door. "Look here! Chips. Knowing Mom, they're healthy chips. Let's see. All natural, no preservatives."

"What are preservatives?" Trey asked.

"Preservatives are used to control, delay or take control of the growth of bacteria, yeast, or mold that exist in or gain entry to the food. They're used to prevent food from spoiling or becoming poisonous."

"That's a good thing, right?" Trey asked.

"I guess it would be okay... only they're in everything we eat. No one really knows if the pool of chemicals swimming inside our bodies from the foods is secretly causing us harm. That's why it's important for us to reduce the volume of foods we're eating that have preservatives, food additives, and chemicals."

"I like these chips, Daddy," Trey said.

"Good, I'll get some when we get back home. Let's finish putting the sandwiches together. Put some more spinach on your sandwich. When you finish eating, you can go in the family room and finish watching the movies your grandpa got for you."

A few hours later, Todd went upstairs to check on Tarrynn. Todd called out to her, "Tarrynn, are you feeling better? Can I come in?"

"Yes, you can come in."

"I just wanted to check on you to see how you're feeling."

"I'm feeling fine."

"Do you feel like going out to eat? Grandma is perfectly willing to cook us something if you don't feel up to going out."

"I'm okay. I don't want any more healthy stuff."

"Go ahead and wash up. I'll go and get your sister and brother ready."

Todd and the kids outvoted Grandpa Holder by selecting Gomer's Country Style Cooking, an all-you-can-eat buffet restaurant in downtown Longview. Todd loved this restaurant. He remembered being able to feast on fried chicken, chicken fried chicken, chicken fried steak, fries, macaroni and cheese, cake and ice cream, and whatever else his heart desired. It was much better than supersizing because he could travel back and forth to the buffet table — two, three, four times, or as much as his stomach would allow. Todd especially favored this restaurant because he could get a lot for his money… $4.99 — all you can eat. Grandma Holder, on the other hand, was concerned because the kids didn't need the temptations of the elaborate buffet.

On the way to Gomer's, the constant chatter of Trey and Trinity with their grandpa was a welcomed sign of acceptance. It was apparent that their grandpa was able to break the ice during their day of exploration. Tarrynn, on the other hand, remained silent during the drive.

As usual, there was a line outside the door, with an hour wait. Todd went back to the car to get some packages of peanut butter on wheat crackers for Tarrynn to eat since she hadn't eaten earlier that day.

"Here are some extra packages in case someone else gets hungry." Todd understood that they needed to eat healthier foods; however, he had no idea what that really meant. After handing out the packages, Grandma Holder began to examine the ingredients listed and nutritional value of what Todd had given the kids. Grandma Holder's recollection of a conversation with her doctor about whole grain foods triggered a thought. *I wonder if these crackers are true whole wheat crackers.* Her examination of the product revealed that the crackers were a fake. Even worse, they were high in calories and loaded with sodium and chemicals.

She whispered to Todd, "This is the last time I want you to feed these crackers to the kids — they are not nutritious at all. They're just a bunch of empty calories that offer no nutritional value," Grandma Holder said, attempting to prepare him for future changes.

"But Mom, they have peanut butter, and you've always said peanut butter is good," Todd said.

"Yes, Son, I know, but these are not. They have this product called partially hydrogenated oil, which is also known as trans fat. There's been a lot of information in the news about it," she said apologetically. "The peanut butter you want says zero trans fat. The main ingredients in a healthy peanut butter are peanuts and salt. Start checking the labels."

"What's partially hydrogenated oil or trans fat?" Todd asked.

"According to the news reports, it's really bad stuff that over the long run can cause major health problems," Grandma Holder explained.

Eavesdropping on their discussion, a man ahead of them in line interrupted by saying, "Excuse me for sticking my nose where it doesn't belong, but I overheard your conversation. The partially hydrogenated oil has a reputation for being the most harmful type of fat — contributing to increased cholesterol levels and heart disease risk. Recent studies indicate that trans fat may pose the greatest risk of heart disease and diabetes. Some say greater than saturated fat."

"Thank you, sir, but we were talking amongst ourselves," Todd said.

"Sorry, mister, I didn't mean to interrupt, but if you're going to eat here today — you're going to take in a lot of trans fat," the stranger announced politely. "This restaurant and others, as well as nationally known fast food chains, fry their food in partially hydrogenated oil. The packaged and baked goods they serve also contain partially hydrogenated oil. About 40% of the products in supermarkets contain this unhealthy oil. Surely for $4.99 you don't think you're getting the top of the line oils such as canola or olive. All you young folks want to do is eat out... thinking you're getting a bargain with those exquisite advertising schemes. A two-piece chicken and biscuit for a $1.49. Two fish fillet sandwiches for $4.00. A chicken sandwich or 3-piece chicken tender basket free with the purchase of a medium fries and drink. Two tacos for .99 cents. A lifetime practice of chasing a deal will result in your own personal health crisis. You will be robbed of a longer, healthier lifestyle. Get in the kitchen and cook sometimes. Cook some real food. Mash some real potatoes."

"If it's so bad, why are you eating here?" Todd questioned.

"Son, I'm 83 years of age. I've lived my life and had a great time doing so. I've had two heart attacks, and those happened in my late seventies. I've traveled the globe many times over. I've lived to see my grandchildren grow up to be successful adults. And now that my wife is deceased, I'm ready to be with her in eternity. The way I figure, my days are limited. You and your family, on the other hand, have many great years ahead of you. I just hope they will be as good for you as they were for me."

Seated at their table, Grandma Holder stared at the pageant of men, women, boys, and girls circling the buffet table. Some had two plates. Others were heading back for thirds and fourths. The kids were excited about the vast variety of foods.

"I want to start out with the chicken fried steak and fries and macaroni and cheese," Tarrynn said.

"I prefer the fried chicken and fries," Trey said with his legs swinging underneath the table.

"I'm going to eat fried fish and pizza," shouted Trinity. "I love the thick crust with pepperoni, sausage and hamburger."

"Todd, do you think we should eat here?" Grandma Holder whispered to Todd, worried about all the trans fat.

"It's just one day. One day couldn't hurt us. We have plenty of time to get on track. And besides, you're planning to cook healthy tomorrow. Let's just enjoy ourselves this evening and let the kids have fun eating their favorites."

The waiter arrived to take their drink orders. "Does your restaurant use partially hydrogenated oil for frying or baking on the premises?" Grandma Holder asked.

"I know we use vegetable oil," the waiter said.

"Is it partially hydrogenated vegetable oil?" she asked.

"Ma'am, I really don't know," the waiter replied.

"Do the prepared foods that your company purchases from the suppliers contain partially hydrogenated oils? I'm talking about the pastries, frozen products...," she asked.

"Ma'am, I really don't know. Are you going to order or what?" the waiter replied.

"Mom, let's just eat here this evening. This will probably be our last time eating here. I have my heart set on a steak," Todd pleaded.

Grandma Holder went along with the family's wishes. The waiter proceeded with taking everyone's drink order, and as usual, the kids ordered soda. After retrieving all of their favorites, Todd and the kids gobbled up all their food choices. The sight of the girls feasting on unhealthy foods that contributed to their already expanded bodies saddened their grandmother.

At home, Grandma Holder thought about all the things Todd had to consider for promoting and encouraging healthier habits among his kids. After he sent the kids up to bed, she encouraged Todd to finish reading the article on pre-teen obesity and do some additional research on the computer. *He needs to understand the impact of trans fat... and the lifestyle challenges that overweight and obese kids face*, she thought to herself.

"When's the last time the children had a physical examination?" Grandma Holder asked, taking a seat at the kitchen table.

"I haven't kept up with it, mom. Joan usually handled those sorts of things," Todd said, sitting beside her.

"Joan's been gone for over a year now! Don't tell me those kids haven't seen a doctor since Joan left. What about their habits? What do they typically eat? Are they involved in any activities in or outside of school?" She further inquired.

"Mom, I mainly work. I give Tarrynn money and a debit card to make sure there's food in the house," Todd said, getting up to get some chips. "What's really helped is that she has her driver's license."

"Are you still eating?"

"Yes, mom. I've got the munchies."

"The munchies are what put weight on people," she said, watching him retrieve the bag from the pantry. "Anyway, you've placed a lot of responsibility on Tarrynn. What do you mean you give her money? Does she cook, do they eat out, what!"

"Mom, they're okay. They eat pizza, hamburgers, and Chinese food. That's what kids eat. Don't get me wrong, I know we have some issues. I'm sure they miss their mother being in the house," Todd said, eating some of the chips.

"When you called the other day, you didn't know where they were. You said they constantly bicker and fight with one another. You said they're disruptive in school and around the neighborhood. Clearly, everything is not okay, Son. You have some serious issues."

"Mom, I was just feeling down and depressed."

"Son, I can't help you fix things if you're not honest about what's going on," she said. "Bottom line, you need to get more involved in Trey, Trinity, and Tarrynn's lives — start spending quality time with them."

"I know, mom. That's why I thought this weekend would be a good start."

"Remember that you are a parent first. You need to sideline that cycling business and get your children on track. Your top priority is the kids. Start taking responsibility. You have two daughters whose health might be in jeopardy. One should be thinking about college and taking the college prep exams. The other has probably started her menstrual cycle, thinking about boys. You don't even know. And like I've stated, a son needs a father to teach him about being a man."

"I'm sure Joan knows about the girls, since she's their mother."

"You don't know what Joan knows. She's not around. You're the full-time parent. You should know everything about your children," she said, watching Todd eat more and more chips. "You should know about their teachers, homework assignments, school activities... who they hang out with, who they text-message on their cellphones, who they blog on the Internet. What kinds of magazines, CDs, and movies they're purchasing. They should be coming to you for comfort, advice, and reassurance. Not their friends."

"Mom, it's not that big of a deal."

"Yes, Sir, it is a big deal. You're so out of touch that you don't know about their experimentation with sex or their pressure to use drugs and alcohol, or participate in other dangerous activities," she said.

"You're right, Mom."

"Your laissez-faire attitude about parenting has endangered your relationship with your children," she said. "Your consumption with your business, lingering self-pity, and now the cycling group leaves your children to raise themselves and rely on friends for support and guidance. It's time for you to connect with your kids. Find out what makes them tick. Start spending quality time with them. Establish some family rituals — start having family talk nights and family dinners without the interruption of telephones, digital cable, video games, or the Internet. And above all, listen to them."

"Mom, I've already started thinking about what I need to do," Todd said. "I know they blame me for their mother leaving. If she wasn't unhappy with me, she wouldn't have left them."

"They probably do blame and resent you, but you've got to work around the unfavorable conditions. Tell them you love them," she said. "Put up the rest of those chips. You've had enough.

Come into the den. I want you to finish reading the article you started earlier."

Todd had never really thought of his girls as overweight or obese. Any staggering thoughts about their sizes were dismissed with "it's just baby fat; they'll grow out of it." Reading the information pertaining to overweight and obese kids, Todd realized that his kids were headed toward an assortment of health problems. Todd was now enlightened — *lack of physical education programs in most schools. Children no longer walking or riding their bicycles to school because of being driven by a parent or themselves. Children spending anywhere from 30 to 40 hours a week watching television, playing video games, text-messaging their friend, or blogging and chatting on the Internet. Children eating an abundance of fast-food.* Speculation of unhealthy habits among his kids, Todd recognized that he needed to become the catalyst for change in his household.

"This is some pretty deep stuff, Mom," Todd said, scanning the different articles. "Like I mentioned earlier, one of the good things about my cycling group is that I've received some valuable information on how to eat healthier foods. Although I eat out quite a bit, I'm making better choices. Contrary to my meal at Gomer's Country Style Cooking, I'm not eating steaks everyday. I know the kids are probably living on take-out, fast food, sodas, cookies, chips, and who knows what else."

"Times have changed. When you were growing up, it wasn't anything for you and your friends to ride your bikes to school — travel from house-to-house playing kickball, dodgeball or basketball. You didn't do much in terms of school athletics, but you were active everyday. Nowadays, kids are not as free. Parents have to contend with worry and fear that their kids might be kidnapped or sexually abused. Unfortunately, today's kids are confined to the indoors, rather than free to explore the outdoors. And because I had a job where I was home at a reasonable hour, you were able to eat a home cooked meal every evening," Grandma Holder said. "Now the challenge for you is how to be creative with helping your kids eat healthier and exercise in a safe, protective environment. You have to figure out how to manage work and household obligations, as well as their school and extra-curriculum activities and everything else in your lives."

"Mom, on top of everything, right now I need to figure out how to reconcile our damaged relationship," Todd said. "The kids see me as a foe, rather than a father. How do I gain their love, trust, and respect?"

"Just be honest with them. Tell them how much you love them. Tell them you've made some mistakes. Tell them they are most important in your life — not the business, not the cycling, not your broken heart.   Ask them to give you another chance," Grandma Holder said. "Bottomline — it's time to change the order of your priorities."

CHAPTER 15

The Road to Restoration

That night, Todd lay in bed contemplating ways to forge a relationship cemented with love, trust, respect, and honesty. He would adjust his work hours to be present when the kids left for and returned home from school. He would schedule regular visits with their teachers and attend more school events. They would eat dinner together at least five nights a week, which would include preparing and cooking the meals together. He would become involved in their academic performance. There would be frank discussions about sex, drinking, drugs, and other unacceptable behaviors. He would change his venue of cycling in the neighborhood to the lake. At the lake, the kids could participate in the various activities offered by the park association. And above all, he would find them a church home. He remembered his mother's favorite saying, "God's power can defeat the wars of life."

The next morning, Grandma Holder rushed through the hallways knocking on bedroom doors, prompting everyone to get up and get ready for church. She and her husband had been faithful members of Trinity Zion Baptist Church for forty years.

Although Todd grew up in the church, he hadn't been back in years. At least not since Trey had been born.

"I didn't bring anything for church," Trinity whispered to her grandma.

"Didn't your father tell you to?" Grandma Holder questioned.

"Yes, he did, but we ignored him because we didn't want to come out here," Trinity admitted.

"We are all going to church this morning, so just tell your sister and brother to put on the jeans and shirt they had on the other night when you arrived," Grandma Holder said. "Come on downstairs when you and your sister and brother are ready."

Todd wasn't aware of the earlier discussion about the church clothes, and became irritated when he saw the kids dressed in demin jeans for church.

"What happened to the church clothes you were supposed to bring?" Todd asked Tarrynn, Trinity, and Trey. He stood in the hallway, dressed in a dark suit.

"We didn't bring any," Tarrynn responded.

"It's okay. The kids look fine," Grandpa Holder interrupted, in an attempt to defuse the potentially escalating verbal exchange. "Go on downstairs. Your grandma has finished preparing breakfast."

Entering the kitchen, the kids found a place to sit at the table. "We're having oatmeal with raisins and brown sugar," Grandma Holder said. "Tarrynn, look in the refrigerator and get the carton of milk before you sit down. The glasses are on the table. Thank you."

"I don't like oatmeal," Trinity replied.

"This oatmeal is going to be yummy and healthy for you," Grandma Holder said.

"I don't like milk," Tarrynn said, frowning at the carton of milk.

"Milk is good for you," Grandma Holder replied.

"We learned in school that milk comes from cows like Grandpa's cows," Trey added.

"You're absolutely right," Grandma Holder said. "That's why your grandpa feeds the cows grass, corn, and hay so they can make good healthy milk. Milk is very important for you. It has what your bones need to help make them thick and strong — and that's calcium. Your bones also become more dense and strong with exercise. That's why your father is going to start getting you and your sisters involved in some physical activity, like soccer, rollerblading, swimming, and biking. Your body needs exercise and all sorts of nutritious foods to grow and stay healthy."

"Honey, we'd better be getting a move on so we won't be late," Grandpa Holder said anxiously.

"When we get back, I'll make you all some smoothies for your road trip. I use soy milk, but you won't even taste the milk with the variety of fruits I'm going to include in the mixture. It will be delicious," Grandma Holder said.

"Thanks, mom, for helping out with the healthy eating and exercise promo," Todd whispered, hugging his mom on the way out the door.

Driving towards the church, Trey and Trinity were amazed by the size and campus-style appearance. Grandpa Holder explained that the church had experienced tremendous growth and major "cosmetic surgery" over the last twenty-five years. He was proud that Trinity Zion Baptist Church offered a variety of amenities that included walking trails, ball fields, picnic areas, prayer and meditation gardens, and an athletic center.

"Your father is going to find you all a church back home, so you can start going regularly," Grandma Holder said. "A church where you all can study the Bible and have fun learning about Jesus Christ."

"I hope it looks like this one," Trey said.

Todd's mother was particularly concerned about Tarrynn. She was withdrawn and noticeably unhappy. She knew Tarrynn would erect a roadblock to mending their damaged relationship. The transition to a household of love and respect could only come by way of spiritual intervention. Tarrynn was at a most challenging and confusing time in life. And with no adult influence to answer those questions about life choices, she was filled with uncertainties. She needed to experience an environment where teenagers and young adults could discover what it really meant to enjoy life and serve Christ at the same time. An environment that offered Sunday School classes, community outreach programs, youth and young adult activities, retreats, and the opportunity for her to grow in God's Word. Tarrynn, Trinity, and Trey all needed an atmosphere where they could meet new friends, learn truths from the Bible, and enjoy the dynamic influence of other Christian youths.

The trip to their grandparents' proved to be exactly what Todd needed to set the stage for parental repair. Reluctant to leave the safe haven his parents had created during the weekend, the time of departure had arrived.

"I'm going to be calling and writing you and the kids more regularly. I want you to send us plenty of pictures. Hopefully, your father can bring you out at least once a month. And we'll come there to visit you, also," Grandma Holder said, walking Todd and the kids to the car.

"Just remember, Todd, if you need me to come out and help you with your whirlwind of responsibilities, I will be happy to do so," Grandma Holder said privately to Todd, while the kids said their goodbyes to their grandpa. "And remember, it's up to you to rescue your kids."

"I will, mom. I've got to start doing what I haven't been doing, and that's fulfilling my role as a parent," Todd admitted. "First step… implement a truce… that's the only way I'll be able to put together the pieces from the brokenness that has occurred. I'll be giving you progress reports on my rebuilding efforts."

The following weeks exposed a house furnished with wall-to-wall secrets, chaos, and confrontations. Todd's attempts at restoration were continuously stifled. The discovery of Tarrynn's involvement with an older guy was explosive. The revelations of her experimentation with drugs were overwhelming. A trip to the physician to determine the girl's participation in sexual activity revealed that Tarrynn had contracted trichomoniasis, a sexually transmitted disease. She was also diagnosed with high cholesterol, and Trinity with high sugar. According to the physician, Tarrynn was one step behind heart disease, and Trinity one step behind diabetes.

"Hey, Todd. How's everything going?" Luke asked, walking into Todd's office. "I've got some papers for you to sign."

"Where have you been?"

"I've been around. I haven't seen you at the lake in the last few weeks. Since we kind of parted on a sour note the last time we had lunch together, I just thought it best…"

"Luke… thanks. You opened my eyes about my relationship with the kids. Anger, resentment, and pain were taking me further away from them. That conversation with you sounded the alarms in my head, and got me to thinking. My household has been a battleground ever since Joan left and probably before… I just wasn't there enough to recognize it. But now, I'm trying to turn things around."

Todd revealed to Luke the woes of his life. "Luke, my girls are sexually active. Thirteen and sixteen — sexually active. And Tarrynn has trichomoniasis," Todd said, feeling powerless. "When we visited my mother a few weeks ago, she was immediately concerned about their health — their weight. I'd never taken notice. They've been doing poorly in school, but I just ignored the reports from the teachers. Trinity skipping school. And drugs. Some drug called Greenades."

"What in the world is Greenades?" Luke asked.

"From what I understand, they're gumballs that contain marijuana," Todd said.

"Todd, man, I feel for you. Why don't you and the kids come with me to church on Sunday?"

"Maybe we'll do it. I promised my mom I would find us a church home. Luke, I just want you to know... you're a good friend. I'm surprised some lady hasn't snatched you up. Why haven't you gotten married?"

"I was engaged a few years ago to Megan."

"I forgot about Megan. I'm so sorry."

"Megan was the woman of my dreams. I don't know if I ever told you, but she died from ovarian cancer. And when she died, I died. I didn't think I could continue. But through God's resurrection powers, I emerged from my paralyzing pit of pain," Luke divulged. "Before Megan died, she made me promise to live a full life. I watched her fight to the end and leave in peace. Remembering her tenacity and strength is what helps me to be the man that I am. So, I know what it's like to lose someone you love. Whether they leave you by choice or by circumstance, it still hurts."

"I didn't know about the ovarian cancer. I guess I was in my own world at that time, and never asked."

"I had the opportunity of a lifetime. I experienced an amazing love. An opportunity some will never experience."

"Was she sick a long time?"

"No. Once she was diagnosed, it was a matter of time. We were planning to join the cycling program together. When she went for her physical, she found out she had cancer. She hadn't been to the doctor in years."

"Is that why you were so adamant about me getting a physical?"

"Yes, it is. I know firsthand how a physical exam can detect a hidden medical problem. I'll never know if Megan's outcome would have turned out differently had she gone to the doctor sooner. An earlier diagnosis might have given the doctors more time to treat the disease. Because the cancer was so advanced, the body, its immune system and chemotheraphy couldn't hold it off. The downhill course was rapid."

"Was she healthy? Ate right and exercised?"

"We were like a lot of people. We mainly ate in the restaurants... fast food... T.V. dinners... loved to eat store bought pastries. The cycling program was going to be our start to getting on track with a healthier lifestyle. Once she was diagnosed, we started eating more fruits and vegetables. Whole grains. Low-fat dairy products, like yogurt — you know, all the stuff you hear we should be eating everyday. I suppose in the final analysis — it was too late. I know it was all a part of God's perfect plan."

After weeks of visiting Grove Missionary Baptist Church, Todd decided to unite. The church was fun and exciting, without compromising the truth of God's Word, the Bible. It was a church where the primary purpose was to share the good news of Jesus Christ, to develop a relationship with Jesus Christ, and to foster a life exhibiting an attitude of worship, praise and blessing.

I know he's going to get tired of hearing it, but I've got to, Todd thought to himself while dialing Luke's telephone number. "Luke, thanks, man. I finally feel like I'm swimming above high water, rather than drowning in it. And it has a lot to do with you being a true friend. That solid foundation I treasured, crumbled from beneath my feet, causing me to plunge into emotional turmoil riddled with anger, resentment, and betrayal. But because of you and my parents, I've discovered a bonafide reason to resurface. A relationship with Jesus Christ and my kids."

"I'm so happy for you, Todd," Luke said. "I know you're concerned about the health of your kids. Take them to Trevor's fitness class on Tuesdays. He can help you with getting them on the right track."

"I will definitely do it," Todd responded. "Thanks again, Luke."

Todd persevered through the tough times. He became involved in his kids' lives. He provided guidance and support for their daily routines. He consulted with their teachers on a regular basis regarding their academics, and their grades were improving. Tarrynn agreed to take the college entrance exams and was starting to think about attending one of the local colleges. Although she had to attend summer sessions to help improve her grade point average, she was optimistic about her future. There were no more reports of disruptive behavior. Todd spent considerable time with them in both household chores and recreational activities. He took them on an educational outing and a sporting event at least once a month. Todd credited their family's transformation to the teachings of Grove Missionary Baptist Church. He rededicated his life to Christ and the kids were all baptized. The influences of the church and his parents gave him the ability to visualize a family rooted in love, trust, respect, and honesty — equipping him with the capacity to assemble the jigsaw puzzle of his life.

"Hey mom! How are you and dad doing? Oh yeah, I just want to thank the two of you for being there these past few months. I don't know how I would have made it without you, Luke, and my new church home."

"You're welcome, Todd," Todd's mother said, sounding pleased about their turnaround. "We're doing fine. What about you and the kids? Are they enjoying your new church home?"

"Yes. We've attended new member's orientation. I've attended the divorce recovery program, and the kids love Sunday School and Wednesday Bible study. And we're doing fitness with Trevor, the fitness consultant at the church, and on our own at White Rock Lake."

"That's good, son."

"We're still struggling with this eating. They want pizza. How can I prepare a healthy pizza?" Todd asked.

"Once again, it's about creativity. Making their favorites healthy and tasty. For pizza, you can make healthy substitutions by purchasing prepared frozen dough at the supermarket, using low-sodium tomato sauce, and low-moisture part skim mozzarella cheese to reduce the calories, fat, cholesterol, and sodium. You can use non-traditional vegetable toppings like broccoli, spinach, and fresh tomatoes. Even fruit like pineapple chunks. The key is to stay away from the high-fat meats like pepperoni, ham, and sausage. You can make your pizza lower in fat and calories than the take-out version."

"Okay, how exactly would I prepare the pizza with toppings like broccoli, spinach, mushrooms, fresh tomatoes and cheese?"

"Son, let me email you the ingredients and instructions. I can't remember everything off the top of my head. The main thing is that you and the kids will be doing it together — having fun."

"I think we can do it. What about Chinese food?"

"I've made some stir-fry dishes at home. Much healthier than what you will find at the neighborhood Chinese restaurant. My recipes integrate chopped chicken with an added mixture of vegetables like broccoli, carrots, celery, and water chestnuts, served with brown rice in a low-sodium soy sauce."

"I like it! Email your recipes for those, also."

Over a period of weeks, Todd's mother guided him on how to prepare a variety of creative healthy meals for breakfast, lunch and dinner. Todd learned how to make fun dishes, like a burrito using a whole wheat tortilla filled with ground white chicken, black beans, whole grain rice, corn, fresh spinach, or mixed field greens and diced tomatoes. He topped it off with a taste of low-fat sour cream. The kids' favorite became known as Dad's Whole-Wheat Waffles. They were nutritiously made with whole-wheat flour, skim milk, eggs, canola oil, vanilla, baking powder, and a dash of salt for taste.

The combination of better eating habits and the involvement in the church's walking club and softball team proved beneficial for Tarrynn and Trinity. Their participation in organized fitness programs resulted in more fit bodies and improved medical reports. Trey became involved in soccer and basketball. For all three kids, the church provided a fun atmosphere in a Christian environment. On Saturday mornings, Todd continued his participation with the cycling group and completed the city-to-city 150-mile ride nine months later.

Todd recognized that his faith, the support of a devoted friend, and his parents had redirected his outlook on life and his role as a father. Through spiritual guidance, he was able to develop a roadmap for their future. He was no longer focused on the failure of his marriage, but on the revitalization of his family.

Superficial or Substance

*L*ife for Todd and the kids was transformed from pandemonium to peace. The seeds of love, respect, communication and honesty eliminated the weeds of resentment, guilt, pain and brokenness that had been choking their family.

"Hi, dad. I've gotten dinner started," Trinity said, slicing tomatoes for the salad. "Mom called. She wants you to call her. She wants to congratulate you on the cycling adventure."

"I didn't know you and your mom had been talking," Todd said, looking through the mail.

"She started calling us a couple weeks ago. She usually calls when we get home from school to check on us."

"Have your brother and sister spoken with her?"

"Just Trey. I told her about your ride and all the neat things we've been doing," Trinity confessed. "She and Chuck broke up."

"Hi," Tarrynn said, walking in the back door.

"Looks like the results of the SAT exam came in the mail today," Todd said, getting some chicken breasts out of the refrigerator to season.

"Great! Where is the letter?"

"Over there on the table," Todd said, pointing to the table.

For weeks, they talked about attending college and taking college entrance exams. Tarrynn was finally excited about going to college. Todd invested in a number of tutoring sessions to make sure she had every opportunity of getting accepted into the college of her choice.

"I hate that I didn't study harder when I got to high school," Tarrynn said, as she began to open the envelope. "I hope I did well. It's a good thing colleges and universities use more than your SAT scores when making admission decisions. Unfortunately, my high school record isn't the best. Neither are my writing skills. At least my history teacher is willing to write a recommendation letter for me, and my involvement in community service activities at church should be helpful."

"Don't worry, honey, you're going to college," Todd said.

"Be quiet, Dad. Let me read this. Reading, I have a score 275. Writing 225. Math 265. That's a total of 765. That's low, Dad. The lowest you can score in each section is 200. After testing for 3 hours and 45 minutes, this is how well I did," Tarrynn said with disappointment.

"Don't worry, honey. You're going to college. You have at least two more opportunities to take the exam. Just consider this one your practice exam."

"You're right. The church is offering free SAT prep classes. Do you think I should register?"

"Yes, honey, I think you should register."

"Okay. They should be doing registration tomorrow night at Bible study."

"We have about forty-five minutes before the chicken is done. Let's sit down and figure this thing out. Trinity, please put the salad in the refrigerator until we're ready to eat. Go and check on your brother."

Todd was excited about his relationship with the kids. A relationship that allowed them to make decisions together. A relationship filled with laughter.

"Dad, telephone, pick up," Trinity yelled out from the top of the staircase.

"Hello."

"Hi Todd. It's Joan."

"Hi Joan... how's everything with you?" Todd said, surprised to hear Joan's voice.

"Everything is going fine. I guess the kids told you that I've been calling to check on them."

"Yep! Trinity told me this evening. Hold on a second," Todd said, moving the telephone away from his mouth. "Tarrynn, why don't you go upstairs and let me have a moment with your mother."

"Okay, Dad."

"Thanks, baby," Todd said, handing the SAT prep book to Tarrynn. "I'm back, Joan."

"Trinity told me about your riding adventure. I'm happy for you — 150 miles — that's awesome. How's the business going?"

"It's going great. I've got more projects than I can handle. I'm in the process of hiring some additional staff."

"That sounds great," Joan said, trying to keep the conversation moving. "Trinity says you cook now."

"Yep! I needed to get the kids on a healthy track."

"What sort of foods do you cook?"

"Their favorite is my whole-wheat waffles. Our favorite dinner is chicken lasagna. Mom helped me with a healthy recipe. A few months ago, I took the girls to the doctor for an annual exam and we discovered that they were headed for heart disease and diabetes if we didn't make some changes. They're exercising, and we're good in spite of..."

"That sounds really good, Todd," Joan interrupted.

"We've also cut out soda and the high sugary drinks," Todd said. "You know my mom is a real health nut. She really got on me about the kids drinking so much soda. I've learned so much about adopting better eating habit. I didn't realize that soda consumption could cause tooth decay due to the high amount of sugars. I found that out when I took Trey to the dentist."

"You've done an amazing job, Todd."

"We've had quite a few hills to climb, but the ascent to happier times has been worth it. Let's cut to the chase, Joan — I know you didn't call to get my cooking recipes. Why are you calling? The kids haven't heard from you in months, until recently."

"I want to see them, Todd. I miss them and I want to see them."

"What does that mean… you want to see them? Do you want to take them out to eat… to a movie… have them spend a weekend with you? What?"

"I have a new home, and I want them to come and spend a weekend with me."

"What about Chuck?"

"Chuck and I are no longer together."

"I thought you guys were getting married a few months ago."

"We decided to go our separate ways."

"I see. Now that you and Chuck are finished you can make time for your kids."

"It's not like that."

"Well, how is it?"

"It was difficult to have them around when Chuck and I were together. I realized that my relationship with Chuck was superficial. I had no future with him."

"Difficult! Difficult! Difficult for you to spend time with your own kids? How does that sound? That's crazy, Joan!"

"I know. I know my actions are inexcusable," Joan admitted.

"I dealt with the pain of losing you for a long time. On that wretched day when you left me, I almost took my life. I was torn between two emotions — love and hate," Todd said. "I thought taking my life was my only option for an escape."

"I'm so sorry for the hurt and pain I caused you and the kids."

"Just when the kids needed a loving and devoted mother the most, you walked out on them. Your departure was devastating. You ripped out their hearts."

"They were young — too young to understand," Joan said, trying to diminish her actions. "I knew you would take care of them."

"Too young! They were seven, twelve, and fifteen!"

"I want to make things right, Todd," Joan said.

"That's just wonderful," Todd said cynically. "I knew you never loved me as I loved you. The only chance I had of keeping you was to make more and more money. I figured if you had the worldly possessions that you so desired… you'd never leave me. But you found another man and left anyway. But, you didn't just punish me… you punished your kids. Oh, I forgot, you never wanted kids anyway. I guess they were for my benefit — incidentals for you."

"I've always loved my kids."

"Funny… you had an odd way of showing it," Todd said, becoming aggravated. "You know what? I can't totally blame you for the discord in our marriage. I admit that I should have been a better husband. I know my passive personality and apathetic attitude caused us to become disconnected. But, to leave your children, that's unforgivable."

"I just got caught up in something."

"Caught up! I guess the kids and I got caught up, too. Tarrynn escaped by running into the arms of a sexual predator. Trinity is on probation for skipping school and doing drugs and alcohol with her friends. Trey cried himself to sleep every night for a year. He's never forgotten those images of you singing to him and rocking him to sleep," Todd said, reinforcing the level of pain Joan had caused. "And the thought of you exposing him to your indiscretions makes me angry all over again. When you left, you placed us all on a path to self-destruction."

"I want to come back. I want to make it up to you and the kids."

"I grieved you everyday. I grieved the abandoned dreams, hopes, and desires. You severed our family ties. A marriage we built for seventeen years. You betrayed me. You broke my heart. And now you want back in?" Todd asked.

"Yes, back in. I'm here now and that's all that matters. I want to be a part of their lives. I am their mother. I want to be a part of your life."

"You forfeited your rights as their mother when you walked out. I won't let you hurt them again," Todd said. "How convenient. Now that you and Chuck have split, you think you're coming back this way. It's been nearly two years — ten telephone calls and five visits. And each time they spoke or visited with you, I saw in all of them a glimmer of hope that the conversations and the visits wouldn't be so far apart. I won't give you the opportunity to shatter those kids' lives again."

"I plan to apologize to Tarrynn, Trinity, and Trey."

"Apologize! Do you think apologizing is going to make two years of pain disappear? You were supposed to be a role model. Someone they could count on. A mother that would love and protect them. A mother that would never hurt or discard them like a bag of trash. What sort of mother cheats on her husband and leaves her family for another man?" Todd questioned. "I've worked too hard to repair the wounds."

"You can't keep me away from my kids. Tarrynn will be graduating soon — going to college. Trinity and Trey need me. I've missed so much in almost two years."

"That's your regret, not mine."

"Todd, I don't want to miss anymore. I want to be around to help Tarrynn make her college and career decisions. I want to be around to help Trinity pick out an outfit for her first date, her dress for the Prom. I have missed milestone birthdays... holidays. I want to make up for my absence," Joan stressed. "I want to hang out with you guys at the lake. I want to be with you in the stands watching Trey play basketball or whatever sport. I want to be front and center in their lives. I know they will forgive me."

"Forgive you! Now that's funny."

"I know you blame me for dismantling your lives, but I know you can do the impossible. Forgive me. Take a shot and make us a real family again?"

"I've already forgiven you," Todd said. "But a shot at us being a family — you've got to be joking. The mean and hurtful things you said. I bored you. How you conned me into marriage. The sex was unfulfilling. Inadequate. He was larger. What happened, did he shrink? Did his money shrink? I have a life. A thriving business. A wonderful relationship with my kids. You know what? Your leaving was probably the best thing to happen to us. We definitely weren't happy. I was walking around in a fog. Now I can see clearly. And to think, I almost took my life because of you. How selfish of me. All I could feel was hurt — pain squeezing the life out of me. So many days I pulled over on the side of the road crying, asking the question — why. Why did she leave me? For weeks, I slept on my office sofa, drinking myself to sleep. I'm embarrassed to mention the countless number of times I drove by your office with my pistol in my lap. The times I thought about driving through a red light hoping to be killed instantly by the oncoming cars. Those times I thought about driving my car off the High Five Freeway. I ached for you for so long. Hanging on to my life with Joan delusion. But I'm grateful that God blessed me with parents and a friend who helped me to emerge from that dark and desolate place inside — that pit of despair. Now, I know that life is precious. A gift from God. And I'm glad I'm alive to experience its greatness with my family."

"I'm so sorry, Todd. I regret every single day of what I did to you and the kids."

"Are those the only words you know? I'm sorry."

"I love you, Todd. I never stopped loving you. You are the best thing that ever happened to me."

"I wonder how many men have had that same song sung to them."

"I'm pregnant, Todd."

"Finally! More truth. Well, at least I know it's not mine."

"It's Chuck's. He never wanted kids."

"Sounds like the two of you were a perfect match."

"I made a mistake. Haven't you made a mistake that you regret?"

"I've made plenty of mistakes. And I have no problem admitting my mistakes. For starters, not being the type of husband I should have been. Not being the type of father I should have been. I'm trying everyday to make up for my mistakes with the kids. But, you know what? I'm not going to sit here on the telephone matching mistake for mistake. I'm working hard everyday at being the kind of father my kids need — a father who nurtures, guides, attends, and shows affection daily. A father, that's involved and supportive. I understand my role as a father, and because of that, my kids have a chance at being emotionally stable. I've worked hard at clearing the remnants of their painful past."

"Todd, just know that things can be different this time."

"Give me some time, Joan. Some time to absorb it all. I don't want the kids exposed to another round of Joan's reign of selfishness."

For weeks, Todd wandered around trying to figure things out. He wondered about the impact of Joan's entrance back into their lives. He wondered about exposing the kids to Joan's emotional barometer. *How do I know if things will be different? One moment, she wants to be a mom, and the next moment, she wants out.* Todd knew his only source of guidance would come from above, and kneeled down to pray alongside his bed. *Lord, Joan desires to return to our family as my wife and as a mother to our children. Both the kids and I have suffered tremendous hurt, and we are now beginning to recover. She is no longer my wife; however, she is still the mother of my children and will always be. I know the kids still love, want and need her, but the love I had for her is gone and I do not wish to reunite with her. I recognize Your will is for both parents to jointly raise their children, but how do I safeguard our kids' hearts, yet allow their mother to mother them? As their father, I have been called to love, support, guide, and protect them from harm.*

Heavenly Father, what should I do? Show me what to do. As always, Lord, not my will, but Thy will be done. Confused and afraid, Todd would wait for divine direction.

"Dad, is everything okay? Did you sleep on the sofa all night?"

"I'm afraid so, honey. How are you coming with your SAT studying?"

"It's good. The prep courses at the church are really helping me."

"I am so proud of you."

"Thanks, dad," Tarrynn said, proudly. "What's the deal on you and Mom? She's been calling here quite often lately. Are the two of you taking a lap around the love track again?"

"No, we won't be taking another lap. However, I do want you kids to have a healthy and happy relationship with your mom."

"I love mom, but I'm apprehensive about letting her in again. How could she just shove us aside? The day you told us she had moved out, I felt like the walls had closed in on me. Even though she was always gone, selling her pharmaceuticals and exercising at the gym, she was my mom and I loved her. After she left, it just seems like everything went downhill. You were never around. I became responsible for looking after Trey and Trinity. The kids at school made fun of me. I was the largest girl in my class. I loathed and despised my life. But, it all seemed to get better when I met Chris on the Internet. He was the only person interested in me. He said he would love and cherish me forever. When I would meet him at the hotels for sex, he filled the emptiness inside me. That day you followed and found us together, I hated you for taking away the only thing I thought rescued me from my horrible life. I hated you for calling the cops, having him placed in jail, and forbidding me to see him ever," Tarrynn confessed. "I wish life had a magic eraser so we could wipe away the last two years of a painful past."

"You kids have had to endure so much in such a short time, and I apologize for that."

"It's okay, dad. At least you figured out a way to make it right. At least you loved us enough. Loved us enough to make us a better family. You and Mom both made mistakes. But, she didn't give you a chance to correct them. Instead, she sought solace with another man."

As the days passed, Joan kept calling. She wanted desperately to be a part of Trey's ninth birthday party. For nearly two years, she had been absent on the day that commemorated the kids' births — no cards, no presents, and no telephone calls. Using Trey and Trinity as her intelligence, Joan asked them to gauge Todd's thoughts on allowing her to participate in the planned birthday party.

"Hi, Trinity," Joan said, trying to get information about the party. "How are you kids doing?"

"Hi, Mom. We're doing fine."

"Did you get a chance to speak with your father?"

"No, Mom."

"What time is the party on Saturday?"

"It's at four o'clock."

"Is it at the house or Diamonds Pizza Palace?"

"It's at the house. Dad says the food at the pizza palace is greasy, artery-clogging pizza, and we don't eat like that anymore. We're going to have our own healthy mini spinach pizzas, fruit smoothies, and healthy chips with a low-fat onion dip."

"What kind of cake and ice cream are you having?"

"I don't know if we're having cake and ice cream."

"Well, don't tell your father that I'm coming. I want it to be a surprise. I want to bring your brother a cake and an assortment of ice cream. Do you know if there's a particular theme to the party or what sort of decorations your dad has gotten?"

"No, Ma'am. I know we're also having chicken tacos made with whole-wheat tortillas. Dad is renting a trampoline and air hockey table, putting up a basketball goal, setting up a volleyball set, and hiring a DJ. I think he's hired a party planner. I know the invitations mentioned something about dressing for fun in the sun, and listed the activities."

"Okay. I'll have my caterer put together something special for your brother. Email me a recent picture of Trey. Do you know what he wants for his birthday?"

"Probably games."

"Okay. I'll plan on seeing you and your brother and sister on Saturday."

Parked across the street, Joan could hear the sounds of excitement coming from the backyard. With tainted thoughts circling inside her head, Joan deliberated over how to move forward. *How can I just waltz back into their lives as though the last two years never happened? I should have at least called more often. Tried to visit them more often. But, Chuck didn't want them around — three kids were too much for him. What if Todd tries to stop my attempts to renew my relationship with the kids? I wish I could change the past, but I can't. This may be my only chance to reclaim our future together. Who am I fooling? The only reason I'm trying to come back is because Chuck doesn't want me. But, I do love my kids. But, I love Chuck more than anything else. If only I hadn't gotten pregnant, Chuck and I would still be together. I just can't have this baby by myself. Todd is a wonderful father now. He would be a great daddy to this baby. And Tarrynn, Trinity, and Trey would love their little sister or brother. If only Chuck would talk to me. If only I could get him to accept this baby. I can't have an abortion. Looks like my only option is to try and get back in the good graces of Todd and the kids.*

Joan braced herself for the reunion. With two cakes decorated with Trey's picture, several gallons of ice cream, and a host of presents, she stepped out of the fully loaded car. Unable to carry everything at once, she proceeded up the walkway through the backyard gate with Trey's presents. Startled by her presence, Trey and Trinity ran and gave her a hug. Todd and Tarrynn watched from a distance.

"Hi, Trey and Trinity."

"Hi, Mom," they both responded.

"Trey, you have a lot of your friends at your party. Help Mommie with your presents," Joan said, beginning to wave at Todd and Tarrynn.

"Thanks, Mom," Trey said, accepting the gifts graciously.

"I have a couple of cakes and ice cream in the car for you. I don't want you to leave your friends. I'll get your father to help me," Joan said, walking with the kids to greet their father and Tarrynn.

"Okay," Trey said.

"Hi, Todd. Hi, Tarrynn," Joan said, stretching out her arms to embrace Tarrynn. "Come and give your mother a hug."

"Hi, Mom," Tarrynn said, reluctant to be hugged by her mom.

"You kids really look great. And Todd... you have muscles bulging every which way but loose. I have a couple of cakes and ice cream in the car for Trey. I didn't want him to leave his guests. Can you help me?"

"Sure," Todd responded. "I'll be back."

Walking to the car, Todd questioned Joan's reasons for not informing him that she was coming to the birthday party. Joan explained to Todd that she didn't want to risk him telling her she wasn't welcome. Todd expressed his disapproval of the cakes and ice cream. He explained how the kids were adapting and accepting their healthier lifestyle. He further explained how most of the parents shared his sentiments about healthier foods, and favored the menu he was serving.

"Hopefully, you'll accept the fact that I'm here, and the fact that I plan on being involved in the kids' lives."

"You're an unexpected surprise. Nevertheless, we'll make the best of the situation. We'll cut the cake in very small pieces and offer a small scoop of ice cream."

The kids enjoyed themselves immensely. The boys played a combination of basketball and air hockey. The girls enjoyed a game of volleyball and jumping up and down on the trampoline, all to the sounds of the DJ's hip hop master mixes. Though Todd expressed his initial concern about Joan's entrance, he agreed to accommodate her request to spend time with the kids.

"Thank you, Todd, for allowing me to spend this special day with the kids," Joan said as she prepared to drive off. "I'll call the kids to let them know I made it home safely."

A couple of hours later, the phone rang. "Hi, Todd. I was just calling to let the kids know I made it home safely. Are they asleep yet?"

"Actually, they are. I think the day simply wore them out. They got up at six o'clock this morning to help get things ready."

"Okay. We didn't get to talk much about us. I just want you to know that I love you. And I want more than anything to be a family again. I know you need time. I'll wait as long as I need to wait. The chance to be a family is worth the wait."

"I'll think about it, Joan."

As he began to hang up the phone, Todd heard a series of clicks. Hesitant to hang up, he paused. He then heard someone dialing a number. A man answered the phone.

"Hello."

"Hi Chuck. It's Joan again."

"Joan, I told you not to call back."

"Chuck, I love you. I don't want to lose you. If you don't want this baby, I'll get rid of it."

"Joan, I don't want you or your baby. I've moved on."

"Chuck, I couldn't bear it if you didn't come back to me."

"Joan, I think you need to accept that this relationship is over. Don't call here anymore. Don't call here about us or that baby."

Horrified by the conversation — her tone of urgency and desperation, Todd had a repulsive reminder of the pain she had caused. It was the sign Todd had asked God for. He had provided solid evidence of Joan's many faces of deception. Any flicker of reconciliation was extinguished. Todd thanked God for protecting him from another round of pain.

Wishing he could rewrite history, Todd was thankful for the lifeline that rescued him from the torment, loneliness, anger, brokenness, hopelessness, and disenchantment that had gripped him. God had shifted his family from the road of devastation to the freeway of hope. Tarrynn was headed to college. With the assistance of SAT prep classes and countless tutors, she was able to score 1,100 on the SAT. Trinity was on the honor roll and participating in gymnastics. And she had satisfied the terms of her probation. Trey was involved in basketball. They were a family that loved and supported one another. Todd never told Joan about the conversation he heard between her and Chuck. And over time, he was able to convince her that the likelihood of the family reuniting was gone. Understanding that her presence was vital to the kids, he accepted her relationship with them.

Listening to the harmonic sounds of birds chirping outside his office window, Todd thought, *Lord, Luke encouraged me to have faith as I navigated my way through the curves of life. And I've definitely had some curves to navigate. Lord, I thank you for piloting and protecting my path from those challenging curves. Above all, I love and thank you for giving me the strength to restore my family and survive the end of my fairy tale marriage.*

Your Guide to Healthier Meals:

Re-Imagine Fun in the Kitchen

*T*his appendix includes the recipes of healthy dishes mentioned throughout the book. You'll discover innovative ways to make your favorite foods nutritious and flavorful by adding whole grains, fresh fruit and vegetables, natural herbs and seasonings, and low-fat dairy products. Creativity in your own kitchen will be the key for your journey to optimal health.

Sarah's Homemade Savory Chicken Spaghetti

From page 58

Sarah has mastered a quick-and-easy savory spaghetti recipe and so can you. She adds her favorite vegetables into the meat sauce to create an irresistible dish that increases her intake of vitamins, minerals, and fiber — whole grains and vegetables that are fresh, fulfilling, and naturally low in fat.

To get started on the meat sauce you will need the following ingredients: one package ground white chicken meat; one-half cup chopped onion; one-half cup chopped bell pepper; one-half cup chopped celery; one clove minced garlic; one and one-half cup of fresh tomatoes; one small can no salt tomato paste; one large can no salt tomato sauce; one large can of water; one tablespoon of basil, cilantro, garlic powder, and oregano; two tablespoons of brown sugar; one-half package of McCormick's spaghetti sauce seasoning.

To start the process, you'll brown your ground white chicken with onion, bell pepper, celery, and garlic over moderately high heat for about five minutes and drain off the excess fat. Add other ingredients and cook on high heat until sauce comes to a boil and then turn it to low and simmer for twenty-five minutes, stirring frequently. This helps the sauce to thicken and not burn.

While the meat sauce is simmering, arrange your pre-cut vegetables (one-half cup of one-fourth inch slices of carrots or baby carrots; one cup of one-inch broccoli florets; one medium zucchini and yellow summer squash quartered and thinly sliced) in a vegetable steamer over boiling water. Cover and steam eight minutes or until slightly tender but crisp, then drain. Once the vegetables are steamed, add them to the meat sauce and simmer for an additional twenty minutes.

Meanwhile, prepare a package of whole wheat spaghetti noodles according to the directions. Then add the cooked pasta to the meat sauce. Presto, you will have your version of a homemade savory healthy spaghetti dish filled with vitamins, minerals, and fiber.

Sarah's Scrumptious Spinach Omelette
From page 99

Sarah combines fresh spinach and mushrooms to create a nutritious omelette for one. The dark green leaf vegetable is a rich source of vitamin A, C, and iron. Always remember, spinach can be added as a complement to any meal. For an added punch, she adds fresh tomatoes, also rich in potassium, beta-carotene (vitamin A) and vitamin C. Plus, she uses Eggland's Best eggs — eggs that are high in vitamin E, contain omega-3 fatty acids, and have less than 25% of saturated fat.

To launch your one-egg omelette, you'll need the following: one egg; two tablespoons of olive oil; two cups of fresh spinach; two portobello mushrooms caps, diced; one-fourth cup of fresh diced tomatoes; one green onion chopped; one-half bell pepper chopped; cilantro, basil and/or other favorite seasonings; and two tablespoons of low-fat mozzarella cheese.

To get started, heat one tablespoon of the olive oil in a large, nonstick skillet over medium-high heat. Add the spinach, mushrooms, tomatoes, green onions, and bell pepper. Sauté, stirring until the fresh spinach wilts. Transfer the spinach and vegetable mixture to a bowl.

Combine egg and seasonings in a mixing bowl. Beat with a fork until combined, but not foamy. Heat one tablespoon of olive oil in a nonstick skillet over medium-high heat. Add the egg mixture to skillet. Allow the egg to set for a few seconds, then start moving a spatula around the edges of the skillet, lifting the set egg so the uncooked portion can run underneath and make direct contact with the hot skillet.

When the egg is set, remove from heat. Add the spinach and vegetable filling along one side of the omelette and fold in half. Top with the low-fat mozzarella cheese and serve with a fresh medley of your favorite fruit.

Jim's Homemade Chili
From page 108

Jim shares the inside scoop on the rebirth of his traditional homemade chili. To get started, you will need the following ingredients: one package of ground turkey or chicken; one-half package of Williams chili seasoning; one cup of water; one cup of fresh diced tomatoes; one can of no salt tomato sauce; one-half cup of chopped onion; one-half cup of chopped red bell pepper; two garlic cloves chopped finely; one tablespoon of cumin; one tablespoon of cilantro; one tablespoon of oregano leaves; one tablespoon of Mrs. Dash; one tablespoon of brown sugar; and one can of Bush's chili beans.

To assemble a flavorful ensemble, brown ground turkey and drain excess fat; blend in remaining ingredients, except Bush's chili beans. Bring to a boil; reduce heat, cover and simmer 15 minutes, stirring frequently. Lastly, add Bush's chili beans and simmer for an additional 10 minutes.

Serve with brown rice and low-fat mozzarella cheese (optional).

Jim's Flavorful Fish Tacos

From page 124

Jim launches another one of his flavorful favorites. He exposes his secrets for intensifying the taste and adding loads of nutrition. You can create a serving of this irresistible dish with the following ingredients: one-half pound of Tilapia or Atlantic Salmon (fresh or frozen); one tablespoon of olive oil, one-half tablespoon chopped cilantro; one-fourth teaspoon of ground cumin, one-half teaspoon of garlic powder; one-half teaspoon of Mrs. Dash (original); one-fourth teaspoon of cayenne pepper; one fresh lemon; one cup of mixed greens; one-fourth cup of fresh diced tomatoes; two tablespoons of mozzarella cheese; one tablespoon of low-fat sour cream; two whole wheat flour tortillas or two corn tortillas; one-half can of Bush's black beans.

To get started, you will need to thaw fish, if frozen, rinse and pat dry with paper towels. Cut fish crosswise into one-quarter slices and season with cilantro, cumin, garlic powder, Mrs. Dash, and cayenne pepper in a bowl, and squeeze fresh lemon juice on fish. Grease a medium sized baking pan with one tablespoon of olive oil, place fish inside pan and bake in pre-heated oven on 375 degrees F for four to six minutes or until fish begins to flake when tested with a fork. Be sure to turn fish halfway through during baking. Atlantic Salmon will take approximately an additional ten minutes.

Meanwhile, heat Bush's black beans according to directions.

Place whole wheat tortilla in a non-stick pan for twenty seconds, turning. Or heat corn tortilla according to directions. Then add a piece of fish, handful of mixed greens and tomatoes, and top with black beans, low-fat sour cream and mozzarella cheese.

Jim and Suzanne's Classic Chicken Macaroni Casserole

From page 167

A collaboration of chicken and macaroni, Jim and Suzanne strikes the perfect balance between 100% natural chicken breast and whole grain elbow pasta. This simple and quick delicious dish for two will keep you coming back for more, but remember portion control.

You will need two pieces of fresh chicken breast; one and one-fourth cups of uncooked whole grain elbow macaroni; one can of low-sodium condensed cream of mushroom soup; one-half cup of low-fat milk; one tablespoon of cilantro; two tablespoons of fresh chopped parsley; and three-fourth cups of mozzarella cheese.

To create a classic of shredded chicken, wash chicken in salt water and clean it as needed. Cover in water and cook thirty to forty-five minutes (until thoroughly cook). Remove meat to cool, strain broth, and place on a cutting board. Using two forks, shred the meat into thin strips.

Cook whole grain elbow pasta according to directions, until macaroni is tender. Rinse and drain. Combine the macaroni, chicken, and remaining ingredients in a bowl and set for five minutes. Set aside enough cheese to sprinkle on top. Place contents in a greased two-quart casserole dish and bake for about twenty minutes at 400 degrees F.

The perfect accompaniment will include a serving of mixed greens and a balsamic vinaigrette dressing.

Molly's Garlic Spinach Mashed Potatoes

From page 180

Now this one you will really enjoy. Molly puts a healthy spin on a traditional favorite. From instant to homemade, you, too, can create a favorable recipe for mashed potatoes that increases nutritional value. To get started, you'll need one large potato, peeled and quartered; two cups of fresh spinach or one (ten ounce) package of plain frozen spinach (cooked according to package); one-half cup skim milk; one-half cup of low-fat sour cream; two garlic cloves, peeled and mashed; one tablespoon of cilantro, and one teaspoon of white pepper.

To get started, you'll cover the potato with water in your favorite heavy-bottomed pan; bring to a boil; reduce heat slightly and simmer until the potato is fork-tender. Drain potato and stir in skim milk, low-fat sour cream, mashed garlic, cilantro, white pepper, and fresh or cooked spinach. Presto, you'll have a nutritious version of a smooth, flavorful, and fluffy potato.

Grandma's Fancy French Toast

From page 223

Todd's mother reveals her old-fashion Fancy French Toast recipe. Light and fluffy, her French toast is packed with nutrition. You'll need the following to create your own version. If it's just you, take two slices of whole-wheat bread; one egg; one-third cup skim milk; one-fourth teaspoon of nutmeg; one-fourth teaspoon of vanilla extract; and one-fourth teaspoon ground cinnamon.

Now the fun starts by beating the egg, milk, nutmeg, vanilla, and ground cinnamon. Dip bread slices in egg mixture until both sides are soaked. Then, spray a skillet or frying pan with cooking spray, toss back and forth until both sides are golden brown.

Top with your favorite fruit or sugar-free syrup. Don't forget about the Eggland's Best eggs.

Grandma's Fruity Smoothie

From page 243

Focused on healthy snack, Grandma Holder blends a collection of fresh fruit. She handpicks the plumpest, ripest of fresh blueberries. She selects the finest of fresh strawberries, bananas, and sliced cantaloupe. You too can choose your favorite fresh fruits to make a tasty, nutritious smoothie. For starters, you can use one banana, four strawberries, one cup of low-fat plain yogurt, one-half cup of Soy milk, and one-half cup ice cubes.

In a blender, combine the fresh fruit, yogurt, and milk, mixing thoroughly. Then, add the ice cubes, cover and blend till smooth. Serve immediately.

Todd's Whole Wheat Pizza

From page 249

Creativity at its best, Todd prepares a healthy and tasty whole wheat pizza. He substitutes unhealthy with healthy products, making his version lower in fat, cholesterol and sodium. To make your fantastic version, you can start by either making your whole wheat dough from scratch or purchasing prepared frozen dough at the supermarket.

For homemade whole wheat dough, you'll need one cup of whole wheat flour; one-fourth cup wheat germ; one tablespoon active dry yeast; one-half teaspoon salt; one tablespoon olive oil; one tablespoon honey; and one cup warm water.

In a bowl, combine the flour, wheat germ, yeast, and salt. Then, stir in the oil, honey, and water until well blended. Beat until mixture is smooth. Let stand for fifteen minutes. Roll out the dough onto a baking sheet for one medium pizza or divide the dough into mini circular shapes. Kids will love the mini pizzas.

You can use any combination of the following non-traditional vegetable toppings, like one-half cup broccoli floret pieces; one cup fresh spinach; one cup fresh tomatoes; three sliced portobello mushrooms caps; one-fourth cup diced black olives; one tablespoon shallots; one-fourth chopped bell peppers; and/or one-fourth chopped yellow onions. Don't forget about your favorite fruit toppings like pineapple chunks. For fresh vegetables, like your spinach, tomatoes, and mushrooms, you can go ahead and sauté lightly in olive oil. Do not overcook. For broccoli, go ahead and steam until partially tender. If you'd like to try sliced cooked venison sausage as a topping, it's okay.

For a tasty pizza sauce, you can combine one can of no salt tomato sauce; one tablespoon of dried oregano; one-half teaspoon extra spicy Mrs. Dash seasoning; two tablespoons worcestershire sauce; and one-half teaspoon Italian seasoning.

Now, you're ready to piece together your work of art. Preheat oven to 400 degrees F. Place your large or mini pizza dough in the oven and bake for about seven minutes. Do not cook thoroughly. Remove baking sheet from the oven temporarily and spread sauce, vegetable and/or fruit toppings, and one-half package of mozzarella cheese sparingly on your large or mini pizza semi-cooked dough. Bake for fifteen minutes.

Congratulations, you've made your pizza lower in fat and calories than the take-out version.

Todd's Sensational Chicken Stir-Fry

From page 249

Todd creates a tasty stir-fry much healthier than what you will find at the neighborhood Chinese restaurant. Rich in vegetables, each bite is filled with a tower of vitamins and minerals. To create your version using fresh natural ingredients, you'll need the following: three pieces of boneless, skinless chicken breasts, cut into thin strips; one and one-half tablespoons olive oil; one cup broccoli floret pieces; one-half cup of shredded carrots; one red bell pepper and onion, each sliced; two garlic cloves, minced; one-half cup of celery; one-fourth sliced mushrooms and snow peas; one small can of sliced water chestnuts, drained; one-half teaspoon minced fresh ginger root; three tablespoons low-sodium soy sauce; and cooked brown rice.

To get the ball rolling, steam your broccoli florets. Next, heat oil and add soy sauce and three-fourth cup of water in a wok or large saucepan over medium-high heat, adding chicken and water chestnuts. Stir-fry until meat is fully cooked. Add the carrots, red bell pepper, garlic, onion, celery, mushrooms, ginger root, snow peas and steamed broccoli, stirring constantly for about five minutes. Serve over brown rice or whole wheat spaghetti.

Dad's Whole-Wheat Waffles

From page 249

Todd's kids love his delectable homemade whole-wheat waffles. His flare for adding flavor keeps his kids wanting waffles every day. All you need is one cup of whole wheat flour, two medium eggs, one cup of skim milk, two tablespoons of canola oil, one tablespoon of vanilla extract, two teaspoons baking power, and a dash of salt for taste.

To get started, combine and beat eggs, milk, and oil. Gradually stir in vanilla and sifted flour. Sift baking powder over the mixture and fold in quickly. Bake in hot waffle iron. To enhance the nutrition value, top with your fresh fruit.

Dad's Whole-Wheat Chicken Lasagna

From page 253

Whether it's chicken, turkey or vegetables, you can make mouthwatering lasagna oozing with nutrition. This recipe will include ground turkey and vegetables. To get started, stray away from the traditional white lasagna pasta and use a package of Whole-wheat lasagna pasta. Don't forget about your fresh vegetables, at least one large zucchini and one large squash (pre-cut into bite sizes). Plus, you'll need a package of ground white turkey; one-half cup chopped onion; one-half cup chopped bell pepper; one-half cup chopped celery; two fresh garlic cloves, mashed; two cups low-fat cottage cheese, one egg, one large can no salt added tomato sauce, and three-fourths cup of shredded reduced-fat mozzarella cheese. You will need a 13X9X2-inch baking dish.

First, brown your ground white turkey with onion, bell pepper, celery, and garlic over moderately high heat and drain off the excess fat. Meanwhile, have your pasta boiling according to package directions and drain. After pasta is cooked, be sure to separate cooked lasagna and lay them on wax paper or aluminum foil to keep pieces from sticking. Next, prepare the cheese mixture by mixing the cottage cheese with the egg, and wire wisk until smooth. Your vegetables (zucchini and squash) should be chopped into bite sized pieces ready to steam until tender.

Now, you're ready for the assembly. Put a small amount of sauce to coat bottom of baking pan, add a layer of pasta, add a layer of meat, add a layer of the veggie mixture, add a layer of cottage cheese mixture, and add some more sauce. Keep on until you finish layering. Top with layer of lasagna and remaining sauce, then sprinkle with mozzarella cheese. Bake in oven at 350 degrees for 40 minutes, and presto, you have a healthy version of meat and veggie lasagna.

I hope these recipes guide you in your pursuit to create healthier meals. I would love to hear how the recipes turned out for you and any recommendations for improvement. Email me your feedback at bridgette@bridgettecollins.com.

Bridgette L. Collins

HEALTH AND FITNESS REFERENCES

Please note that some of the web-addresses have been hyphenated. Do not include this hyphen when typing in your browser address bar.

NUTRITION
Eating Breakfast – American Dietetic Association – www.eatright.org

Tips for eating Mexican food - American Heart Association – http://www.americanheart.org/presenter.jhtml?identifier=1100

Sodium in Processed Foods – The Center for Science in the Public Interest - http://www.cspinet.org/new/200511081.html

Nutrition Fact Label - U. S. Food and Drug Administration - Center for Food Safety and Applied Nutrition - http://www.cfsan.fda.gov/~dms/foodlab.html

Trans Fat – American Heart Association - http://www.american-heart.org/presenter.jhtml?identifier=4776

Portion Distortion - National Heart, Lung, and Blood Institute - http://hp2010.nhlbihin.net/portion/

Dietary Supplements - U. S. Food and Drug Administration - Center for Food Safety and Applied Nutrition - http://www.cfsan.fda.gov/~dms/ds-oview.html#what

Vitamins and Minerals – National Institute of Health - Office of Dietary Supplements –

http://ods.od.nih.gov/Health_Information/Vitamin_and_Mineral
_Supplement_Fact_Sheets.aspx
Iron Deficiency – National Institute of Health - Office of Dietary
Supplements – http://ods.od.nih.gov/factsheets/iron.asp

Kids and Breakfast – KidsHealth -
http://www.kidshealth.org/kid/stay_healthy/food/breakfast.ht
ml

Diet and Cancer – American Cancer Society - http://www.can-
cer.org/docroot/ped/content/ped_3_2x_common_questions_abo
ut_diet_and_cancer.asp

Diet and Cancer - American Institute for Cancer Research -
http://www.aicr.org/site/News2?abbr=pr_&page=NewsArticle&
id=10261

Nitrite and Cancer – U.S. National Library of Science Medicine
and the National Institutes of Health -
http://www.nlm.nih.gov/medlineplus/ency/article/002096.htm

WEIGHT LOSS
Counting Calories – American Cancer Society – http://www.can-
cer.org/docroot/PED/content/PED_6_1x_Calorie_Calculator.asp

Effective Weight Loss – U.S. Department of Health and Human
Services – Office on Women's Health -
http://womenshealth.gov/faq/weightloss.htm

Quick-Weight-Loss or Fad Diets – American Heart Association –
http://www.americanheart.org/presenter.jhtml?identifier=503

Fad Diets - American Academy of Family Physicians –
http://familydoctor.org/784.xml

Weight Control – American Academy of Family Physicians -
http://familydoctor.org/197.xml

Body Mass Index (BMI) – Department of Health and Human

Services - National Institute of Health - http://www.nhlbisup-port.com/bmi/bmicalc.htm
Body Mass Index (BMI) – Department of Health and Human Services – Center for Disease Control and Prevention - http://www.cdc.gov/nccdphp/dnpa/bmi/index.htm

ILLNESSES/DISEASES
High Blood Cholesterol – National Heart, Lung, and Blood Institute - http://www.nhlbi.nih.gov/health/dci/Diseases/Hbc/HBC_WhatIs.html

Healthy Cholesterol Levels – American Heart Association - http://www.americanheart.org/presenter.jhtml?identifier=183

Stroke – American Stroke Association - http://www.strokeassociation.org/presenter.jhtml?identifier=3030387

Osteoporosis - U. S. Department of Health and Human Services National Institutes of Health - National Institute on Aging - http://www.niapublications.org/agepages/osteo.asp

Anemia - National Heart, Lung, and Blood Institute - http://www.nhlbi.nih.gov/health/dci/Diseases/anemia/anemia_whoisatrisk.html

Urticaria – American Osteopathic College of Dermatology - http://www.aocd.org/skin/dermatologic_diseases/urticaria.html

Urticaria and Histamine – American Academy of Dermatology - http://www.aad.org/public/Publications/pamphlets/Urticaria-Hives.htm

Menopause – Mayo Clinic - http://www.mayoclinic.com/health/menopause/DS00119

Lupus – National Institute of Arthritis and Musculoskeletal and Skin Diseases - http://www.niams.nih.gov/hi/topics/lupus/shades/

Pre-Diabetes – American Diabetes Association -
http://www.diabetes.org/pre-diabetes.jsp

Diabetes – American Diabetes Association -
http://www.diabetes.org/about-diabetes.jsp

Diabetes and Kidney Disease – National Kidney Foundation -
http://www.kidney.org/atoz/atozItem.cfm?id=37

Alternatives for Taking Insulin - National Institute of Diabetes and
Digestive and Kidney Diseases - National Diabetes Information
Clearinghouse -
http://diabetes.niddk.nih.gov/dm/pubs/insulin/

Insulin Pumps – American Diabetes Association -
http://www.diabetes.org/diabetes-forecast/may2004/pump.jsp

High Blood Pressure and Kidney Disease – National Kidney
Foundation - http://www.kidney.org/atoz/pdf/hbpkidneys.pdf

Cancer – American Cancer Society - http://www.cancer.org/doc-
root/CRI/content/CRI_2_2_1x_What_Is_Cancer.asp?sitearea=

Breast Cancer – American Cancer Society -
http://www.cancer.org/docroot/CRI/content/CRI_2_2_2X_What
_causes_breast_cancer_5.asp?sitearea=

Tobacco and Cancer – American Cancer Society -
http://www.cancer.org/docroot/PED/content/PED_10_2x_Tobac
co-Related_Cancers_Fact_Sheet.asp?sitearea=PED

Sodium Intake – Mayo Clinic -
http://www.mayoclinic.com/health/sodium/NU00284

Salt and High Blood Pressure – American Stroke Association -
http://www.strokeassociation.org/presenter.jhtml?identifi-
er=3027283

High Blood Pressure - National Heart, Lung, and Blood Institute - http://www.nhlbi.nih.gov/health/dci/Diseases/Hbp/HBP_Who IsAtRisk.html

Heart Surgery Overview – Texas Heart Institute - http://www.texasheartinstitute.org/HIC/Topics/Proced/

DISORDERS
Emotional Eating – Mayo Clinic – http://www.mayoclinic.com/health/weight-loss/MH00025

Sleep disorders – National Sleep Foundation – www.sleepfounda-tion.org

OVERWEIGHT/OBESITY
Overweight Kids – Department of Health and Human Services – Centers for Disease Control and Prevention - http://www.cdc.gov/nccdphp/dnpa/obesity/index.htm

Costs Related to Obesity – American Obesity Association - http://www.obesity.org/treatment/cost.shtml

Economic Impact of Obesity - Department of Health and Human Services – Centers for Disease Control and Prevention - http://www.cdc.gov/nccdphp/dnpa/obesity/economic_conse-quences.htm

Obesity – National Center for Health Statistics - http://www.cdc.gov/nchs/pressroom/06facts/obesity03_04.htm

GENERAL
Antihistamines – American Academy of Family Physicians - http://familydoctor.org/857.xml

Erectile Dysfunction - American Academy of Family Physicians - http://familydoctor.org/109.xml

Vagina Dryness – Mayo Clinic -
http://www.mayoclinic.com/health/vaginal-dryness/DS00550

Radon Gas and Cancer – American Cancer Society -
http://www.cancer.org/docroot/NWS/content/NWS_1_1x_Rado
n_Gas_Confirmed_as_Second_Largest_Lung_Cancer_Risk.asp

ABOUT THE AUTHOR

Recognizing the pitfalls of misplaced priorities, Bridgette Collins launched MAC Fitness (Making-A-Commitment to Fitness) in 2002 to educate, coach, and motivate individuals who struggle with implementing healthier lifestyle habits. She is skilled at creatively crafting solutions to help her clients overcome the physical, financial, and emotional consequences of physical inactivity and poor nutritional habits.

Bridgette has worked as a certified personal trainer, both privately and for Bally's Total Fitness, and she holds a personal trainer certification through Aerobics and Fitness Association of America. Combining her fitness training and passion for healthy living with nearly twenty years of human resources and program development experience, Bridgette delivers practical health and fitness solutions.

Understanding that the quest to incorporate a healthier lifestyle is often hampered by daily demands and obligations, she equips her clients with a collection of lifestyle tools that helps to close the gap between understanding and doing what is right to reduce the risk of disease and illness.

A motivational speaker and facilitator, Bridgette travels throughout the country delivering a message that empowers audiences to make positive lifestyle choices. She writes a health column for *Crux Magazine*, a spiritual lifestyle magazine, and has also served as a fitness coach for an Internet radio station and an online lifestyle management program.

Bridgette has been an avid runner for more than 10 years, participating in a host of 5K and 10K races and completing four marathons and two half-marathons. In an effort to share the benefits of a consistent running program, she has coached several group training programs to provide beginner walkers and runners weekly instruction for improving their fitness level.

A native of Houston, Bridgette resides in Grand Prairie, Texas, where she is an active member at Golden Gate Missionary Baptist Church. She enjoys running, watching football, traveling, and going to movies and stage plays. She has a degree in business administration.

Bridgette would love to receive your feedback on *Imagine Living Healthier*. To contact her, please write or email:

Bridgette L. Collins

P.O. Box 542671

Grand Prairie, Texas 75054-2671

bridgette@bridgettecollins.com

For more healthy living tips and information
on Bridgette's other book, visit:

www.ImagineLivingHealthier.com

"*Imagine Living Healthier* allows the reader to vicariously experience the life challenges facing three adults. Immersed in day-to-day events, each character avoids confronting issues that if left unresolved emerge as uneasiness on all fronts: mental, physical, social, and familial. Resolution comes when Sarah, Suzanne, and Todd listen to their inner voices, seek the help of professionals, and embrace the support of friends and family. A must read for today's high stress, high achieving and highly competitive society."

　　—Eunice Stanfield, MD
　　　Medical Director of Dallas County Employee Health

"This is not your typical health book. In this novel you'll learn about Sarah, Suzanne, and Todd, who have not made the correct choices and find themselves battling some serious problems. Readers will be empowered as they recognize themselves in many instances. Ms. Collins' passion for healthy living is clear as she offers solutions and provides invaluable information that is well-researched and interestingly presented."

　　—Cheryl Smith, **Dallas Weekly**

"Ms. Collins has fashioned a book of parables that highlights health crisis and medical facts, as she unveils what unhealthy lifestyles do to the mind, body, and soul. *Imagine Living Healthier* is intended to inspire and empower readers to rearrange their priorities, shift their thinking, and unleash the spirituality that lies within."
　　—The RAWSISTAZ Reviewers

"Using fictional stories along with non-fiction information and a little witnessing, Collins was able to write a self-help book that will grab your attention beginning with the first page. *Imagine Living Healthier* is the best book I have ever read that does not preach to you, but encourages you with true facts and ideas on how to begin to live healthy."

     —Sharel E. Gordon-Love, APOOO BookClub

"*Imagine Living Healthier* seeks to remind us that the cure for our ills lies not in the food that we eat, but in the lifestyle choices that we make. Collins does an impressive job of properly framing the problem of obesity, showing that its root causes are really psychological in nature."

     —Nisha Powell, Apex Reviews